November in Salem

The Bargain of Witches

L.C. Russell

iUniverse, Inc.
New York Bloomington

November in Salem
The Bargain of Witches

iUniverse books may be ordered through booksellers or by contacting:

iUniverse
1663 Liberty Drive
Bloomington, IN 47403
www.iuniverse.com
1-800-Authors (1-800-288-4677)

ISBN: 978-1-4401-1898-2 (pbk)
ISBN: 978-1-4401-1900-2 (cloth)
ISBN: 978-1-4401-1899-9 (ebk)

Library of Congress Control Number: 2009921065

Printed in the United States of America

iUniverse rev. date: 02/19/2009

To Bob,

the real Mr. Whoozi-What's.

Thanks for believing in me.

Acknowledgments

Many friends and family have given their time, advice and support during the writing of November in Salem. It goes without saying that any mistakes or errors concerning facts or interpretations are mine and mine alone.

My editorial specialist, George Nedeff, was not only brilliant, but helped me to climb the steep learning curve that is first-time publishing. Thanks, too, to everyone else at iUniverse, especially Natalie Chenoweth who was patience personified and who went 'the extra mile' with the finishing touches.

I'd particularly like to thank Conner Miller for not only taking the time to read the earliest drafts, but for his enthusiasm and encouragement through the long writing process. I'd also like to thank Dr. Leslie Chilton for reminding me that hay was stored loose and not baled in 1701.

I am very grateful to my sister and brother-in-law, Linda and Bill Perkins, who read November's story aloud to each other on long trips between Northfield and Milmay—must have been some ride!

Finally, to Marsha and Dennis Gilliam (the real Aunt Marsha & Dynnis) who not only convinced me this was a book worth writing, but who provided day-to-day help, practical support and companionship well beyond the call of duty—to you I bow in deepest gratitude.

And to my husband, Bob. His love, support, and inspired suggestions—not to mention all those dinners cooked while I wrote—made all the difference, as they always have and always will.

Prologue

The Bargain

Salem Village, Massachusetts

November 11, 1701

The moon was in its last quarter in the house of Gemini. This would prove to be important on another such night in Salem Village. But on this night, six solemn-faced men sat round a rough-hewn table, in the tiny rectory of the Meeting House, arguing over the neatly penned words of an ominous document.

Their raised voices drowned out the sound of the rising wind that shook the windows and blew sparks from the flue of the woodstove in the corner, and the sudden howling of the neighborhood dogs, that echoed into the cold night. The strong gusts of frigid night air were forceful enough to move the heavy brass bell hanging in the tower. Its iron clapper sounded eight times as the men continued to pound the table and shout before the door to the Meeting House flew open, causing them to jump to their feet in surprise.

Two figures, one tall and wide as the door frame, the other half his size, stood just inside the threshold. Time seemed to stand still as all sound ceased both inside the building and out. It could have been an instant or an eternity that held each man in the room frozen in the posture he'd assumed just as the door was flung wide.

The giant figure, wrapped in a deep purple cape, broke the spell by striding into the meeting room, his footfalls making an odd tapping sound as if he wore hobbled boots.

"Good evening, gentlemen. It appears there are some concerns regarding our...agreement." His whispery voice matched the sounds of the brittle autumn leaves that had blown through the doorway behind him and his companion, and were now scuttling across the dusty, pine floorboards. Once inside the circle of light thrown out by the large oil lamp, he pushed back his hood and an intake of breaths could be heard round the room.

Except for the elderly man seated at the head of the table, none of the others in the group had ever met the two strangers with whom they were about to seal the most important deal of their lives. But even at his advanced age and with all his worldly dealings, he had never noticed the strange shape of the big man's pupils before, as they reflected the flickering lamplight. Almost vertical, they seemed to have the power to immobilize.

The newcomer nodded to his assistant who produced a razor-sharp quill from beneath his own cloak and laid it atop the vellum document on the table. Rubbing his hands as if to warm them, the large man indicated the pen. "Gentlemen, I believe we have business to tend to."

Outside, a sudden snow squall had come up, the fierce wind whipping the heavy white flakes until they resembled sheets flying on a clothesline on a black, blustery day. The snow collected quickly on the frozen ground and window sills of the sleeping village. At this hour no sensible man was anywhere but beneath several layers of goose down quilting. So no one in the village saw the white stuff pile deeply everywhere except on the roof of the Meeting House, where it hit the glowing cedar tiles like drops of water on a flame. And much later, no one but the large brown and gray hawk riding out the storm in the belfry saw the shadow of a figure bury a wooden box beneath a sapling in the churchyard.

Chapter One

A hospital structure—plain and simple but complete in all of its appointments—shall crown Hathorne Hill, with its wealth of pure water and purer air and its broad landscapes of beauty stretching out on every side.

—Clement Walker, medical advisor, State Lunatic Hospital, Danvers, Massachusetts (1875)

Danvers, Massachusetts

November 8th, The Present

"SO WHAT DO YOU THINK THEY'RE GOING to do with the old insane asylum?" Jeff asked as we walked down Maple Street past the gargantuan boarded-up structure. On this dark afternoon, the deep burgundy buildings making up the main complex sat shuttered and guarded, like a group of moody old trolls—nasty, dirty, and dangerous.

"Tear it down and make condos," Hawk replied as he fiddled with the adjustment buttons on the "Dune Buggy," his nickname for his wheelchair. I walked along behind him, holding onto the handles because Aunt Marsha had asked me to make sure he went slowly down the steep sidewalk, especially because there was still snow on the ground. I wasn't sure I was the best choice for the job, because I'd always had this weird kind of feeling when I was around someone in a wheelchair—like I was a kind of jinx or something. Besides Hawk, there had been only two occasions when I'd been close to someone in a wheelchair—and both times that someone had died. Oh, I was assured each time that it wasn't my fault. But I knew that if I had been more attentive—a better daughter, a better granddaughter—things might have turned out differently.

"Where'd you hear that?" Jeff pulled me back to the present by picking up a stick and throwing it over the temporary chain-link fence, erected to keep out the vandals and homeless people. I tightened my grip on the chair's plastic handles. Well, it wasn't going to happen again. I glanced down at the back of my cousin's head.

Hawk, apparently satisfied with the speed of the wheelchair, looked up at the asylum. "Heard Mom reading it to Aunty Gin from the paper this morning. You know, that place was originally called the State Lunatic Hospital when it was built in 1875," Hawk said.

"Here we go," Jeff said over his shoulder. "The rolling encyclopedia is going to give a lecture."

"*Lunatic hospital* is not exactly a politically correct term," I said as I helped steer Hawk away from a high pile of plowed snow.

"No, but that's exactly who it was built for," he continued. "Insane people—lots of them. Guy by the name of Kirkbride built it to test his new theory of beautiful surroundings and fresh air as a cure for mental illness. It's 300,000 square feet and sits on over five-hundred acres. That's why we can see it from so far away."

I looked up at the forbidding exteriors of the three-story Gothic buildings. They gave the impression that a vampire bat might fly down from one of the steep eaves at any moment.

"Beautiful surroundings?" I muttered.

Hawk heard me. He had the hearing of a cat. "Well, it didn't always look like that." He waved his hand toward the buildings. "I've seen pictures of the original structures on the Internet, and it was really pretty nice back in the day. It's the perfect example of Victorian Gothic." He really did sound like an encyclopedia.

"So what happened?" I asked. I couldn't help but be intrigued. We usually didn't take this route home, but the sidewalks on the other side of Maple were too icy for Hawk's chair. Although the buildings were far off in the distance, the fact that they sat on top of a hill made the sharp roof lines visible almost all over town.

"The place was abandoned in 1992, and it's been vacant ever since." Hawk was just getting warmed up, and we listened patiently as he prattled on about the architect who built it and the statistics surrounding its size and design.

Hawk's real name is Stephen Atwood, and he and his identical twin brother, Jeff, are my cousins—their mom being my dad's older sister. Thirteen years ago, Hawk was born with a spinal cord disorder and has always needed the aid of a wheelchair. But where his body is limited, his mind is not. His nickname comes from Stephen Hawking, the famous physicist, because Hawk's greatest love is quantum physics and, like Hawking, his IQ is reported to be somewhere in the stratosphere. He has a photographic memory, and whatever he reads, and that's plenty, he retains—completely.

Jeff, on the other hand, is as athletic as Hawk is brainy. Aunt Marsha calls them "mirror twins," because each has a small mole at exactly the same spot on opposite cheeks, like someone looking in a mirror. But beyond their faces, the similarities stop. Jeff is an avid sports nut. His big love is baseball, and he dreams of a career in the majors; but lately, his grades have kept him from playing on the baseball team at school. Still, he's fun to be around and has a keen sense of humor and a fierce devotion to his "baby brother" by four minutes.

I had never met either of them, or my two aunts, before I came to Danvers that September. And if I was honest with myself, I would have to admit that my heart sank the first time I saw Hawk in his Dune Buggy. *Death.* The word echoed through my mind as if it had been breathed into my ear, causing me to stumble awkwardly through the introductions and earning me a sharp look from my stepdad, Frank.

Frank is a representative of the State Department in our home state of Arizona, and he and my mom were spending the next year in Antibes, in the south of France, as emissaries for the United States.

My real dad, a pilot, died when I was eight, after a lengthy illness resulting from a plane crash. So I'd never really gotten to know his side of the family.

When my mother suggested I might "like to try living with a *regular* family and attend a *public* school," I thought she was attempting some kind of tasteless joke. I had never seen a day of structured school in all of my twelve years. First, Mom homeschooled me and then, after she married Frank, they hired my nanny, Miss Toni, to travel with us.

Until two months ago, my only knowledge of what kids did in public school consisted of what I had seen in movies and on sitcoms. I had always accompanied my parents when they traveled. I'd already filled three passports and was looking forward to cracking the spine on a fourth when Mom and Frank hatched this plan.

"You know, November needs to experience real life," I overheard Frank tell my mom as I stood poised, toothbrush in hand, over the sink in my bathroom. There was no better intercom in the world than the heating vent in the floor of my parents' bedroom.

"She's thirteen and she's never really been away from us. What I guess I'm trying to say is that she should spend some time around a normal family. She's pretty much seen the world, and yet she's never really experienced life."

"Well, I'm not so sure what's considered *normal* anymore," Mom said. "But I get your point, and, in this case, I'm inclined to agree." My chin almost hit the sink. "But I'm not sure *she* will," she finished.

No kidding.

"Well, I think we should take your sisters-in-law up on their offer." Frank's voice came through loud and clear, but it was hard to hear Mom's reply as she walked across the cavernous room that was their Owner's Retreat, as the master bedroom was called in our gated community. Leave it to Frank to say the plural form of sister-in-law correctly. Because I was concentrating on that, I missed Mom's answer. So the next morning when she brought the subject up, I pretended to be surprised. Still, even with a surprise attack, no amount of whining or pouting or storming upstairs would change their minds. They had convinced themselves this was in my best interest.

So after the holidays, Miss Toni was given a six-month severance, and I was packed and bundled off to Danvers, Massachusetts, to live with my Aunt Marsha and her sister, Ginny, in their old colonial house on Preston Street for the remainder of the school year. It would be *a good experience—a chance to get to know Dad's side of the family; a good look at what public school was all about.* I looked first at Hawk, then at Jeff, picking up rocks and heaving them over the chain-link fence.

So far, I liked my cousins well enough, and my aunts were nice. And the public school? Well, I had only been going to Putnam Middle School for a couple of months, and even though my cousins were in eighth grade, like me, we didn't have many classes together, so that made it kind of hard to fit in. This was the East Coast and I was from the West. I was pretty much an outsider, and the kids let me know it.

So the jury was still way out on what, if anything, I would learn from public school and from my relatives in Danvers. I had a strong feeling that it would not be much and that whatever it was, it couldn't be nearly as exciting as Antibes.

"Hey, let's race!" Jeff shouted and started to run, snapping me out of my thoughts.

Race? Before I could say the word, Hawk hit the fast-forward on the Dune Buggy, and the chair jumped out of my hands. Were they nuts? We started downhill on an almost complete sheet of ice.

I watched with my mouth open as Jeff shot ahead, his Reeboks sliding sideways along the icy pavement, with Hawk's wheelchair fishtailing madly from side to side, right on his heels.

"Wait!" I tried to run and almost went over backward on a patch of ice. "Are you guys crazy?" I managed to shout, as I whirled my arms like a deranged aerobics instructor and tried to keep my feet beneath me as I slid headlong down the steep incline.

We were almost at the bottom when I realized that Hawk was overtaking Jeff, and, just when I thought we would all make it down the hill in one piece, Jeff looked to his right and saw Hawk next to him. In an insane attempt to keep his lead, Jeff veered to the right, and Hawk's left front wheel caught on his twin's right heel. I watched in horror, as I slipped and slid some twenty feet behind them, as Jeff's left leg went out from under him, and he was thrown up and into Hawk's lap. The weight of Jeff's body threw the careening machine over onto two wheels, and it hurtled, with both boys flailing like stricken pelicans, off the sidewalk, straight toward a gigantic oak tree at the edge of someone's front yard.

"Watch out!" I called helplessly and promptly landed on my backside as I slid the rest of the way to the bottom of the hill. I managed to make it to my feet in time to see the wheelchair hit something at the edge of the sidewalk and go airborne. I screamed until I had no breath left as I watched Jeff fly out and then Hawk right behind him, as if they were some mad team of brothers demonstrating being shot from a cannon simultaneously. They flew in tandem, headfirst, right into a snow bank, mere inches from the base of a black oak tree. The chair hit the tree, rebounding off to the right into the snow-covered yard, where it lay drunkenly on its side, its rear wheels still spinning as if not yet ready to give up the race.

I could see Hawk's shoulders moving as I made my way, slipping and sliding, to the pair and silently thanked the powers that be that he was still alive and able to move. Then I noticed Jeff's shoulders moving the same way. Were they in shock? Having a fit? I started to run. I would have given anything at that moment to have a cell phone. This clearly was a good example of why kids need cell phones. I was going to press that point when we got home—*if* we got home. And just how was I supposed to help them, anyway? What if they needed an ambulance? I wasn't exactly medically inclined. In fact, my only other attempt at first aid was with my goldfish, Alice, and she died. I started looking up and down the street for help. The only vehicle on the road was a black SUV, just turning the corner and heading in our direction. I glanced back at Hawk and Jeff. The shoulder shaking had grown more intense. Seizures. I waved at the SUV and watched the driver, a middle-aged woman with a cell phone to her ear, smile and wave back as she hit the gas to beat the yellow light at the intersection. A deep cough and a ragged breath brought my attention back to my cousins, and I made my way toward where they lay hunched in the snow. It wasn't until I was almost upon them that I realized they weren't having seizures at all—they were laughing. In fact, they were laughing so hard, they couldn't talk.

Jeff sat up and wiped his eyes on the back of his hand and then took in his brother. "Gentlemen, I believe we have liftoff." His voice caught on the last word, and he collapsed in hysteria. Hawk rolled onto his back and howled along with his brother.

I stood there, looking at the two of them. They could have both broken their necks, and they thought it was funny. *Funny!* I felt like finishing the job.

"Oh yeah—ha, ha. I just made an idiot of myself!" I shouted at them. I realized I looked like my mom, with my hands on my hips, but there is something fundamentally necessary about that pose when you're about to really ream someone out.

Jeff was up on all fours now, trying to give Hawk a hand sitting up. "Did you see that, Emmy?" He was trying to diffuse the situation by using my nickname. It wasn't working. I wanted to throttle them both.

"Oh, yes, I saw it, alright. Were you trying to kill just yourself, or did you plan to take Hawk with you when you made *liftoff*?" At the stressed word, they both lost it again, and Hawk fell back into the snow, kicking his feet as Jeff bent over him, head hanging down as if in prayer as his shoulders shook his entire body with the force of his mirth.

I stood there in stony silence until they regained some composure, and then I said, "Well, now I know why Aunt Marsha wanted me to walk behind Hawk's chair, for all the good it did." I glared at Hawk who was now waving away any attempts at help from me or from Jeff. He was still chuckling as he managed to get over onto his elbows as Jeff went off to get the chair.

"Oh, November, you should be used to these stunts by now. But I admit, that one was a—" He broke off what he'd been about to say and suddenly clawed at the ground around the root of the oak tree.

I leaned in. "Do you need help getting up?"

Hawk shook his head. "No. Wait a minute; there's something here." He continued to push away the snow and dig his hands under the tree root. "Here. Give me a hand." He directed his left hand toward the large gnarled root that grew out of the base of the tree.

I pulled back. "Hawk, I'm going to help you into your chair, and then I'm going to get you back, hopefully in one piece, to your house. But there isn't anything in this world that will make me put my hand inside a nasty hole under that old root." Maybe the hard landing had rattled something inside his head. I looked up at Jeff who had righted the wheelchair and was bringing it back to the sidewalk. It seemed none the worse for wear. I motioned him to join us.

Hawk was still on his belly, digging away under the root. When Jeff approached, Hawk ordered him to help dig. He turned enough to see us both look at each other and then said, "There's something in there! I can just make it out. It looks like it might be a … box of some kind, but my arm isn't quite …" He strained to reach into the hole up to his shoulder.

"Here, let me." Jeff dropped to his hands and knees and then bent down and peered into the hole under the root. Then, as Hawk moved away, Jeff stuck his own arm in.

"There *is* something, and you're right. It feels like … it's some kind of …" Jeff stopped. "I need something to dig it out with." We looked around, and I saw a silver rod sticking out of the snow bank where the wheelchair had landed. It turned out to be a piece of pipe from under the seat. I picked it up and brought it back to where Jeff and Hawk were now both clearing a larger opening under the root.

Jeff took it and finished digging around the outside. "I think I've broken it free," he announced as he wiggled the pipe around and then reached in the hole once more. After a few grunts, he pulled his arm from within the root and reached down with both hands. "Got it!" He pulled a dark box, about two inches deep and a foot long, from the frozen ground. It was covered in wet dirt but, as Jeff brushed the top, some of the grime fell away and the grain of very old wood showed through.

"Let me have it," Hawk commanded. When Jeff looked like he wouldn't relinquish it, Hawk said, "I'm the one who found it."

Rolling his eyes and heaving an exaggerated sigh, he handed it over and Hawk used his sleeve to wipe away more of the dirt. Jeff and I crowded around, trying to see.

"Hey, what's going on here?" a deep voice boomed, making us all jump. A tall, beefy man with gray hair that stood on end stepped out the front door of the house where Jeff and Hawk had come in for a landing. He made his way across the yard toward where we were crouched by the tree. "Somebody hurt?" he shouted, cutting across the snow-covered grass, stepping high, like he was walking through deep water.

Jeff and I stood up, and Hawk, clutching the box, motioned toward the wheelchair, "November, my backpack."

I took two steps backward and grabbed the backpack, which by some miracle was still hanging on the handles of the Dune Buggy, tossing it to him as Jeff stepped forward and greeted our guest.

"Uh, hi," Jeff said, shoving his hands in his pockets.

Hawk stuffed the box into the backpack and then threw it back to me, jerking his head toward his left shoulder in the direction of the wheelchair. I slipped it back onto the handles just as the man appeared from around the tree.

"Hello, sir." Hawk greeted the big man, who stepped around Jeff as if avoiding a shrub. "I'm afraid I've had a bit of an accident." Hawk's angelic smile caused the man to halt and then look suspiciously at both Jeff and me.

"Why hasn't one of you gone for help?" he accused, then to Hawk, he asked, "Are you injured?" He knelt next to Hawk, who was now shivering from being wet and sitting in the snow for so long. Before he could answer, the man began shouting orders to Jeff and me.

"You! Go into the house and dial 911." He pointed a finger as thick as a banana at Jeff. "And you." He looked at me. "Go with him and bring me the throw cover on the back of the sofa." When we didn't move, he bellowed, "Well? What are you waiting for?"

"Sir?" Hawk interjected. "I'm fine—really. I just need to get back into my chair and go home. I'm just wet and as soon as—"

"No." The man sat back on his heels. "I'm afraid not, son. You've taken a nasty spill on my property and if something should be broken, or you've got internal injuries or whatever ..." He threw up his hands to indicate there could be no end of things that could be wrong with Hawk. "Anyway, I can't just let you get into that wheelchair and go home until I'm sure you're all right. I don't want you moved." He looked at me and then at the chair to see if I got his meaning. "Girl, why aren't you doing as I say?" His shout had the effect of a bullwhip, causing me to jump again. "I said go in and get this boy something to help keep him warm until the EMTs get here!"

I turned in the direction of Jeff's retreating back as he made his way slowly toward the house.

Oh, crud. Now we were in it. I had sometimes wondered what it would be like to have a brother or a sister. My friends in Phoenix used to tell me how lucky I was that I didn't. My best friend, Beth, had five brothers, all younger, and she said they were nothing but ticking disaster sitting on a cracker. I now knew what she meant.

Darkness and hard cold were starting to settle around us. I noticed that Hawk was shivering so badly now his teeth chattered; so I hurried toward the house for the blanket.

Just then, a badly rusted '85 Chevy station wagon pulled to the curb, and a small wiry woman in a navy L.L. Bean coat and matching woolen hat got out and started toward us.

"What seems to be the problem?" Aunty Gin called out. I felt like the cavalry had just arrived.

"Hey, Aunty Gin!" Hawk called out. "Had kind of an accident!" he shouted, as she made her way with surprising speed across the snowy lawn to where he sat.

I left Hawk to the explanations and introductions as I raced to the house to catch Jeff before he called the paramedics. Inside, I spotted him hunched on the sofa, staring dejectedly at the floor, the throw cover I'd been sent to fetch clutched in his hands.

"Did you call them?" I asked, and Jeff shook his head then looked up at me. "What should I do, November? My mom will have a fit if they take Hawk to the hospital. We don't have any health insurance, and the last time Hawk took an ambulance ride, it cost so much we couldn't eat anything but frozen veal patties for a month." He shivered. I couldn't tell if it was from being cold and wet or from the thought of the veal patty.

"Well, don't worry about it," I said. "Aunty Gin just pulled up out front."

"What?" Jeff sprang to his feet and looked out the front window, then started for the door. "Oh, man, we'd better get out there. Aunty Gin's unpredictable on a good day, and right now it looks like she's about to blow."

He ran to the door, flung it wide, and raced down the icy walkway toward where an argument was clearly taking shape. Although I couldn't hear what the man was saying, his agitation told me he was none too happy with my aunt. She looked like a marine captain confronting the enemy: hands at the ready, eyes boring into the face of her foe, feet planted firmly, and a grim expression that said she was not going to be moved anytime soon.

I caught the end of his sentence as I came within earshot: "… needs to have medical attention."

"Let me assure you, Mr. …?" Aunty Gin paused, but when the man didn't supply a name, she continued, "… whatever." She made a waving gesture that I had only ever seen done by the Queen of England on TV, then started to help Hawk up from where he sat looking back and forth between the two adults, like he was referee at a tennis match.

"I'm the boy's aunt and guardian," she continued, as she struggled to help Hawk toward his chair, "and I also happen to be a licensed medical practitioner. I assure you that he doesn't need an ambulance. And what's more, he's been sitting on frozen ground, which is more likely to harm him than simply getting him into a heated car and taking him home." She spotted Jeff and me and motioned for us to help. Jeff took Hawk's left side while I steadied the Dune Buggy.

As they placed a shivering Hawk into the Buggy, the man went into what my Grandma Bran might call a "tizzy." He began shouting and waving his arms like a windmill. "I want you to know that I'm not going to be held responsible if you move that boy and something serious results!"

After making sure Hawk was safely seated, she turned to face him and stood like an oak tree in a hurricane under the onslaught of spittle and bad breath. Except for blinking once, she might have been made of granite.

Hawk sighed as he sank gratefully into the chair. "Thanks for getting me off the ground," he said. "My butt was beginning to freeze to the spot."

He turned and waved me closer. As I leaned down, he whispered in my ear, "Go along with me for the next few minutes, or we'll never get out of here." When I looked puzzled, he continued, "Don't worry. Jeff knows the routine, so, no matter what happens next, just go along with it, okay?"

I nodded, somewhat reluctantly. Now what? These two had more tricks up their sleeves than Thing One and Thing Two and were about as predictable.

"Control yourself!" Aunty Gin shouted and raised her arms, as if to throw a lightning bolt. The man took a step back. I must admit I was surprised such a big voice could come out of someone so small. And that stance—she resembled Mickey Mouse in *Fantasia*.

Suddenly, Hawk started crying and howling and clutching the arms of his chair. "I wanna go home," he wailed. "Please, please let me go home! I want my mom! I'm so-o-o cold! Please, *please* take me home, Aunty Gin. I want my *mommeeee*!" He thrashed around in the chair, alternately grabbing his head and stomach and grasping wildly for either Jeff or me. If this was an act, it was a darned good one. I could feel the hair stand up on my arms at the sad, high-pitched pleading in his voice.

Jeff stood beside the chair, stroked his brother's head, and looked intently at Aunty Gin. "Oh, please, Aunty, we need to get Stephen home *now,*" he implored, leaning down and covering his brother's body with his own. "It's two hours past his medication time, and you know what happens if he misses it!"

The man and Aunty Gin ceased their standoff and looked over at Hawk. Aunty Gin's face first registered confusion, then understanding. She stepped over to Hawk's chair and placed her hand on his forehead. "Oh, *Stephen!*" she said, in a perfect stage voice. "We've got to get you home *now.*"

Turning back to the man, she said simply, "My name is Virginia Atwood, in case you want to make note of it, and, as I've previously stated, I'm the children's aunt and guardian. I'd like to thank you for your concern, but now it's time to be taking my niece and nephews home. If you have a problem with that, you can call the police or the ambulance or the governor of Massachusetts for all I care!" And with that, she took hold of the Dune Buggy and started for the car, with Jeff running ahead to open up the back of the station wagon, and me opening a door for Hawk to get into the aged Chevy.

The man still stood there, looking like he wasn't sure what had just happened, as we pulled away from the curb.

I had to admit I was not so sure myself, until I realized Jeff, Hawk, and Aunty Gin were all laughing. Hawk tossed back and forth, snorting with glee. Jeff slapped both his and Hawk's knee in the backseat, and my aunt chuckled as she drove into the darkening afternoon. I sat next to her in the front, not getting the joke.

Aunty Gin said over her shoulder, "*Stephen* needs his medicine?" and they all laughed like she had just delivered the punch line to a hilarious joke.

"Clearly, I'm missing something," I began, as Jeff mimicked, "I miss my *mommy?*" and coughed into his hand.

Then she turned to me: "You know your Aunt Marsha and I don't usually approve of the twins' pranks and shenanigans," she said, "but sometimes their antics can prove helpful in a sticky situation." She tossed her head toward the place we had just left before focusing her attention back on the road.

The darkness was almost complete now and, but for a few leftover snickers from the backseat and the music playing on the radio, we rode in silence.

I watched as we passed by houses now twinkling with lighted windows in the gathering darkness and thought about what Aunty Gin had said about sticky situations—and when Jeff had said she was "unpredictable." Was she unstable? I looked over at her, and she turned and gave me a smile.

These questions began to form other questions, and suddenly I began to feel very unsure of where I fit in. After all, what did I really know about my aunts and cousins? Not much. And I was sure my mom and Frank knew even less. I stared ahead at the traffic coming toward us, the lights making funny shadows, first on the dashboard, then on us as we sped past. The three people in the car with me were like those shadows—appearing to be one thing one moment and something else the next.

Aunty Gin looked over at me again, as if reading my mind. "You know we're happy you've come to stay with us, don't you?"

"I guess so," I said.

"Well, we are. Aren't we, boys?" She lifted her chin so her voice could carry to the backseat of the station wagon.

"Yeah, sure," Hawk and Jeff both said, as if in stereo.

Aunty Gin negotiated a hairpin turn before continuing. "And if we all seem a bit strange, well, I guess it's because we are, somewhat. But we're a tight-knit group and whether you realize it or not, you are as much a part of this family as any of us." When I didn't reply, she asked, "Do you know anything about your dad's past? Or about the Atwood family?"

I had to admit that I didn't know much—just the few stories my mom had told me about when she and Dad first met.

"Well, sometime soon we'll have to have a nice chat, and Aunt Marsha and I can fill you in on the other branches of your family tree."

"Yeah, I'll bet there's a treasure hidden under those roots, too," this from Hawk.

I heard a light slap and some rustling, then, "Hey, quit elbowing me."

Aunty Gin called over her shoulder, "You two knock it off back there—none of that."

"He started it," came the reply from two different voices at once.

But I was thinking about the long, cold months that lay ahead, and Aunty Gin's comments about my not knowing my dad and his family, and the fact that Jeff and Hawk seemed to be able to communicate almost without talking.

Death. The dreadful voice I'd heard on my first day in Danvers broke into the middle of the song on the radio.

"*THE DEVIL hath been raised amongst us, and his Rage is vehement and terrible, and when he shall be silenced, the Lord only knows.*"

I looked at my aunt. Eyes on the road, she hummed a tune as if unaware of the strange pronouncement. Then, sensing that I was staring at her, glanced over at me.

"Something wrong?" She smiled.

"Did you just hear that?" I indicated the radio.

"Hear what? Oh, you mean the song—well it's an oldie, but I just can't help humming along."

I glanced into the backseat. The twins both had their iPods on. Hawk looked up and smiled, then went back to nodding to the music coming through his earbuds.

"Another golden oldie from James Taylor," the radio announcer chirped, as the soulful sound of a guitar filled the old station wagon and a gentle voice began to sing,

When you're down and troubled ...

And all at once I felt a hand on my shoulder, and a voice I hadn't heard for a very long time spoke the last line of the song directly into my ear:

You've got a friend.

Chapter Two

The thorny witch is in the wood. Cross
your fingers and be good!
—Norah Hussey, *The Wood Witch*

We didn't get a chance to look at the box hidden away in Hawk's backpack until after dinner and homework that evening. Aunty Gin examined Hawk when we got home and pronounced him fit. And after relating the entire incident to Aunt Marsha, they both proceeded to lecture us about responsibility, Jeff and me for the safety of getting Hawk home in one piece, and Hawk about personal responsibility and the liability of others.

"I don't get it," Jeff said later when we all had gathered in the room that he and Hawk shared. "Aunty Gin says for us not to let anything happen to Hawk, and then she yells at Hawk about being careful so we don't have to be responsible. So which is it?" Hawk sat on his bed, digging in his backpack. "Are we responsible for you or are you responsible for us?"

"Here it is," Hawk said, ignoring the question and tugging on the box that had become tightly wedged inside the pack. Pulling it loose, he laid it on the bedspread. Small clods of dried dirt fell in tiny sifting piles from the edges onto the powder blue bedcover. Without regard, Hawk brushed more from the top. "It has some sort of design on it," he said, leaning in for a closer look. Jeff plopped on the foot of the bed next to the box, causing even more dirt to loosen as he too peered closely at the lid.

I noticed it had a metal clasp held tight with a small padlock. I got on my knees by the side of the bed to examine it more closely.

"It's an elephant with a castle on top of it," Hawk said.

"There are letters, too." Jeff joined his brother in brushing away the dirt from the top.

"And there's a pretty sturdy padlock," I replied, tugging at the ancient rusted metal loop that held the clasp tightly closed against any intruders.

Jeff blew some soil into my face.

"Hey!" I jumped up.

"Look!" he exclaimed. "The letters spell out HMS BLESSING. Wonder what that means."

Hawk still scrubbed furiously at the top with the corner of his pillowcase.

"His Majesty's Service—Blessing. The *Blessing*. It's the name of a ship." He looked up, grinning.

"Ship?" Jeff said. "That box came from a ship? Let me see it." He picked it up and began to shake it. Specks of dirt and old wood flew in all directions but what held our attention was the sound of something rattling softly inside.

"Let's open it." He began to tug at the lock.

"Wait a minute," Hawk said. "November, hand me the toolbox from the bottom drawer of the desk." He motioned me toward the old battered roll-top against the wall next to the window. When I returned with the case, Hawk opened it and removed a small velvet drawstring bag. Inside the bag was a flat plastic case with several thin screwdriver-like tools with pointed ends.

He smiled up at my questioning face. "Lock picks," he said simply, choosing one and inserting it into the tiny keyhole. He worked it around for about thirty seconds, and then we heard a soft click and the lock released.

"Wow. I didn't know you knew how to use those," Jeff said, looking at his brother with admiration.

Hawk slowly lifted the latch. "Started practicing the day they arrived in the mail. What did you think? That I was just a poser?"

More caked dirt fell on the blue spread as he slowly lifted the lid, and we all leaned over to see what lay inside.

Taking up almost the entire space inside the box was a soft leather document-folder, tied round the middle with two narrow straps. Reaching in carefully, Hawk removed it, shaking off the carcass of a long-dead spider. The leather was the color of old blood and riddled with tiny cracks and creases, like wrinkles on an aged face.

Hawk began trying to untie the matching leather strips that were wound several times around the folder. They were knotted together over the front and the hardened leather refused to budge.

While Hawk patiently worked at the knot, I picked up the box. It was empty except for some strange-looking lines gouged into the bottom and a couple more fossilized bugs, which I shook out before tilting the box toward the light to get a better look. The lamplight revealed that the grooves dug deeply into the wood at the bottom of the box were actually crude letters. Moving closer to the lamp, I held the box just beneath it and read them out loud.

"R–A–C–E."

Jeff looked up. "What'd you say?"

"That's what's carved into the bottom." I handed the box over to him, and he held it up above the lamp to capture more light from the 75-watt bulb.

"You're right," he said, lowering the box, as Hawk still struggled very gingerly with the ties on the binder.

"Well, Mr. Wikipedia, what does R–A–C–E stand for?"

Hawk stopped picking at the ties for a moment and thought. "I don't know." He shrugged. "Race?"

"Oh, thank you, oh, great one!" Jeff bowed low. "That was truly awesome, oh, head of great knowledge."

"Shut up, weirdo." Hawk went back to work. "I'll try to figure it out later. Right now I'm … it's starting to come loose!" His fingers worked more quickly now as the old leather started to give way. "Here we go." Hawk pulled the ties free and started unwinding them.

"Hurry up," Jeff urged. "You're not opening a birthday present."

Hawk lifted his head, as if to give a snappy comeback, but his face froze along with the rest of his body as he looked over my shoulder.

Jeff and I spun around.

"Whoa!" both boys said at once.

I stood staring, as if my eyes were playing tricks on me. I had not seen this figure since I was a small child, and when I'd heard him repeat the last line of the song from the radio that evening, I'd dismissed it as just my imagination. But now …

I turned back. Jeff had leaped across the room to where Hawk sat on the bed. I pointed to the little man standing in front of the closet door. "You can see him?" Before they could answer, he spoke.

"They can see me, November. Think back. When you were just a wee child, you asked me once if I was real? Do you recall my answer?"

"As real as the moment I am in," I replied softly. It had been a long time since I had heard that phrase.

"Well, it's as true now as it was then—maybe more so." He nodded toward Jeff and Hawk, who now sat side by side, like a couple of bookends on a very dirty shelf. "Would you like to introduce me to your companions?" he inquired politely, as he picked an invisible speck from his pale blue coat.

"You really can see him?" I asked my cousins again, just to make sure. Two identical dark blond heads nodded in unison. "Okay, then," I said, extending my right arm toward the bed.

"I'd like to introduce my cousins, Jeff and Hawk Atwood." I turned back to the figure standing just inside the closet door. "Jeff and Hawk, meet Dynnis, my imaginary friend."

Chapter Three

Who goes there through the open-crack door, sliding without a sound across the carpeted floor?

—Robert Fisher, *Hallowe'en Fright*

Hawk gathered himself enough to say, "Your what?"

"Very pleased to make your acquaintance, young sirs." Dynnis gave a slight bow.

It was no wonder they were both speechless. Dynnis did make an unusual picture, standing there outlined against the closet door, not yet fully materialized. I could almost make out the wooden panels through his figure. But I somehow doubted that was what had my cousins spellbound. It was more likely the fact that Dynnis looked something like a troll.

He was about three feet tall. He liked to say he stood a full meter, but I had my doubts. He had a small, pointed, rosy-cheeked face, dominated by big liquid-brown eyes encircled with several layers of wrinkly, leathery skin. His hair was … well, it was troll hair, just like the troll dolls you see in stores, except that Dynnis' hair wasn't a bright pastel color. Pure white, it stuck out and flew up from his head like it was electrically charged, then fell to just below his shoulders. The same fly-away hair was on the backs of his hands and in his very bushy white eyebrows. He was also what he liked to refer to as "portly," with a protruding potbelly, knobby knees, and somewhat bowed legs.

But his most outstanding feature had to be his hat. It was almost as tall as he was and was as red as a freshly picked apple. It was made of flannel or a soft material, molded around a long cone that fit snugly around his head and ended in a point at the top.

The first time I saw him I thought some little kid in our neighborhood was playing a trick on me. But as soon as he opened his mouth, I realized no kid that I knew would be capable of knowing, much less doing, some of the things he could do. And then, there was his unsettling habit of suddenly popping up when and where I least expected.

My parents had tried to convince me that Dynnis wasn't real. At first they went along with my tales and descriptions of him. They even set a place for him at the table, which was really his idea, and they never could figure out where the food went that I insisted they put on a plate for him. After a while, they got tired of the game and began to talk about my growing up and how I needed to have real friends and stop this nonsense.

But Dynnis helped me through a pretty bad time. He appeared not long before my dad died, and he stayed with me through many long, dark nights when I couldn't sleep because I could hear my mom crying in the next room.

He told me stories about my dad as a boy, and he answered hard questions that I couldn't ask my mom, or anyone else, for that matter. He was even okay with the times I was so sad I couldn't even cry.

"Tears will fall when your heart is full," he said; and then he told me the story of the night I was born. It had been unusually hot that September, even for Phoenix, but the night winds blew clear and dry and cool. At eight minutes past eight, just as I came kicking and screaming into the world, the blue star Eltanin, in the constellation Libra, exploded like a fireball across the star-struck sky. It was the eighth sign and eighth constellation from the vernal equinox. According to Dynnis, when the sun enters the sign of Libra, days and nights are equal all over the world.

Almost immediately after I was born, my dad hiked to the top of Papago Buttes, a rocky hill outcropping just outside the Phoenix city limits, and lit a candle beneath the brilliant heavens.

As he told the story, Dynnis sat in the small rocking chair at the foot of my bed. I lay on my back, staring up through the tears that filled my eyes and spilled down both sides of my face, as he began to sing a song he said was from long, long ago, in the land where his people came from. The strange thing was, his song was accompanied by a flute. I never saw him do anything but rock and sing as I fell sleep, but the music was there, just the same. I remember the last thing I saw before closing my eyes that night was Dynnis, sitting and rocking, rocking and singing—an imaginary man singing to music that wasn't there.

Not long after I turned nine, he stopped coming around. One day I realized I hadn't seen him in a while, but I was busy with music lessons, traveling, and friends. I had gotten on with my life, and Dynnis was gone. Until today.

I looked at the small, round figure materializing right before my eyes. He was dressed in dark brown pants that puffed out at the top, then tapered to fit snugly just above his brown-stockinged knees. His snowy white dress shirt with long, loose sleeves was topped by a robin's egg blue jacket with embroidered pictures of various fish. He wore dove gray boots made of fur. And of course, there were the rings; each finger sported a different kind, some gold and very ornate, and others, simple silver or gold bands. As I watched him take solid form, I suddenly realized how much I had missed him.

Jeff found his voice first. "You're really November's imaginary friend?" He sat stock still on the bed, holding onto the headboard as if at any moment the bed was going to float out the window and keep on going right down and into the sea.

Dynnis nodded. "Well, I suppose you could call me that. But are you imagining me? In which case, I'm your imaginary friend, too."

I saw Hawk's eyes narrow. "Well, if we're all hallucinating, then you could be appearing to all of us at the same time."

"Ah, ever the scientist, eh, Stephen?" Hawk's face showed surprise at the use of his first name. "Well, you might be right about that." Dynnis walked over to the roll-top desk and picked up a Lucite paperweight with a scorpion in the center. He threw it into the air and caught it with his other hand. "On the other hand," he said, hooking it to Jeff, who caught it just before it hit him squarely on the nose, "events that you perceive as being *real* might just be shadows, whereas those things you can only witness as imaginary are startlingly real." At that, Dynnis dissolved, and two things happened at once. Hawk lifted off the foot of the bed and floated across the room, landing gently in his chair—and Dynnis reappeared in front of it.

My cousins exchanged stunned looks.

"Dynnis, why are you here now?" I was used to tricks. I had seen him do much more.

He walked over to the bed and picked up the folder Hawk had dropped. "I'm afraid you've set a series of events in motion by finding this ..." He held up the folder and then tossed it into the box I'd placed on the desk. "... events that cannot be easily stopped and that perhaps should not be stopped at all."

"I don't understand," I said.

"Nor do I. Not fully," Dynnis answered. "But the very fact that I am here is an indication that something is starting to gather around you." He looked pointedly at the three of us. "All of you." His normally crinkly, happy troll face had taken on an expression I had never seen before—a mixture of fear and uncertainty. "You are being surrounded by a vapor of darkness, November, much darker than the last time I came to you. I do not mean to alarm either you or your cousins, but unless we can discover what is at the heart of the events that are about to unfold, I'm afraid you are all in for a pretty rough ride."

Jeff and Hawk exchange a look I couldn't decipher; then Hawk spoke. "So what is it you think we should do?"

Dynnis walked to the table, picked up the box, then turned to Hawk. "I suppose we had best begin by discovering what is in the folder."

Chapter Four

Riddle me; riddle me, what is that, over
your head and under your hat?
—Robert Fisher, *The Old Woman of Riddles*

We all crowded around the Dune Buggy as Hawk slowly opened the leather folder and took out a stiff, yellow brown piece of paper. It had been folded in fourths, and it crackled with age as he spread it across his lap.

"Vellum. Paper made from sheep's skin. Important documents were written on it long ago." Hawk held it up, and Jeff took hold of the wheelchair handles, moving his brother closer to the only lamp in the room.

Hawk leaned over the desk and unfolded it carefully. "It's in pretty good shape, considering how old it is." With his nose to the document, Hawk began to read, first silently and then aloud. "The handwriting is really awful, but I'll do my best. It says:

'Three Seals, the three Echoes and the New City,
To three stones
(where'er hid, scattered and dispersed),
To be gathered by He who has the Foundation Stone,
Who is elected in secret for the New City.'"

Hawk stopped reading and looked up. We all shrugged and he continued:

"When the Moon of Storms is risen,
To lead you out of your bed and into the darkness,

Where the Sprites keep their Strong Hold,
Binding and putting out the eyes of those
Who try to take their treasure,

"Be mindful!
Such are the subtle wiles of them
That steal and draw away the minds of anyone they seize,
And seduce them,
So that they cannot get up and shake off the earthly dust.

"One square stone inlaid on the great Foundation Stone
Will give forth a luster,
As if so many bright Suns had been there,
And will light the way
To the path of the other two.

"Because the three stones are at present,
Lying amongst the Rubbish of Confusion,
Who in due time are to be linked together,
You will need to keep close counsel
As to your whereabouts during Hollantide.

"One does not venture abroad on Hollantide,
If one is Wise."

Hawk stopped reading and sat back.

"Weird. Is that all there is?" Jeff said.

"No, there's more, but the writing is so cramped that it's killing my eyes." Hawk ground his eye sockets with the knuckles of each hand.

I leaned over his shoulder and continued:

"Lying 'neath the ..."

"The letters that look like long "F's" are really "S's," Hawk supplied, still with his eyes closed.

"Hill of Hathorne,
Under the protection of Our Lord,
Is the answer to the way
To that which has been carried
To the New City at great peril.

"Go beneath the stones of Hathorne,
On the Eve of Hollantide,
And retrieve the Looking Glass of All Mysteries.
For under its seal,
Lies the door to eternity."

Hawk was right. The scribble was so crabbed that I could barely make it out, and those archaic letters were maddening. I continued, "It ends with:

'Signed and sealed this Eleventh Day of November
In the second year of the reign of our Sovereign
King William III.'"

I stopped and looked up. "I can't make out the signature, and there's a blob of dark red."

"Sealing wax," Hawk supplied, sitting up and wheeling himself toward his dresser, where he reached up and took down a slim notebook computer.

"What's Hollantide?" Jeff asked Dynnis, who was pacing back and forth, from the door to the window, pulling on his beard. He spun around and faced us:

"Autumn's gone and winter's come,
'Tis Hollantide, old Hollantide.
Tonight the witches' magic brooms bestride,
And goblins, dwarfs and elves with glee
Will dance around the chimneyside."

When none of us responded, he walked to the bed and hefted himself onto it, bouncing up and down a bit on the soft mattress. His feet didn't touch the floor, and he looked like a child in a Halloween costume who couldn't wait to go trick-or-treating.

"Hollantide," he finished, "is All Hallow's Day."

Jeff asked, "You mean like Halloween? But the paper said November 11th; Halloween's on October 31st."

"It says here," Hawk looked up from his laptop, "that on old Hollantide Eve, the eleventh of November, it is believed that magical beings roam at night. It's also called 'Troll Night' on the Isle of Man."

The laptop was Hawk's most prized possession. He had won it in a trivia contest sponsored by the local mall last summer. Aunty Gin bought him a wireless router and, with Jeff's help, they had configured it to locate any Wi-Fi signal up to three miles away.

"Also, by my calculations, the eleventh year of William III was 1700." He continued as his fingers flew over the keys.

Dynnis shook his head at the computer. "Those gadgets never cease to amaze me. But you're right, Hawk, on both counts. Old Hollantide was a merry time indeed and was celebrated on November 11th, the last night of the Celtic year, with a festival. In the Isle of Man, it was known as Hollantide Eve or Hop-tu-Naa. Boys went from house to house, knocking at all the doors with turnips or cabbages on sticks, singing a special song, until they were given potatoes, or herring, or bannocks. And then there were the dumb cakes."

"Dumb cakes?" I asked.

"Dumb cakes were baked and eaten in silence by young ladies on Hollantide Eve," Dynnis explained, and Jeff gave a loud snort. "It was made from flour and water," Dynnis continued, as if he hadn't heard him, "without leaven, and baked in hot turf ashes. A piece was to be eaten while walking backward toward the bed. The young lady's future husband was supposed to appear in her dreams that night."

Jeff couldn't contain himself any longer. "Hawk, quick! Google the recipe; it's already the eighth, and November's very future may depend on it! We don't want her to be a dried-up old maid!" He fell back against the bed, totally enjoying himself and jostling Dynnis to the floor.

I shot him a hard look and turned my attention back to Dynnis.

"While going from door to door, the boys would sing out, 'Trolla-laa,' which means 'Troll Night.'" Dynnis walked over to where Hawk was busily punching keys. "You're correct on your other point, too, Hawk. 1700 would have been the eleventh year of the reign of William III, King of England, Scotland, and Ireland. But I am afraid it is not the year that has me concerned." He walked back to the middle of the room and stopped for a moment, deep in thought. "It is the date itself. I am not at all sure I like the fact that this *Looking Glass of Mysteries* is to be retrieved on Hollantide."

"Because of the trolls?" Hawk asked.

"Is that why you know so much about Hollantide?" Jeff added. "Because *you're* a troll?"

In all the time I had known Dynnis, I'd never seen the look he now turned on Jeff. His eyes widened to double their size, and his cheeks turned the color of hot cinders. Taking a deep breath, hands in balled fists at his side, he grew to his full height. Although he only came up to my chin, hat and all, he was such a forbidding-looking character at that moment that I took a step back and Hawk, looking up from the computer screen, froze.

"Young—and I *do not* mean that word as a compliment—man, *never*—and I mean *never*—call me that *again,*" he hissed through his teeth as he advanced toward Jeff, who quickly retreated up onto the bed and against the wall. "I am a *gnome.* And for your information, there is a *big* difference between a troll and a gnome. Let me demonstrate." He raised his left hand and extended his first and second fingers toward Jeff.

"Dynnis, no!" I shouted. I wasn't sure what he was capable of since I had never seen him so mad before, but I didn't want him taking out his anger on my cousin—especially since all along, I'd thought he was a troll, too.

But I was too late. A light emanating from his fingers traveled in a straight line to the bed. In less time than it takes to gasp, a creature as large as Jeff sat on the bed next to him, breathing, belching, and scratching himself in several unsavory places.

He had long, skinny arms and legs, big bare feet, a prominent nose, long ears, and a long, hairy, untidy tail that fell onto the floor. But what really stood out about him was the smell. He reeked of unwashed flesh and hair, and when he opened his mouth, I could have sworn I saw a cloud of stink swirl out from between his green teeth.

Chapter Five

Troll sat alone on his seat of stone, and munched and mumbled a bare old bone.

—JRR Tolkien

JEFF LEAPED OFF THE BED AND HEADED toward the door as the thing reached out for him.

"Dynnis!" I shouted. "Get rid of it!"

Just as quickly as he had erupted, Dynnis deflated like a blow-up toy that had lost its plug. He snapped his fingers three times and the thing disappeared with a loud pop, like a bursting balloon. He stood for a moment, shoulders sagging, looking at the floor, then straightened and turned to where Jeff and I stood by the door.

"I apologize for that outburst, Jeffery," he tucked his hands behind his back and looked sheepish. "I do not know what got into me. It is just that trolls are so … so … well, they stink and have no manners. They are also incredibly stupid. To be mistaken for one is the worst insult you can throw at a gnome. But that creature I conjured just a moment ago could not have hurt you. I'm afraid my powers extend only to conjuring up three-dimensional images of things."

"But that smell," I said.

"Oh, that was just power of suggestion I threw in for good measure." He gave me a weak smile.

"Dude, that was really freaky!" Jeff said, sagging against the door with his hand still on the knob. "That thing was just like the creature I'm fighting in World of Warcraft." He looked at Dynnis for a split second before continuing. "*Just* like the creature."

Dynnis looked properly repentant. "Actually, it was the same creature." He shrugged his shoulders. "I simply took it from your memory bank."

"Awesome," Hawk said, in reverence.

Jeff moved away from the door then. "Sorry. Didn't mean to insult you."

"Well, if you will forgive me, I will forgive you." Dynnis brushed his hands together briskly. "Anyway, no harm done. You see, the difference between trolls and gnomes goes far beyond just mere appearance and ... well ... hygiene." He cleared his throat. "Over the last several hundred years, we have been pretty much forgotten by humans, except in stories and fairy tales. But some of our ancestries go so far back that our families are still connected to those humans we had been close to in the far distant past." Dynnis paused. "Such is the case with us, November," he said, and then looked at Jeff and Hawk. "And with both of you, too. My family, the Bartholomews, and your ancestors, the Atwoods, have a very special tie. I haven't time to go into it here, but one day I will explain how we were given guardianship of the Children of Avnova." He looked back at me.

"It is why I came to you just before your father passed on, and it is why I am here now. But we need to focus on the task at hand." He nodded at the box and the documents laid out on the desk.

"Any idea what it means?" Hawk looked over his shoulder.

Dynnis stepped forward pursing his lips as he leaned over the document. "'Neath the Hill of Hathorne' is a direct reference to John Hathorne, one of the judges of Salem Village. 'Neath the hill' would most likely be beneath the hill on which his house stood."

"Stood?" I asked. "As in, it doesn't stand anymore?"

"Precisely," Dynnis answered. "Judge Hathorne's house was torn down sometime in the mid-eighteenth century."

"So what does that mean?" Hawk asked. "Can you decipher what the letter says?"

Dynnis frowned and squinted at the faded writing again. "Well, I am not very good with your written language, but from what I heard read aloud, this is a message to someone regarding something of extreme value that has been hidden."

"You mean, like a treasure?" Jeff asked.

"Yes, I suppose it would be by now—and a buried one, at that."

The three of us exchanged glances.

"So where are we supposed to look for it?" Jeff asked.

"Well, as I said, the judge's house once stood on Hathorne Hill," Dynnis answered. "But it was torn down—"

"Hathorne Hill?" Hawk interrupted. "But that's where—"

"The old insane asylum is," Jeff finished, his eyes widening.

"You mean that insane asylum we go by on our way to school?" I asked. A shiver snaked its way down the middle of my back, as Dynnis, Jeff, and Hawk all nodded like so many bobble-head dolls standing in a row.

"Well, that ends it." I folded my arms. "There is no way I'm going into that old building at all—especially not to dig up something buried underneath it."

Dynnis picked up the box and removed the dark red folder. Tipping it upside down, he shook it gently. A gold-colored disk fell out and plunked heavily on the floor.

Jeff picked it up. "What's this?" He examined it closely. "Looks like some kind of coin."

"Let me see." Hawk held out his hand, and Jeff gave it over. "1675," Hawk read. He bounced it in his palm. "It's heavy. Feels like gold."

"It is," Dynnis said. "It's a guinea, an English coin,"—he put out his stubby palm and Hawk dropped the coin into it—"and if I'm not mistaken, it is from the reign of Charles II of England."

"Is that what the letter is trying to say?" Jeff asked. "That there are more of those coins buried?"

"I think there is more to it than just that," Dynnis said, handing the coin to me. "Although these coins are very valuable—probably worth a fortune in your currency—there is something even more valuable hidden under the stones of Hathorne."

I gave the coin back to Dynnis, and he put it into the folder, along with the carefully refolded document; then he put both inside the box and returned it to the desk.

"The treasure the document speaks of is far more important than mere gold coins." Dynnis went to the window and gazed out into the night. "It is something that has been guarded jealously for over three hundred years and which will not be given up easily. The guardians of this treasure know you have found the message, and they now know you are the ones who must right the wrongs that were done all those years ago."

"You mean *we* have to find the buried treasure?" Jeff asked, and I heard Hawk sigh.

"But that means we have to go beneath—" I started.

"Exactly," Hawk finished. "It means we have to go under the Danvers Insane Asylum."

A sudden knock at the door made all of us jump.

"Just me," Aunt Marsha said, poking her head in. "You three need to be getting ready for bed. It's after 10:30. Tomorrow is a school day." She looked across the room, her eyes widening. "Why is that window open? You're letting the heat out."

The three of us turned toward the window. The curtains waved out into the cold autumn night—and Dynnis was gone.

Chapter Six

The Witch! The Witch! Don't let her get you! Or your aunt wouldn't know you the next time she met you!

—Eleanor Farjeon, *The Witch! The Witch!*

THE NEXT MORNING WAS OVERCAST AND BITTERLY damp. As we rounded the corner onto Hazen Avenue, the towers of the Danvers State Asylum rose dark and empty-eyed on the hill under a bank of charcoal clouds that billowed and scudded across the sky, like angry goblins circling the sharp rooflines. I zipped the collar of my parka tighter under my chin and noticed Hawk pulling on his gloves.

Jeff slid on patches of black ice, the worn-smooth soles of his sneakers allowing him to skid long sections of the walk with his back to the asylum. He seemed to be purposefully avoiding looking at it.

"There it is," Hawk said unnecessarily, but neither Jeff nor I made comment. We finished the rest of the walk to school in silence, each of us in our own thoughts. Most of the way was uphill, and this morning's cold was making it especially treacherous. Several times, the motor on Hawk's chair revved as it struggled up the steep, icy grade, and either Jeff or I had to steady it without losing our own footing. When we had almost reached the top of the hill, I stopped and looked back. It was as if the old asylum watched us, or maybe something inside the long-abandoned institution was standing in the dark, deserted halls, watching three figures make their way along a quiet road in the early morning mist.

***

The library was a warm, brightly lit haven after the long walk through the dark morning. It was almost empty, too, with just a few kids either milling through the book aisles or sitting at the computer carousel, typing last night's assignments.

My cousins and I found a spot in the far corner near two tall windows, the dark sashes of which framed the menacing sky like spectacles over puffy, bruised eyes. We threw our packs on the table and sat. Jeff picked at a thumbnail, and I looked around the library, as if I had never seen it before.

"We have to figure out what to do," Hawk said at last.

"About what?" Jeff's voice was a monotone.

Hawk sighed and slumped in his chair. "About everything—about last night. About the box and *The Vellum*." He leaned forward over the table at Jeff. "Denial is not an option here." He turned to me. "And we all know it."

Jeff shifted uneasily in his chair, and I said, "So where do we start?"

"I was hoping you'd tell us, Em," Hawk said. "I mean, you know Dynnis better than we do."

Jeff nodded agreement.

Now it was my turn to sigh. "You know, all those years ago when Dynnis showed up, he never acted like he is now. I don't know; I mean, maybe he did and I was too little to notice or understand." I picked up a mechanical pencil just to have something to do with my hands. "Look," I said with a shrug, "I really don't know any more about him than you guys do. I wish I did."

Jeff still had not said more than two words since we left the house. Now, he got up and walked to the windows. He stood very still, hands in his pockets, gazing at the rain that had begun to fall, the way you might watch fish in a tank. After a few moments, he returned to the table. "Do you have the box with you?" At Hawk's nod, he sat back down.

"Why?" Hawk asked.

"Just didn't want Mom or Aunty Gin finding it is all." He slumped down in the seat, hanging his head. Then he looked up. "Look, you guys, this is really creeping me out." He sat up straight. "If what Dynnis said is true—if Dynnis is real and not some … some group halloo …"

"Hallucination," Hawk finished.

"Yeah, that," Jeff continued, leaning forward on his forearms. "If all he said is true, then this … power or whatever is guarding some secret treasure, and *we're* meant to go get it." He leaned back, hugging himself like he was cold.

"Well," Hawk said, "whether that's the case or not, I think we'd better have another look at the manuscript." He took his backpack off the handles of the Buggy.

"Here?" I asked, glancing around the room. "Isn't that a little bit risky? I mean, it's a great big piece of old parchment—"

"Vellum," Hawk corrected.

"Whatever. It's big and crackly—and it's bound to attract attention with us poring over it."

Hawk looked around the library and then out at the rain. "So what do you suggest? We can't exactly leave school and sit in the grass. And would we be any less suspect if Mom or Aunty Gin came in our room while we're trying to decipher it?" He plopped the pack on the table and started digging through it.

"He's got a point," Jeff put in. "I mean, Aunty Gin's like a hound dog when she's on a scent."

"Besides," Hawk continued, with a superior smile. "Jeff here is going to go tell the librarians that we're working on an old document for our mom's family reunion in Boston next summer. That ought to keep them at bay for a while."

Jeff took a lung full of air as if about to protest but expelled it and then said, "Oh, all right—I guess that'll work. Anyway," he said, brightening, "I'm always pretty good at getting ol' Mrs. Ritter to do things for me. She thinks she's keeping me from becoming some kind of dropout criminal or something, since we 'don't have a father figure' in our lives," he intoned, in a pretty good imitation of the librarian's deep British accent; then he grinned wickedly. "Last month she did all my research for that Greek mythology thing Ms. Bird gave us and then practically typed the whole thing for me, too!" He laughed out loud, and the library aide looked up from her computer desk and frowned.

"Well, you'd better not talk too loudly, or you'll blow a good thing," I said, laughing along with him.

Hawk busied himself, spreading out the stiff vellum across the study table, as his twin headed toward Mrs. Ritter's desk.

He had brought along a magnifying glass, two mechanical pencils, and a yellow legal pad, which he laid alongside the document.

By the time Jeff returned, Hawk had slowly made his way through the tight script, and I was busy taking notes. We decided that Jeff's job would be to research those things we had never heard of or did not know the meaning of. From role-playing games, he had developed an extensive knowledge of databases concerning historical names and places. We were so engrossed in our tasks that we were surprised when the first bell sounded, warning we had five minutes to get to class.

"Let's go," I said, grabbing the pencils and notes and shoving them into Hawk's pack.

"Just one second more." Hawk continued to squint at the document. "Look here." He pointed to a tiny symbol drawn about a third of the way down the page. I leaned over to get a better look.

It was a circle within a circle that contained fourteen symbols on the outer edge. The center held three other more elaborate symbols.

"What do you suppose it is?" I asked.

"Looks like a map." Jeff had come back to the table and leaned over the indenture. "See, there are two different paths." He pointed to the top and bottom figures in the middle of the circle. "The top symbol has one starting point and three ending points. The bottom has one starting point, and then it kind of curves around, and X marks the spot." He looked up as if it was the most obvious thing in the world.

"Then what's the middle figure supposed to be? And why would you have two starting points?" Hawk asked.

"How should I know?" Jeff grabbed his pack, just as the warning bell rang. "Guess that's for us to figure out." He spun on his heels and headed for the door. "Later," he called over his shoulder. Clearly, he had gotten over his earlier mood.

I glanced at the windows as I helped Hawk stow the document and the other things. The sky had lightened, and the sun was beginning to peek from behind the clouds.

Hawk wheeled toward the doors of the library. "You know, that lunkhead just might be right," he mused. "And if he is, then we've got ourselves a map to a treasure." He smiled up at me and then pushed harder on the wheels of the Dune Buggy. "See you in fifth hour, November."

As I left the library I thought about what Jeff had said. Could the symbol really be a map? We wouldn't know for sure until we had deciphered the document. And where had Dynnis gone? Neither Jeff nor Hawk had mentioned his disappearance. He said he had come here for a purpose that involved all three of us and maybe even my aunts, too. But what was it?

The sun retreated behind the clouds again, and it started to sleet. I lowered my head and hurried to my first-hour class. As I rounded the last building and started toward the classroom door, I noticed a flash of red behind the soda machine. I stopped, and a small bearded face appeared for just an instant before a kid stumbled into me, pushing me toward the door—but not before I saw Dynnis give me a merry wink.

Chapter Seven

Into the houses hustle and run. Here is mischief and
here is fun! Break the china and slam the doors.
Crack the windows and scratch the floors.

—Ruth Bedford, *The Witch's Song*

My cousins and I had only one class together, fifth-hour math, but we usually sat together in the cafeteria. Jeff and I each grabbed extra stuff for Hawk, who normally insisted on going through the line himself. But today he was busily going over my notes. We didn't dare try to bring out *The Vellum* during lunch. The tables were crowded, and it was so noisy that we would not have been able to even hear each other, much less have any space to write where it was safe or clean enough.

I was just putting my tray down and handing Hawk a baloney sandwich that had known better times when Josh Bixler, the most obnoxious of the football jocks, reached over and grabbed the papers from Hawk's hands.

"What have we here, nerds?" He held them high as if to read them aloud to the grinning faces crowded tightly together up and down the long portable tables. Several people hooted, and Tommy Camburn, who was usually joined at the hip with Bixler, said, "A love letter from Mrs. Ritter, maybe?" and everybody laughed. "Always heard she was partial to twins," he sneered.

"Give them back," said Jeff, in a level voice, coming up behind them with his tray.

Bixler looked around, as several people said, "Oooooo."

"Well, well," he said, holding the papers higher, "if it isn't little Jeffrey Atwood, the junior varsity wannabe. What's the matter? You don't want me to read all the juicy details of your love affair with Mrs. Prune Face to the rest of your friends?"

Several people laughed aloud as Jeff carefully put his tray down, then turned to face Josh. I could tell by Jeff's face that this was not going to end well. Hawk said, "Give them back, Bixler. They're just notes."

"Oh, I just bet they are." Josh was clearly playing to the crowd now. "Like, love notes? Dirty little words you and the librarian whisper to each other in the book stacks? Or, I know; these are notes about the positions—"

"I'll take those." Mr. Roth snapped the papers from Bixler's hand as he waved them over his head. He had come up behind Josh and was now standing there with one jet black eyebrow raised, his mouth set in a grim line. "Still having trouble with the concept of sharing, Mr. Bixler? I thought even you would have mastered that skill by now. Perhaps you should go back to kindergarten and learn your manners from the ground up." He tilted his head back and looked down his long straight nose at the eighth-grader.

Several snickers could be heard up and down the table. When he turned, Josh Bixler had a worm's-eye view of Mr. Roth's nostrils because, even though Josh was one of the biggest kids in the school, he had to look up at the math teacher, who was easily the tallest man on campus, maybe even in the whole town. Mr. Roth loomed over his classes. Built like a powerhouse, he had blue black hair, worn short enough so he needn't worry about brushing it, and matching black eyes so dark you couldn't see the pupils. When he looked at you, it was like he was seeing into your soul. The kids called it his "laser scan."

Mr. Roth was one of the few teachers at Putnam Middle School who never had to send anyone to the office. No one, not even the likes of Josh Bixler, ever defied his authority. He was giving Josh one of the *lasers* now. "I believe some grass drills are in order for this afternoon,"—Roth leaned forward, his voice a near whisper, his face inches from Josh's—"since you have so much … energy." Bixler collapsed into his seat with a groan. "What did you say? I didn't catch that." Mr. Roth raised both eyebrows but not his voice. You could have heard a cotton ball drop in the cafeteria now.

"Yes, coach," he mumbled.

"What?" Roth said louder.

"Yes, coach, sir," Bixler said, louder, staring straight ahead, as if at attention.

Mr. Roth seemed satisfied with the response and looked down at the papers. He shuffled through them, quickly scanning each until he came to the last page where he paused, looked up at Hawk, Jeff, and me for a long moment, then folded them and put them inside his sport-coat pocket.

Just then, the bell rang, and everyone jumped to their feet. Josh Bixler got up slowly, looking over his shoulder at the teacher. With a nod from Mr. Roth, he grabbed up his tray with one hand, his backpack with the other, and beat it, with Tommy Camburn close on his heels.

Over the din of metal chairs being pushed out, trays being slammed onto countertops, and all the chatter, Mr. Roth's voice carried clearly to the three of us. "I will return these to you after class today." Without another word, he turned and headed out of the cafeteria.

***

Mr. Roth made no mention of the notes during algebra class that day, but he seemed to be preoccupied through the entire lesson. Once, while writing a long equation, he stopped and looked out the frosted windows, like he had been struck with an idea; then he finished the equation as if he had never paused. And several times as he let us work the problems out at our desks, I caught him staring at either Hawk, Jeff, or me. He wasn't giving us the laser scan or anything; he just sat at his desk with his fingers together in a point in front of his lips, as if we were unique specimens on display. Even when I caught him staring, he did not look away.

After the bell, as the others gathered up their things and headed out of the classroom, Mr. Roth motioned for the three of us to stay behind. He came around in front of his desk and leaned back on his hands against the edge. "I took the liberty of looking at your notes," he began, and when none of us responded, he continued. "Looks like some kind of research."

After a moment, Hawk said, "It is."

Mr. Roth nodded. "Mind telling me what you're researching? Is it for a class assignment? Another teacher, perhaps?" He seemed oddly nervous—or maybe anxious was a better word.

"Well, no, we just found an old—"

"We just found an old story about some big old house that looks a lot like ours," Hawk interrupted Jeff.

Mr. Roth looked first at one twin and then the other. "I see." He nodded his head slowly, once. "I just have one more question," he said, standing up and walking back behind the desk, where he opened a drawer and took out the folded yellow papers. He flipped to the last page and pointed to the sketch of the circles with the symbols I had copied from The Vellum. "Can you tell me where you found this?"

Jeff stood with his mouth open like a landed trout; Hawk licked his lips like he, too, needed water.

"I dreamed it," I said, and the black eyes zeroed in on me.

"Indeed."

"Yes … uh, yes. I had a dream about a person getting a tattoo with an ancient symbol on it, and when I woke up I just … got up and wrote it down … drew it, I mean … so that I could show it to my cousins." I held up my hands and shrugged my shoulders. "Thought it might be a good thing to try painting in art class." I smiled my most disarming smile; the one my stepdad always calls my "high-wattage."

Mr. Roth seemed to consider my explanation for a moment. "I see. It is a very interesting figure—almost a mathematical drawing, really." He seemed about to say something else, then changed his mind. "Well. Thank you for sharing that with me. You can take your notes. You're free to go." He turned back to the chalkboard. "Good luck with your … research," he said to our retreating backs.

The hall was deserted as we made our way down the long corridor.

"I wonder what that was all about," Jeff said, as we reached the end, and he shoved open the doors to the next one, holding them so I could push Hawk through. "Do you think that symbol is a math symbol, like Roth said, and do you think he knows what it means?"

"Oh, I am sure he does," said a familiar voice on the other side the door. Hawk and I went through, with Jeff close behind. There stood Dynnis in the deserted hall, leaning against the water fountain with his arms crossed. "And so do others." His smile was grim. "My friends, I am afraid it has begun."

Chapter Eight

I dare you to spy through the dust on his window pane. They say those who dare to enter his lair have never been seen again.

—Gareth Owen, *The Alchemist*

An icy-hot jolt ran down both of my arms and the middle of my back simultaneously.

"It's begun?" Hawk repeated.

Dynnis stood straight and nodded. "Things are starting to move into place, and events will undoubtedly begin to pick up speed in a short period of time."

"You know, you talk in riddles most of the time," Jeff said impatiently. "Why can't you just tell us what's going to happen, and then we can figure out how to deal with it."

I looked at Jeff in surprise. At times, he could be surprisingly rational and to the point.

Dynnis picked at a speck on his trousers. "Well, to begin with, I do not know what is going to happen. I only get a sense of things." He scanned the hallway for a moment, as if searching for inspiration. "In a way, it is like seeing someone's shadow coming toward you. You know that it is a person, you know he is bigger or smaller than you, but you cannot really tell who he is or what he intends. It is like that with me." He stuck his hands behind his back and rocked back on his heels, which by now I knew to be a sign that he was trying very hard not to show us how unsure he was. "I can see shadows but not the clear picture." He looked at us solemnly. "I only know that powerful forces are at work here and that by opening that box, you have also opened the door to a path that must be traveled—and it must be traveled by you." Dynnis nodded at the three of us as we stood just inside the open doorway to the west hall of Putnam Middle School.

"So what should we do?" I asked.

"Well, I think you should begin by going back to the tree where you unearthed the box. I have the distinct feeling that you didn't find everything that is buried there."

"Oh, great," Jeff said. "And old man Whoozi-What's is going to come tearing out the door to invite us in for cookies and hot chocolate when he sees that we're back, digging around his tree."

"I agree with Jeff. I don't think it's such a good idea," I put in.

"We have to," Hawk said. "Dynnis is right. Besides, I'm not sure we got everything either. And one of us can be the lookout for Mr. … what *is* his name, anyway?"

We all shrugged.

"Okay, then," Jeff clapped his hands in a sudden shift of mood. "What we need is a plan."

Hawk and I glanced toward each other. This ought to be good.

On the way back to the house at the bottom of the hill, Jeff laid out his plan. I was to go to the door and ring the bell. If Mr. Whoozi-What's was there, I would say that I wanted to apologize for the upset we'd caused yesterday and to thank him for trying to help us. Then I was to act like I was feeling dizzy and ask him if I could come in the house and sit down until I felt better, maybe get a drink of water or use the bathroom—whatever would stall him long enough for Hawk and Jeff to have a look under the tree root. If he wasn't home, I was to sit on the steps and keep watch in case he came home.

"In the meantime," Jeff instructed, "Hawk and I will dig beneath the tree and look for anything else that might be buried there." He looked over at Dynnis, who was slipping in and out of the bushes and shrubs in each yard like a wisp of smoke.

"If I didn't know he was there, I would think he wasn't there," Jeff said.

Hawk looked over his shoulder at me. "Ever hear of Yogi Berra?"

"Wasn't he a baseball player a long time ago?" I said, wondering why Hawk was talking about baseball now, of all times.

"Never mind," he said, shaking his head. "Dynnis is following us, and he said when we get to the tree, he's going to keep watch along the street from some hidden point."

We had arrived at the edge of Whoozi-What's yard, and Jeff went into army stealth mode. He motioned me to my post at the front door, then took Hawk's chair, maneuvered him into the shadows behind the giant black oak, and squatted down next to him.

As I made my way up the walk to the front door, I spotted a blur in the bushes that moved ever so slightly, as if a tiny wind had rippled through them.

I climbed the front steps and rang the bell. After several seconds with no response, I punched it again. Glancing through the large picture window, I could see lights but the living room was deserted. Just for good measure, I pushed the bell a third time and then knocked. After several seconds of silence, I turned and gave the high sign to Jeff and Hawk. After that, there was nothing much for me to do but sit on the front steps and wait.

Time seemed to drag and I glanced at my watch—3:57. We had been there less than fifteen minutes. I was tempted to go see how my cousins were making out and had just lifted my bottom from the step when a thunderous voice said from behind me, "You! Young lady, what are you doing here?"

I was so startled that I hopped up in the air and off the front steps, spinning into the yard, my hands flying to my chest in order to keep my heart from leaping out. "Oh, Mr. Whoozi-What's!" I gasped. "You scared the living—"

"Mr. what?" he demanded.

"What?" I said, then froze when I realized what I had called him.

"That's what I asked." He had evidently come around from in back of the house and was stomping quickly toward where I stood in front of the steps. He was so large and menacing that I half expected him to start saying, "Fe, fi, fo, fum."

"And *what* were you doing on my steps?" he roared instead.

"Oh. I was … well, I called you … I mean I rang the bell. …" I stopped and gasped as much air as I could into my depleted lungs. "I was just … just where did you come from anyway?" I finished, leaning over and holding onto my knees like a runner after a marathon.

"Look, young woman, I don't need to answer to you. I'm the one asking the questions here." He was now right in front of me, with arms folded and eyes reduced to slits.

"I don't know what kind of game you're playing, but I'm not going to go through this every day. Now either you give me some answers as to why you're on my property for the second day in a row, or I'm going to go inside and call the police."

This was clearly not going the way we had planned, and I still didn't know his name.

"Well, you see, Mr … uh …" I began, in the hope that I could reawaken the pity he had felt yesterday.

He interrupted me with, "Hold on. What's that?"

Oh, no! He must have seen Hawk and Jeff. But then I realized he was looking the other way.

"Is that …?" he paused, squinting toward the shrubbery at the end of the drive. "It can't be!" He took a few tentative steps before shouting, "Good Lord, it is!"

"What?" I too found myself squinting as I followed his gaze.

"A tufted titmouse!" he said, with reverence. "I can't believe it." He spun around and stared at me as if he had never seen me before. "Wait here!" he ordered, turning back to look one more time at the tall shrub at the end of the driveway. "Don't move! I'm going to get my 'nocs." He spun on his heels and raced up the steps into the house.

I stood frozen, literally by now, next to the steps. His knocks? Was that some kind of weapon? And what the heck was a tufted titmouse anyway? I started looking around on the ground. Maybe it was infesting the neighborhood, and he was going to get his gun in order to shoot it.

Mr. Whoozi-What's returned almost immediately with a pair of binoculars and a cell phone. Without further explanation, he began stalking the infected shrub. Even though most of the snow had melted on his lawn, he still took those high, knee-lifting steps, like he was walking through the jungle grasses of the deep Savannah. I stood mesmerized, watching him step oh-so-quietly up to the bush, open the cell phone, and then—snap! The cell's camera flash went off in the fading light and a small blue-gray bird flew out of the branches and into the darkening afternoon sky.

Mr. Whoozi-What's turned with the look of a minor celebrity who had just been handed an Oscar. Clutching the phone to his chest, he looked at me and said, "You are a charm, young woman. I have been trying to get a glimpse of that bird in different places around the world for over forty years, and because of you, I now have him." He tapped the tiny phone lightly on his massive chest. "Right here. Forever. Thank you."

Because of the fading light I couldn't be sure, but I would almost bet those were tears in his eyes.

"You're welcome," I said simply.

Just then, Hawk called from the sidewalk. Jeff was pushing him as though they'd just arrived, down Maple Street.

"Glad we caught up to you!" Jeff's cheery voice rang out. "Thought you'd left us behind at school!"

Mr. Whoozi-What's looked up. I waved at my cousins and then turned back to him.

"Just stopped by to say thanks for helping my cousin yesterday," I said hurriedly, "and … glad to have been of help."

Mr. Whoozi-What's' face broke into a wide grin. "No, young lady, it is I who thank you. Say, would you kids like to come in for some cookies and hot chocolate?"

"Oh, no, no thanks all the same," I said, looking back at the twins, now getting ready to cross at the corner. "We really have to be getting home now. My aunts, they … well, you know, they worry."

"Yes, I understand," he said. "You run along home now, but don't forget to stop in now and then when you're passing by. Door's always open."

I nodded a smile, then took off to catch up with Hawk and Jeff as they crossed the street.

"Did you find anything?" I asked.

Hawk nodded. "A stone."

"A stone!" I glanced back. Mr. Whoozi-What's was making his way back inside the house, still clutching his binoculars and cell phone. "You looked under a tree root and found a stone? Will wonders never cease." My sarcasm fell on deaf ears.

"It is not just any stone, November." Dynnis slipped out of the hedge along the sidewalk. "What your cousins have found is a lodestone."

Chapter Nine

In the wood there burns a fire, and in the fire there melts a stone, within the stone a ring of iron.

—Kathleen Raine, *Spell of Creation*

We didn't examine the lodestone right away that evening as we gathered in my cousins' room after dinner. We had arranged with Dynnis that it would most likely be safer for him to join us after 8:00.

"My mom will be watching CNN until at least 10:00, and Aunty Gin will be making her rounds," Jeff said.

Aunty Gin's rounds were her patients. She is a midwife with a large number of clients. When I asked her how she started her practice, she told me that when she was only eleven years old, she had to help deliver a baby in a Boston elevator during a blackout.

"It was the middle of July, and the electricity went out in our building," she explained one night in the kitchen, while she helped me dry dishes. "I was on my way downstairs before the outage to get some ice cream. Being in a hurry, I left before everybody else, so my brother and the other kids who lived in my foster home had to take the next elevator. It was just me and this big, pregnant lady." She held her hands out in front of her belly. "We got on the elevator at the fifteenth floor, the power went out on the fifth, and she became so frightened, she went into labor. Well, of course, I was only eleven years old and didn't really know how babies were born, much less how to deliver one. But there was no one else, and that poor woman was scared out of her wits. All she kept saying was, 'Dear Lord, dear Lord.' Then she said to me, 'Child, you're going to have to help me bring this baby into the world.'" Aunty Gin smiled at the memory.

"All I can remember is that once the baby started coming, I just felt like someone was guiding my hands. That little baby boy popped out screaming his head off, pretty as you please, and not a moment later, the power went back on, and we lowered him and ourselves to the ground floor." She chuckled. "Boy, were those people in the lobby surprised when the elevator door opened that night!"

Aunty Gin said the woman named her son *Yeketi*, which means "lift up" in Wolof, the language of her native land, Senegal.

"Oh, I get it," I smiled. "Lift up, as in elevator?"

Aunty Gin nodded. "Exactly. Anyway, after that, word spread around the building that I could deliver babies easier and better than any doctor and much cheaper, too." Her eyes clouded for a moment as a memory emerged. "Of course my foster parents saw an opportunity to make some money from my talents and took me out of school to 'market my skills,' so to speak." She finished drying the last pot and stowed it away in the cupboard.

"So how did you come to live with Aunt Marsha's family?" I already knew that Aunty Gin was not Aunt Marsha's biological sister; that was evident from simply looking at them. Like my dad's eyes, Aunt Marsha's were the color of faded denim. She had a rosy pink complexion and long, pale hair that she wore pulled back, letting it tumble down between her shoulder blades. In contrast were Aunty Gin's smoky brown eyes, razor-straight, chin-length black hair, and flawless chocolate latte skin. And where Aunt Marsha was tall and full-figured, Aunty Gin was small and slender as bamboo.

"My parents were the Atwoods—not to be confused with the two people who produced me physically and then left me and my baby brother to fend for ourselves in the basement of an old tenement building." Her beautiful mouth shaped the bitter words like she had just sampled fresh lime. "My brother, Alvis, was adopted first. A couple who only wanted a baby took him, so that left me in foster care for two more years, until my parents adopted me just before my thirteenth birthday. Marsha and I had become inseparable friends at school—sisters, even then. George and Lillian Atwood were good people—good parents. They told me once that they had room in their lives for many more children than they had been blessed with by nature. They already had five when I came along, but they took me into the heart of their home, as if I had always been there, and you know what?"

I shook my head.

"Sometimes I felt like I always had been." She tossed her dark head as if to throw off the past and bring herself back into the now. "Anyway, the rest is history, as they say. The adoption was final exactly nine months to the day after I came to them. Mom always said it was the easiest pregnancy she ever had!" She folded the damp towel and hung it on the hook that was shaped like a cow's head; then she turned back to me. "And as for becoming a midwife? Well, I never considered doing anything else."

***

Before Dynnis arrived that evening, Hawk spread The Vellum on the desk along with the letter. The lodestone was holding down the yellow notes we had written in the library. When Dynnis joined us, we were deep in discussion about what we needed to do next.

"I think we should finish deciphering The Vellum completely before we do anything else," said Jeff. He lay on his back on the bed repeatedly tossing a pillow shaped like a soccer ball up to the ceiling and then catching it as it bounced back. "I mean, we don't even know what that symbol thing means."

Hawk pursed his lips as he bent over the large document with a page magnifier. He and I had been working through the complicated text for the past hour-and-a-half while Jeff played Warcraft on the laptop.

"We?" Hawk repeated. "You mean, as in all three of us?" He threw a pink eraser at Jeff just as his brother caught the last ceiling ball. The rubber wedge sailed past his nose and bounced off the wall. "Who's been doing the deciphering, Jeff?" Hawk lowered the magnifier and pushed back from the desk as Jeff sat up, looking sheepish. "I think we have enough information here to make some kind of a reasonable decision about our next move." Hawk smiled as Dynnis made his way out of the shadows toward where we huddled in the glow of the single desk lamp. "It seems that the coin in the box was part of a larger stash that was given to a …" He looked down at the notes. "Samuel Parris by Captain Hobs."

"Very interesting," Dynnis said. "I once knew a Captain Hobs, a long time ago when I was a child. Nasty fellow." His eyebrows drew together as he shook his head, causing his beard to sway back and forth like a fluffy cat's tail. "And Reverend Parris. Now there is a name I've not heard in a very long time." He motioned for Hawk to continue.

Hawk looked down at the notes. "When this was written, gold was being minted into coins. The king of England at that time was Charles II." He turned back and faced us. "If the gold the document speaks of was in the form of gold coins, which weighed approximately a quarter of an ounce a piece, then thirty-six ounces would be—"

"One-hundred thirty-two coins," Jeff said, and then shrugged his shoulders as we all looked at him in surprise.

"Good with figures," he said simply.

"Hmmm." Dynnis seemed deep in thought.

Jeff jumped off the bed and grabbed the wooden box. Opening it, he removed the folder and took out the thin gold coin. "You mean the gold this letter talks about might be one of these coins? You think gold coins are what's buried underneath the insane asylum?"

Hawk was tapping at the computer again. "I don't know why I didn't do this in the first place," he muttered to himself. "Hah! Here it is." He turned the screen so we all could see. There, flickering in the semi-lit room, was an image of both sides of the coin that Jeff held in his hand: A gold guinea with the bust of King Charles II of England, surrounded by the letters CAROLVS II DEI GRATIA.

"*Dei Gratia*: by the grace of God." Hawk's knowledge of Latin allowed him to interpret: "MAG BR FRA ET HIB REX: of Great Britain, France, and Ireland king."

I held out my hand, and Jeff dropped the tiny golden disk into my palm. It was surprisingly heavy and felt warm and smooth. I looked closely at it and then at the computer screen. It was the same coin, all right. "Dynnis, is Jeff right? Is this what's buried beneath the asylum?"

Dynnis shrugged. "Don't know, but I have a strong feeling that even if it is, there is more to what is underneath that old pile of lumber than mere gold bullion. Whatever it is down there has been watching over something sacred for centuries, and whoever is doing the watching knows we're coming." He walked over to the box now laying on the bed, lifted it, and held it beneath the glow of the desk lamp. "The symbols scratched into the bottom of this box are Elfin." He looked up at us. "Dark elves have lived beneath the hills and mounds of these parts for centuries. They are known to be jealous guardians of ill-gotten gold, and they are sinister and stealthy. If whoever—or *whatever*—is guarding that which is buried beneath the Danvers Asylum and Judge Hathorne's house has anything to do with *that* group"—he motioned toward the box Jeff now held—"then you can bet there is more at stake than mere gold coins."

"Like what?" Jeff asked.

"Souls," Dynnis said softly.

Chapter Ten

When storm winds shrieked and the moon was buried and the dark of the forest was black as black, she rose in the air like a rocket at sea, riding the wind, riding the night, riding the tempest to the moon and back.

—James Nimmo, *Space Traveller*

At the last word Dynnis uttered, a clap of thunder just outside the window slammed into the ground so hard and loud that it felt like the old house shook clear down to its basement stones. We all jumped, and Dynnis grabbed the bedpost in order not to fall. As he was righting himself and securing his hat, something caused me to glance at the desk. The lodestone was moving. At first I wasn't sure if my eyes were playing tricks on me. But as I watched, the fist-sized black stone began to vibrate, slowly at first, then picking up speed as if its own movement was causing it to gather energy. The others in the room followed my gaze. Hawk's eyes widened.

"The lodestone's moving!" He pointed to the desk with one hand while pushing his chair toward it with the other.

"Not only that, it's starting to glow." Jeff stated the obvious.

The lodestone turned the color of molten lava as it shook and hopped atop the pile of yellow notes.

"It's going to catch the papers on fire!" I looked around for something to throw over it.

"I don't think so." Hawk pushed himself closer to the gyrating rock and reached out his hand.

"Hawk, don't!" Dynnis and I shouted, but we were too late. Hawk's hand covered the stone and it stilled. Looking back at us over his shoulder, he smiled. "It's not even hot."

We all crowded around.

"Good heavens!" Dynnis breathed, as Hawk lifted the stone from the paper. There, burned into the middle of the page, exactly where the lodestone had sat, was an intricate symbol—one that was not on any of the documents we had taken from the folder:

Beneath it were seared the words:

THE SOULS ARE FORSAKEN—*the bargain* IS STRUCK

Thunder still rolled in the distance and except for that, the small bedroom was silent. Hawk placed the now-quiet lodestone on the desk next to the papers, and we all stared for what seemed a very long time at the symbol and the ominous words.

Jeff asked Dynnis, "Do you know what that means?" Jeff's voice had never sounded so small.

Hawk turned the paper around in his hands as he spelled out the letters printed in the outer circle. "A–S–T–A–R–O–T–H."

Dynnis' face had lost all color as he backed to the bed and grabbed onto the post again, as if expecting another crack of thunder. "Astaroth." He whispered the word.

"Who's Astaroth?" I asked, knowing I was not going to like the answer.

With a hand from Jeff, Dynnis managed to seat himself on the bed. He swung his feet for a few seconds, as if trying to gather his thoughts. "Astaroth." He licked his lips before saying the name, as if it had a bad taste. "When I was a child, I remember a story told 'round the fire on long winter nights about a misbegotten British ship sailing from the African coast to America." Dynnis shifted his position on the bed, took out a large red handkerchief, and blew his nose loudly into it. "It seems during a particularly nasty squall off the Guinea coast, a middle-sized ship in His Majesty's naval fleet had been forced to drop anchor offshore in the middle of the night. Once the storm passed and the sea had calmed, the sailors decided to wait the night and set sail at daybreak. As the story goes, the full moon came out from behind the clouds, and seeing as how the fresh fruit supply was long gone, three sailors decided to row ashore and gather some wild fruit by moonlight. No one knows how far inland they ventured, but by daybreak they still had not returned. Since the ship was not a large vessel, the captain could not afford to lose three of his crew, and so sent a search party of two men to look for them.

Along about dusk, one lone figure emerged from the deep undergrowth of the jungle, screaming and tearing at his clothes and hair. The others managed to get him aboard and in between fits of hysterical laughter and shrieks of terror, he told the story of his group going into a cave that was lit from within. The first thing they spotted was a long, wide vein of gold, so pure and soft that when one of the sailors pressed a farthing into it, it held fast. In their greed they followed the vein deeper into the tunnel, wondering at the source of the light that seemed to guide them.

"When the light suddenly went out, they were left in utter and complete blackness deep inside the cavern—but not for long. Soon, a soft glow returned and the men saw that it came from a large lantern, but the figure holding it was like nothing they had ever seen before. That is where the story ends—almost."

Dynnis stopped and cleared his throat. Jeff grabbed a bottle of water from the nightstand and offered it to the gnome, who accepted it gratefully and took a long swig. "As the rest of the legend goes, the *thing* that held the lantern was a demon straight out of the inferno—a creature so fearsome that a single glimpse of him could drive a man to madness."

Hawk asked, "So was that Astaroth?"

"Yes, but that is not all. The name of the ship anchored off the coast on that fateful night was the *Blessing*. It sailed out the next day with the one crewman who had made it back on board, but he would never be the same again. Jumping ship in Barbados, he would spend the rest of his life telling the tale over and over to whomever would take the time to listen."

"Wait a minute!" Hawk interrupted. "The Vellum mentions a ship called the *Blessing*." He grabbed the manuscript. "Right here: *'also to accompany this miserable voyage on the* Blessing *was his honorable Reverend Samuel Parris and his family and his two island slaves.'*"

"Right you are," Dynnis replied. "And why do you suppose that voyage was so 'miserable'?"

"Are you saying that the demon was aboard the ship?" I asked. "That Astaroth was on board all the way from Africa?"

Dynnis chewed the inside of his lip. "When I was only seven, I remember my grandmother saying that something wrong had come into our village; something bad from the ship docked in Salem Port. *'The elves are talking amongst themselves, and what they say is getting passed on to us. There is great trouble ashore in Salem Town. Great sorrow will follow the unification of the elves and the Dark One.'*"

Dynnis shook his snowy head. "I didn't understand it all then, but I do remember my father's face when the troubled times began some three years later. I remember asking him why he seemed so worried, and he said that he wished he could read the human's language in order to know exactly what was happening, but that there was one thing he did recognize. My father pulled from his coat pocket a piece of torn flour sack that had been scorched with the symbol you now hold in your hand."

Dynnis motioned toward the page that Hawk held. "He called it a *sigil*, the sigil or symbol of Astaroth." He paused, his eyes filled with sorrow. "I was ten that year—the year our town erupted into madness. It was as though every possible evil had been unleashed on the tiny settlement of Salem Village—anger, accusations, hatred, cruelty, greed, madness, revenge … and murder." His shoulders slumped. "It was humanity at its ugliest."

"What year was that?" Jeff sat beside him, and Dynnis shook his head.

"It was 1692, the year Astaroth reigned in Salem Village." His face was grave. "This is the beginning I spoke of—the start of the dark times." He indicated the mist pressing against the bedroom window.

"I'm afraid this heavy fog and violent storm is only a warning. What has lain dormant for all these centuries has been awakened, and the entire town will pay the price, as it did all those years ago, unless it is put to right."

"What price?" Hawk asked.

"The down payment will be the lives of the direct descendants of the original families of Old Salem Village. The payoff will be the collection of their souls, as well as the souls of many others. This will satisfy the last payment of a deal that was struck with Astaroth in 1701 in exchange for power and wealth." Dynnis removed his hat and laid it carefully on the desk, then ran his fingers through his thick white hair before picking up the box.

"I've spent the last few hours speaking with others of my kind who remember those days more vividly than I, and they tell me there is another box somewhere—no one knows where. The legend says there will be:

> *'three who will find the first box. One of them will be a maiden of the Eighth Sign. It is she who will need to find and open the second box in order to release those souls already collected and held in chains, and those whose lives are in immediate danger.'"*

Dynnis placed the box back on the desk.

My arms had goose bumps. "Three who find a box?"

Dynnis nodded. "The three of you."

Suddenly something didn't feel right. The whole scene—Jeff, Hawk, and Dynnis talking, the wind whistling around the eaves of the house, the sound of the train in the distance, the clock in the front room chiming the hour, even Dynnis standing over the box, tracing the strange design on the lid with his index finger—it was all oddly familiar, like a memory or a really strong sense of déjà vu, yet I could not quite grasp it. Then, all at once, it was there, rushing back, vivid and so much "in the moment" that I smelled the very place and time. But this was no ordinary memory; at least, it was unlike any memory I had ever had before.

I was hiding inside of a darkened space, like a closet or a small room, peeking through a door made of rough wood, but I wasn't alone. Someone I knew very well and, I realized, loved very deeply knelt next to me. *Thomas.* I knew I had not spoken, yet the boy next to me answered.

"Be silent, Doe."

He leaned close, his touch meant to reinforce the command, causing me to lean back into the circle of his arms as we silently observed the two people speaking on the other side of the door. At first, I couldn't make out what they were saying because I could not understand them. They seemed to be speaking a foreign language, and then I realized they were using an unusual form of English.

"Aye, and then you'd be sayin' that on the Hollantide, some three-hundred and five years hence, there be a chance for redemption?"

A tall man with shoulder-length dark brown hair, wearing a long black coat with a white ruffle at his throat, was speaking to someone I could not see. *"On a narrow time alone,"* came the reply. This voice was deep, like a recording being played too slowly.

"And that would be?" the man in the black coat asked hesitantly, as if he were afraid of the figure to whom he spoke.

"Whilst the constellation Leo is obscured. Only then."

The man in the black coat looked confused. *"But how will they know this? Surely there can be some other—"*

"Only then!" roared the voice, and the man fell to his knees, covering his ears.

Thomas gasped and released me. "Doe, we must maketh haste. Doe?"

Why was he calling me that?

November!

I was suddenly pulled out of the darkness and into the wonderfully messy, familiar bedroom, with Jeff and Hawk staring at me as Dynnis stood shaking my hand like we had just met.

"Did we lose you for a minute?" he asked, jiggling the hand a few more times, concern showing in the gray eyes beneath the shaggy brows.

"I … don't know." I closed my eyes and shook my head to clear it. "For a second there, I … I think I left the room." I expected laughter from my cousins but when I glanced over at them, they were anything but amused.

Dynnis grasped my hand tighter and pulled me toward the chair. "Perhaps you had better sit down and tell us about it."

I thought about the dark closet and the strange men on the other side; and then, I thought about Thomas, the boy who I had yet to meet and who, I knew, was as much a part of me as my very soul—the boy who had called me "Doe."

Then I looked at the three expectant faces.

"I was listening to what everyone was saying and watching Dynnis trace his hand over the box. Then it was like I was remembering a different time." I paused and the others waited while I cleared my throat and collected my thoughts. "It was as if I was being drawn back to a different life—a different me." I had my cousins' rapt attention, but they looked confused. The expression on Dynnis' face, however, was one of understanding.

"What did you see, November? What memory took you back to that other time?" His voice was soft but urgent.

I decided I would share what I had heard and seen on the other side of the rough-hewn door, but not the part about Thomas—he belonged to me.

"Two men were talking about … redemption. I mean, there was one man I could see and the other I could only hear. The man I could see was asking the other one about a specific time period when something would be redeemed."

"And what was to be redeemed?" Dynnis' voice had become hypnotic.

"I don't know. They didn't say. But the time period for the redemption seemed to be the issue."

"Do you remember what it was?"

"I think so, but it doesn't make much sense."

Dynnis signaled Hawk, who grabbed the first thing he could get his hands on to write with, then nodded for Dynnis to continue.

"The voice of the one I could not see said that it would be on Hollantide, three-hundred and five years hence, '*whilst the constellation Leo is obscured*.' He was really definite about that."

Hawk scribbled every word I said, like some mad court reporter being forced to take shorthand because his machine had gone on the blink. When he was done, he handed it to Jeff and said, "Three-hundred five years hence. Three hundred five adds up to—"

"Adds up to the number eight," his brother supplied. "And the legend mentions something about the *eighth sign*. Hollantide is November 11th," Jeff continued, "and today is November 9th."

The two brothers spoke as one, finishing not only each other's sentences but each other's thoughts as well.

"But the constellation Leo—what does that have to do with it?" Jeff turned to Dynnis.

Hawk was already at his computer. "The Leonid constellation is very visible in November. In fact, there is a meteor shower this year that coincides with ..." He stopped typing and sat staring at the computer. "Hollantide. It is visible to the eye just past midnight." He consulted his watch. "That gives us roughly thirty-nine hours to find the other box."

Jeff let out a low whistle.

"But wait," I said. "The voice also said that the constellation had to be obscured."

"The moon," Hawk said simply and began scrolling down the page. "It says here that the full moon is only a few days before the eleventh and that it could block the view of the meteor shower connected with the sighting of the constellation of Leo in the northeastern part of North America."

"Of course, that's if we buy into the legend." Hawk turned from the computer, folding his arms across his chest. "This could all still be a really big coincidence."

"And I, along with *this,* could just be figments of your collective imagination." Dynnis held up the sigil of Astaroth. "You just said it yourself, Hawk; in thirty-nine hours you will find out, one way or another. It is up to you *how* you will find out."

The grandfather clock in the front room struck ten.

"Well, if we get an early start in the morning, we can have a look around the old asylum," I suggested.

"And lose eight, maybe ten hours? No way," Jeff said suddenly, standing up and grabbing his backpack. "I suggest we start now. Tonight. Hawk, are you up for it?"

I couldn't help my involuntary gasp. The thought of Hawk having to go all the way to the asylum at night in the cold, much less attempting to get inside it, made me cringe.

I tried to think of a gentle way to suggest that he stay behind while the rest of us scout out the place, but his hardened expression at my reaction made me hold my tongue.

"Hand me my backpack, dude," he ordered Jeff, never breaking eye contact with me. "Get the flashlights, and don't forget the extra batteries—we're going to do this."

And so, just before midnight, we began our trek toward Hathorne Hill. The old asylum, its ancient timbers creaking and muttering against the cold night wind, slumbered—waiting for us to arrive.

Chapter Eleven

Who goes there, stopping at my door in the deep dark dead of the moonless night?

—Robert Fisher, *Hallowe'en Fright*

IT HAD BEEN SURPRISINGLY EASY TO ESCAPE from the house, considering the hour and all that was going on. We left the Dune Buggy at home and took Hawk's manual wheelchair because we did not want to take the chance of having the aunts hear its motor. As we made our way down the long hallway leading to the front door, we heard Aunt Marsha and Aunty Gin discussing something in soft tones. A few pieces of conversation floated out the door of Aunty Gin's bedroom as we passed.

"Don't need to know …"

"… find out anyway …"

Hawk and Jeff did not seem to notice, and Dynnis had taken another route out of the house. But I didn't have time to reflect on the meaning of my aunts' conversation, because as we opened the door to the outside, the cold night hit me like a slap. Again, my cousins didn't seem to notice the sharp air that engulfed us. What they did make comment on was the thick mist swirling around us like cotton candy as we made our way to the sidewalk.

"Man, this fog is creepy enough," Jeff muttered, "even if we were going someplace fun—which we are not," he added, as if that was news to any of us.

"A cold front is colliding with warmer air from the ocean," Hawk said. "It is really no creepier than simple science."

"Well, we've got to be Simple *Simons* to be out in it," I grumbled, as I pushed Hawk over the rough pavement. The fog was so thick that it obscured any light that might have come down from the night sky. Since there were no lights along the streets, it was up to Jeff to lead the way with his flashlight, beam pointed toward the ground, in order not to reflect off the pea soup and further hinder our progress.

Nobody would say what I knew we were all thinking—that we should just turn around and head back home. As we made our way slowly down Preston Street to Hazen Avenue, I thought about my home in Arizona. With the three-hour time difference it would only be a little after 8:00 p.m. This time of year was what Phoenicians waited for all summer—temperatures in the mid-80s during the day and the low 70s at night.

I pushed the wheelchair with one hand while I pulled my coat collar up around my neck. The mercury must have dropped thirty degrees since the afternoon, and I used to think it was a cold night when it hit 50. I hunched my shoulders and dipped my chin inside my coat as I trudged behind Hawk. Out of nowhere, a huge root growing out of the blacktop caught the front wheels of Hawk's chair, bringing it and me to an abrupt halt. If Hawk hadn't been holding onto the arms of the chair, he would have been tossed out. As it was, I was thrown into his back and partway over his shoulder.

"Steady there." Dynnis appeared out of the mist, took hold of the handle, and righted the tipping wheelchair and me along with it.

"Ugh!" I said in disgust. "This is awful. It's so cold and damp, and we can't see where we're going." Dynnis had taken over the handles of Hawk's chair. "This is ridiculous. We should just go back and wait until daylight."

Jeff turned around, and Hawk looked over his shoulder at my outburst.

"You want to go back?" Jeff asked, like he was hoping I would say yes.

"Yes."

Dynnis stepped back to look at me too. He rolled his tongue inside his cheek for a moment and then said, "Well, then let us go back." He turned on his heels and started off in the opposite direction. "After all, we can just as easily sit at home and watch it all unfold on the telly." His hat disappeared into the mist first, and then he was gone. "Well, what are you waiting for?" His disembodied voice floated back.

"I didn't get a vote," said Hawk.

Dynnis' head poked back through the fog into the circle of light cast by Jeff's flashlight. He looked expectantly at Hawk.

"I say we go on." Hawk faced forward in the chair. Jeff let out a soft moan.

Dynnis looked at Jeff and me. "Well, what is it to be?"

I thought about the long walk, the cold that was only getting worse while we stood there, the long night, the things that might be living around that old asylum, the asylum itself, and what might be living *inside*, and I suddenly realized it wasn't the cold or the fog or the long walk. It wasn't that I was going to lose a night's sleep in a nice warm bed. It wasn't even that I would most likely encounter spiders, night creepy things, and bats. It was the Danvers State Asylum for the Insane.

"We have to be *insane* for even thinking of doing this," I said suddenly, in a panic. "I mean, we're kids, for Pete's sake! What can we possibly do about any of this?" I waved my arms around as if there was something more to see in the distance besides fog. I was not even sure in which direction the asylum stood. I had never before in my entire life been so afraid. The feeling of dread that enveloped me at that moment was what I always thought facing death would feel like.

When I was five, I fell off the back of a boat my parents and I were on with friends, and I almost drowned. I had dropped Beast, my favorite stuffed animal, overboard and was trying to catch him before he hit the water. Instead, I followed him into the lake. Even though I was wearing a life jacket, I still remember how empty it felt to watch the boat pull away with my parents on board, not even knowing I was gone. I was too young to know that I could die, but I knew a sense of hollowness and loss that felt like it emptied my soul. Then I panicked and started screaming. The boat turned, and I was soon pulled into my mother's arms.

I felt like that now. The dark pressed around me like the waves of that lake, trying to suck me down into its murky depths. My parents were someplace this time where they could not reach me, even if I called out to them.

Dynnis whispered softly, "But I am here." I knew I hadn't spoken a word. "I have always heard you, and I always will," he said.

Then he stood in front of Hawk's chair and spoke to all of us. "Whether you realize it or not, you three are special: a chosen trio whose path has been preordained by those who have preceded you. You are the Children of Avnova."

"Avnova?" Hawk repeated. "I've never heard of that."

"Me, neither," Jeff added. They both looked at me and I shrugged.

"Loosely translated, it means Children of the Mist. The ancient Celts believed Avnova was goddess-protector of the forests and rivers, most specifically the Black River. Her name translates down as *mist* or *fog*, if you will." Dynnis spread his arms wide to indicate our present situation. "So, you can see that it is entirely appropriate for you to be setting out on your journey in this."

"Wait a minute," Hawk said. "What do you mean we're the *Children* of Avnova? What does an old Celtic legend have to do with any of this?"

"Yeah, I thought the Atwoods were English," Jeff put in.

I blew on my hands and stuck them inside my sleeves as I stamped my feet to put some feeling back into them. "You know, guys, we really need to decide if we're going or not because I am about to freeze to this spot if we don't do something."

"November is right," Dynnis said. "I can just as easily explain your family connection to Avnova while we're walking. So. What say we choose a direction, eh? Which will it be, forward or back?" He stood along the edge of the road, his arms spread wide in either direction.

Hawk still faced forward. "I'm for going on," he said.

Jeff and I exchanged looks silently behind his back. I opened my mouth to suggest retreat, when a pair of headlights pushed through the fog, followed by the hood of a dripping wet, dark blue SUV that slowed and came to a stop next to where we stood. The passenger's side window slid smoothly down, and Mr. Roth's face appeared.

"What are you children doing out at this time of night? The fog is so tight I almost didn't see you. Do you need a lift somewhere?" The light was on inside the car so we could see him better than he could see us.

Jeff answered first. "No, thanks, we're just going for a walk."

Mr. Roth looked at me.

"Yes. I mean no, we don't need a ride. We're just going 'round the block." I held the wheelchair handles and nodded toward Hawk's back. "Fresh air, fresh night air is good for my cousin. I mean, cousins," I stammered.

Mr. Roth looked unconvinced. "Are your parents aware you're taking this … nocturnal sojourn?" When we didn't answer, his mouth set. "Apparently not. Well, I would strongly suggest that you let me take you home. This is no night to be out walking along unlit roadsides." He opened the car door.

"Quick!" Dynnis urged. "Step into the shadows of these trees." When we didn't respond, he grabbed the wheelchair handles. "Now!" he demanded. "And be quiet!"

Jeff and I responded as one, while Dynnis pushed Hawk into the underbrush that grew along the roadside, then hustled us behind him into the bushy branches.

We watched in silence as Mr. Roth came around behind the SUV and stopped. Clearly puzzled, he stepped alongside the passenger's side, glancing both ways before looking down at the ground where we had been. Surely he would see the tracks from the chair, but he gave no indication that he did. Then he stared into the trees right where we stood, as if we were spotlighted on a stage.

"Well, I guess they didn't need my help after all," he said, as if speaking to an audience. He waited for a few seconds more, staring right at me, his black eyes locking with mine, making it difficult to blink, much less move.

"Run, Doe, run!" The shout rang through my head, repeating over and over like an air-raid siren. "But I was frozen, much like the proverbial doe held by the headlights of a semi truck bearing down upon it.

"Hope they're not lost." Roth's deep voice was soft but his projection was such that it could have been heard in the back row of the largest theatre. "Not a pleasant thing to lose your way." His mouth turned up in a slight smile as he headed back to the car.

"Whew!" Jeff said after Mr. Roth had returned to his car and driven away. "Talk about weird. What was *that* all about?"

"Yeah," chuckled Hawk. "Old Roth acted like he was performing a bad rendition of Count Dracula." His voice dropped into the accent of the vampire himself. "I vant your blooood!"

Dynnis pushed Hawk's chair out of the gravel and onto the edge of the road, then addressed me. "Shall we go on then?"

"Yes," I nodded without hesitation and watched Jeff's eyebrows go up in surprise. "We need to do this."

"And you know this because …?" Jeff questioned.

I could still feel the math teacher's eyes boring into mine. There had been a fleeting moment, like that spell I'd had earlier in the evening, where a memory—a very bad memory—floated just on the edges of my mind. "I just know, is all." I stepped behind Hawk's chair.

"Then press on, MacDuff; time's a-wasting." Hawk gripped the arms of the chair like he was readying for takeoff. "Let's go, already."

Chapter Twelve

Who goes there in the clothing of a dream, in the breath of fear with no noise ever near, ever near—who goes here?

—Robert Fisher, *Hallowe'en Fright*

The entrance to the grounds of the Danvers Asylum was probably less than a mile from our house but with the fog and the uneven pavement, it took almost forty-five minutes to arrive at the long drive leading to the main building complex.

As we made our way along, the tall red towers of the Kirkbride Building suddenly loomed out of the fog. I thought about "Paul Revere's Ride," the poem we had read in English class last week, and the description Longfellow had given of the Old North Church:

As it rose above the graves on the hill,
Lonely and spectral and somber and still.

As if hearing my thoughts, Hawk said, "Did you know there's a graveyard in this place?"

"Yippee," Jeff mumbled.

We continued on in silence, and as we neared the buildings, Hawk put his hands down and stopped the wheels of the chair.

"Do you hear that?" he asked, sitting stock still and looking up at the tallest tower atop the main building.

"Hear what?" Jeff glanced around, then frowned at his brother. "Are you trying to creep us out on purpose, or are you just naturally a ghoul?" Hunching his shoulders from either the cold or the effect of our surroundings, Jeff tried cramming his hands inside his pockets while holding the flashlight. This caused him to drop the light on the blacktop with a resounding crash. The reverberating sound was followed almost instantly by the sound of mighty wings taking flight. I didn't even have time to look up before something very big swooped low over our heads.

Jeff scrambled for the flashlight that had rolled down the drive, so he was already bent over when the huge form plunged toward where we stood. But he was quick enough to grab the light—miraculously, still shining—and point it to where the creature had landed.

As the beam swung up into the gnarled old oak tree, we saw a majestic brown bird as big as a swan perched on a stout, leafless limb. But this was no swan; this bird's beak was curved down menacingly like a meat hook and, as we watched, the magnificent creature spread its beautiful gray brown wings the entire length of the branch. After flapping them a few times, it settled back on the arm of the tree and peered down at us with bright brown eyes, as if we were exotic creatures put on display solely for its entertainment.

"That's a red-tailed hawk," Hawk said, pointing to the bird. "*Buteo jamaicensis*." The Latin name rolled off his tongue as if he used it in conversation every day. "It's one of the largest birds in North America, and he's a really big one, even at that." Hawk reached around for his backpack. "My camera," he said, more to himself than to me, as he pulled the bag into his lap and began digging inside of it.

"Hawk, you can't take a flash picture," I gasped. "What if someone sees it?"

"Yeah," Jeff added, "and anyway, I don't want to spook him into dive-bombing us again. Look at those claws."

"Talons," Hawk corrected as he held the tiny digital up to his eye. "Don't worry," he whispered. "Night-vision lens. No flash." I heard a tiny click, and Hawk lowered the camera. "And besides, if someone was going to see us, don't you think the flashlight would be even more of a draw?"

"Whatever." Jeff took a few steps back. "But I'm not going to turn my back on that thing." He kept a somewhat steady beam on the bird as he walked backward toward the entrance to the asylum.

Without moving, the hawk continued to stare, and I noticed that Dynnis had not moved either. He still stood in the exact same spot as when we had first come upon the bird, and his expression was that of someone who had just heard something surprising.

As I watched, he pursed his lips and made a noise that sounded like it rose up from his throat and ended in a whistle. He stood several seconds making these sounds that varied in tone and pitch. The great hawk watched him intently the entire time, and when Dynnis quieted, the bird made one up-and-down movement of its head, screeched three long cries, then lifted lightly from the branch and flew out of sight toward the high square tower.

Dynnis turned back to the rest of us. "Well," he said matter-of-factly, "that takes care of that." At our questioning faces, he explained, "You are correct about the bird being a red-tailed hawk, Hawk." Dynnis smiled at the play on words. "But I'm afraid that you're wrong about its being a *he.* The female hawk is most always the larger bird, and this one is a very royal member of the hawk world as well."

"Royal?" Hawk looked confused.

"Yes, she told me she is the Queen Huntress; her realm encompasses the rivers and forests of most of the Northeastern American continent. She has been waiting for our arrival—or, I should say, for *you* three to arrive.

"Wait a minute." Jeff had stopped walking backward and rejoined the group. "You mean you actually talked to that bird and he—*she* answered you?"

"We gnomes have long ago made friends with the nocturnal creatures of the forests. We had to learn their language in order to do that."

"So, why was she expecting *us*?" I asked.

"She is one of your guides. She knows this place very well—has a nest in one of the cupolas. You've only to call her name, and she will help in anyway she can."

"Call her name?" Jeff and Hawk asked in concert. "What's her name?"

"*Avnova.*"

"*Avnova!*" Hawk and Jeff were still in stereo. "You mean like—?"

"Just like." Dynnis then explained, "In the Old World it was possible for lower deities to change back and forth from animal to human: shape-shifters, for lack of a better term. And since those deities are immortal"—he looked up to where the hawk had flown—"it is quite possible that we have just encountered one of your family's ancestors from that long-ago time."

Dynnis went on to tell us that Avnova had instructed him to lead us in the direction she had flown, and there we would find an open entrance to the asylum. So with him in the lead, Hawk and I following, and Jeff bringing up the rear with the flashlight, we entered the overgrown path to the front entrance.

Dynnis stopped and turned. "Avnova said we will find a set of double doors, one standing ajar, just beyond those bushes." He indicated a badly neglected group of shrubs that had grown to the sills of the boarded-up second-story windows. "She also suggested that we take care with our footing. The doors lead down into tunnels." He motioned toward Hawk and me. "We will need to proceed with extreme caution; there are bound to be some slippery spots along the way."

Hawk and I nodded our heads simultaneously, and I heard Jeff swallow hard.

Dynnis took a deep breath. "Okay, then," he said, squaring his shoulders. "Jeff, since you have the torch, you lead the way. Let us begin."

The hawk had indeed led us to the right spot. As we made our way around the hedges, the glow of the flashlight shone on two badly rusted metal doors. One swung in, hanging open like a drunken host propping himself against the wall, inviting guests inside. Silently, we followed Jeff into the inky blackness, stepping around puddles on the slippery concrete floor. I held tightly to the chair handles, both to keep Hawk safe and to help keep my own footing. It was so dark that the flashlight beam itself seemed to shrink with the gloom. And if I thought it was cold and damp outside, it paled in comparison to the dank underground world we now entered. I looked overhead for signs of bats; I was not a big fan of the creatures. Remembered stories from when I was little made me wish I had a hood on my coat.

The words that had been burned into the yellow notepaper by the lodestone suddenly sprang to mind: THE SOULS ARE FORSAKEN—*the bargain* IS STRUCK!

The phrase seemed more ominous in this dungeon. Were we entering the Hill of Hathorne right now? I supposed we were. The floor had a definite, downward slope. And what about the people who had been sent to live here in the asylum? Whatever became of them? My mind filled with questions as I gazed around at the moldy gray walls that looked as if they might have once been white. Old paint hung down in strips like fly-paper coils. Jeff swung his light left and right and then back onto the floor to see where the puddles lay. Even when it was new, I don't think I would have had high hopes for any length of time upon entering this place. My only hope now was that we could get to the end of this quickly—and in one piece.

All at once a loud crash, as if the metal door had swung shut with great force, resounded through the tunnels, repeating over and over again, causing my stomach to lurch—and causing Jeff to stop dead in his tracks and Hawk to cover his ears against the reverberating noise. Although I wanted to do the same, I hung onto the wheelchair and clenched my teeth, wishing, not for the first time, that Hawk had stayed home.

Dynnis was first to speak as the sound faded away down the tunnel. "The outside doors have closed." It was obvious he was shaken but determined not to show it. "And even if we could make our way back up that slippery walkway, we would need much more strength than any of us has to open them, so …"

He held out his hand for the flashlight, which Jeff surrendered. Dynnis swung its beam down the long corridor ahead of us. Although the batteries were fresh and the beam strong and steady, the gloom of the moldering basement absorbed its rays until it shone only a few feet ahead of where we stood. But even with that limitation, we could see several archways ahead, curving slightly and seeming to go on forever—downward.

Turning, Dynnis shined the light on the backpack Hawk still had in his lap. "We are going to need something else to help us find our way into the hill—and more importantly, out of it."

Before he could explain further, a long drawn-out noise filled the tunnel, like the sound of a ship's sail being ripped in two by giant hands. Before I could determine the source, a pinging sound joined in, and Jeff shouted in pain.

"Something hit me!" he yelled as he doubled over, holding his left arm, just as another *ping* hit the wall not far from my head.

"Hawk, down!" I shouted. Hawk bent double, putting his face into his knees and covering his head with his hands. Crouching alongside the wheelchair, I glanced at Jeff. He was down on one knee in the water, and I suddenly realized that Dynnis no longer held the flashlight. It simply hung in the air like a helicopter set on hover, shooting its beam upward toward the tops of the walls. Back and forth it swung, as if suspended from some kind of invisible thread, twisting this way and that.

The ripping grew louder, and whatever whizzed through the air increased in intensity until the walls seemed to hum like they were being bombarded by millions of angry bees. Several projectiles landed in the puddles at my feet, and I reached out and picked one up. As the flashlight swung in my direction, I got a momentary glimpse of what looked like a small, yellow, arrow-shaped stone. It was smooth, with extremely sharp edges.

"Jeff!" Hawk cried, as his ashen-faced twin tipped forward, fell face first into the murky water—and then lay still. Before I could move toward him, another ping hit the flashlight, causing it to fall, making a *kerplunk* as it hit the water, plunging us into total darkness.

Hawk and I both shouted Jeff's name at the same time, causing our voices to echo off the thick tunnel walls. The ripping sound and the pelting of the stones had stopped, and now quiet settled around us, except for the sound of dripping water from the walls and ceiling. I was barely aware of it, however, as I searched frantically on my knees for Jeff, in darkness so complete it seemed to suck the very air from the tunnel.

"Jeff, answer me!" I didn't need to shout now, but my frantic calls received no reply.

"Where is he, November?" Hawk sounded as frightened as I felt.

"I don't know." I crawled around helplessly in the muck, trying to feel my way to my cousin. "Dynnis! Where are you?" My voice echoed back at me.

"Jeff!" Hawk said, then I heard something between a grunt and a groan.

"Hawk, what's wrong?" I knew it wasn't a good idea to bring him along.

"I'm going to find my brother."

"No! Don't try to get out of that chair." I didn't know what to do next—try to get to Hawk or keep looking for Jeff. And where the heck was Dynnis?

"I'm going to help Jeff." I could hear Hawk beginning to maneuver himself out of the chair. If he got down in that water, I didn't know how I was going to get him back up—provided I could even find the wheelchair in this pit. If he died in this horrible place, it would be my fault. Once again, I would have to live with the knowledge that I'd failed someone. I'd been given one more chance to get it right, and now I was going to lose both my cousins.

As suddenly as it began, my fear turned to anger—white-hot rage against the injustice of it all. I started splashing around. Nobody was going to die in this hole—not tonight, not if I had anything to do with it. "Hawk, *don't move.* That's an *order!*" I said through clenched teeth, like I was talking to a bad little kid.

The rustling ceased, and I heard him say, "Damn this thing!" and his fists hit the padded armrest, as I continued to feel around for Jeff.

My knees were almost numb now with the wet cold, and my jeans were completely soaked up to the waist. I kept seeing Jeff in my mind as he'd fallen, face first, into that filthy black water, and so I kept crawling and sweeping my hands through the thick darkness. *It's too long. I'm taking too long.* The words were doing a round-robin in my head. *Too long, too long. Got to find him, got to find him—sweep, sweep, swish, swish.*

"I have him," came Dynnis' voice out of the void.

"Dynnis, the flashlight!" I said—if only I could see Jeff and make sure he was all right.

"I have that, too," Dynnis said grimly. "It's broken."

"Jeff!" Hawk called, and when his brother didn't answer, he asked, "Dynnis, is he okay?"

"He's alive," came the reply, "but I'm afraid he is far from okay."

Chapter Thirteen

Let no lamenting cries, nor doleful tears be
heard all night within, nor yet without.

—Edmund Spenser, *Epithalamion*

"What do you mean?" Hawk's voice was tight.

Dynnis didn't answer right away. Instead, it sounded like he was trying the button on the flashlight. He sighed, and then I heard what I assumed was his dropping it back in the water.

"Dynnis?" Hawk prompted.

I began crawling toward Hawk's voice.

"Jeff has been hit by Elf-shot." Dynnis' voice suggested he was moving something heavy. "And," he panted, "he's unconscious right now. I'm trying to …"—the sound of water sloshing against the walls indicated he was attempting to move Jeff to higher ground—"move him to the side," he grunted, which I took to mean that he had been successful.

"Dynnis, can you see at all?" I asked. I bumped my head on something hard. Hawk cried out, and I said, "It's just me." I felt around to determine if I was in the front or the rear of the wheelchair, and my hand met warm flesh that pulled away from my touch like I was a water moccasin.

"November, I hope that's you." Hawk reached out and grasped the material of my coat in his fist.

"Gnomes can see in the darkness nineteen times better than humans," Dynnis said, in answer to my question. "But the blackness in this crypt is so solid that even my abilities are severely limited. And we are going to have to move soon because something is causing water to run into this passageway. I have moved Jeff to a high spot, but it will not remain that way for long, I fear. I judge at the rate the water is seeping in here that we have less than ten minutes to get out of this corridor and up to a different level."

"What's Elf-shot? Is he going to wake up soon?" Hawk's tone suggested he was not going anywhere until he had a full report on his brother.

"Elf-shot, sometimes called Elf-arrow or Elf-dart, is a small, very sharply pointed arrowhead that is almost always tipped with some type of poison. It is usually fatal, but in Jeff's case, it must have only grazed the skin."

"So he's going to be okay, then?" Hawk pressed.

The water was now running freely inside the tunnel, and I stood up. It was at my knees and rapidly rising.

"We are going to have to hold the questions for later," Dynnis stated. "We need to be moving on—and quickly."

"But we can't see!" I cried. "And besides, we don't even know where the entrance to the upper level is. How are we going to know which way to go?"

"We will simply have to go forward. This is an old building. There are bound to be some loose bricks and places where some light might filter in." Dynnis was trying to reassure us, but his voice betrayed his words.

"Wait." It was Hawk's voice in the darkness now. "My watch. It has an LCD display that comes with a night-light. When I push the button on the bottom right of the dial ..."

Suddenly, a small sphere of dim light lit up the tunnel, showing Hawk sitting hunched and looking down at his left wrist, Dynnis standing not three feet away against the wall, and Jeff semi-propped against the dingy walls as water rushed over him up to his chest. Hawk spotted his brother as the light faded to black, and his mouth dropped open in horror.

"I can keep hitting it as we need it," he said. "I'm pretty sure the battery will last long enough to help us get Jeff out."

"That is wonderful," Dynnis said with false optimism. "I'll tell you when you should press the button, and between us, we just might get this young man to safety."

I heard Dynnis grunt and then there was a lot of sloshing. "Okay, Hawk, turn on the light," he commanded.

When the tiny watch face illuminated, we saw that Dynnis was carrying Jeff on his back as he began making his way through the ever-rising water that now reached the midsection of his body. It was like watching an ant move an acorn.

I took that opportunity to grab the handlebars of the wheelchair and push Hawk after the retreating figure. I had to hustle to keep up. It was amazing how fast Dynnis could carry the limp figure. My unconscious cousin had to outweigh him by at least fifty pounds.

By the time we reached the end of the corridor, Hawk had hit the light several more times, and the water was up to Dynnis' shoulders and my waist.

Hawk held his arms above his head to keep the watch dry. The icy water was now to his chest, and I heard him take sharp breaths in order to bear it.

The chair was almost impossible to push with the debris that floated by in the swift current. Chunks of plaster and the odd shoe, as well as sticks and small branches from the outside, rushed past, jamming up the wheels as it swirled into us with ever-increasing speed.

When I thought the water would surely swallow us, I heard Dynnis' voice. "Hawk, the light. I think I've found the door."

Without a word, the sphere of light glowed, and sure enough, there was another set of badly rusted double metal doors. I prayed they would release, and at the same time wondered how Dynnis meant to open them while holding Jeff.

"November, push the handle on the left door," Dynnis instructed. Even though I doubted I had the strength to be successful, I let go of Hawk and waded toward the doors. As I reached out my hand, Dynnis added, "And push in—hard."

I grasped the peeling handle and turned it while slamming my body against the door for added leverage. Nothing. It wouldn't budge.

"Try again," Dynnis said, puffing as the water swirled just under his chin.

Pulling back as far as my arm could reach, I grasped the handle once more and rammed my shoulder into it with all my might. The door held fast. Again, Hawk lit the watch and again, I threw myself at the door. I could feel the water as it rushed past, throwing spray into my face from the swirling debris, but I knew the water in my eyes were tears of frustration.

As Hawk hit the light one more time, I saw he was in water up to his chin, and Dynnis was holding his head back in order to keep his face free to breathe.

"One more time; there's the girl," Dynnis said gently, as if we had all the time in the world.

Hawk's light flared once more, and then I felt huge claws grasp my shoulders and the weight of a large body settle onto them. Before I could even react, I heard the sound of enormous wings flapping above my head, and in sheer terror, I reared back, grabbed the handle, and ran into the door like it was made out of crepe paper. The sound of hinges, frozen from long disuse, screeched loudly, as if joining in a chorus with me as I screamed my way through the entrance, while high water surged in behind me, carrying Dynnis, who, once he had his footing back, ran past me with Jeff up a long ramp to higher ground.

As the water reached Hawk's nose, I watched in wonder as the gigantic hawk, Avnova, settled onto the wheelchair handles and lifted it into the air as if it were made of Styrofoam. Dynnis was already halfway up the ramp to the second level, so he didn't see Avnova fly through the doorway and over our heads, carrying Hawk to the top of the next level, where she deposited the chair gently on the floor before flying back and slamming the door against the flooding waters with her enormous, outstretched feet.

Somehow, I had managed to stumble up the ramp as the massive bird flew to the rafters of the tall corridor. The windows along one wall testified to the fact that we were no longer below ground. Avnova settled herself on a large pipe and began preening as if nothing of any consequence had just occurred, but as I passed under her, she stopped and looked down at me.

"Thank you," I whispered, my voice hoarse from my screams. The great bird inclined her head once, then resumed her grooming.

The near-full moon produced just enough light through the filthy windows to make out where Dynnis had deposited Jeff. Hawk wheeled his chair over and sat shivering as he spoke quietly to Dynnis. I had never before been so cold that my teeth chattered, and so I found it a strange sensation when I couldn't stop my lower jaw from vibrating up and down, causing my teeth to clack together furiously. I seriously doubted I would ever be warm again. As I approached the others, sitting beside the entrance to a steep stairwell inside a metal cage, I could see that Dynnis had found several old manila folders full of papers, which he now used to make a crude pillow for Jeff's head.

Hawk leaned forward toward his brother. "Jeff! Jeff." He reached out and touched his twin's shoulder. When there was no response, he looked up at Dynnis. "We have to get out of here and get him home," he said. "Aunty Gin will know what to do for him."

"Yeah, like send him to the hospital." They both looked up at me.

"Hawk is right," Dynnis replied, ignoring my sarcasm. "Jeff needs to be seen to." He indicated the stairwell that ascended at least two more stories inside the wired cage. "The bad news is that we are going to have to get him up to the next level in order to find another way out." Turning to Hawk, he continued, "I can carry your brother up that flight of stairs and get there faster, but you and November are going to have to go through that door."

He pointed to a single, peeling metal door with a small glass window in the upper half. Like the ones we had just passed through, it, too, had a rusted metal lever as a handle. I could see there was something printed on the door just below the window. Walking closer, I read the words aloud: "Extreme Precaution."

"Excellent advice," Dynnis said, as he lifted a still-unconscious Jeff onto his back once more and made for the stairwell. "I intend to do just that, and I advise you to follow suit. I will meet you at the next floor, and I would also advise not tarrying." He nodded his head in the direction of the water seeping under the doors.

I walked to the door of the stairwell cage and looked up. It was too dark to see all the way to the top, but the tall, barred windows rising as far as I could see let in enough light to make out the steepness of the stairs and the treacherous footing of the metal mesh steps. The cage door screeched in protest as I swung it wide for Dynnis and Jeff, leaving it standing open as I watched them go up the steps. They resembled some kind of misshapen monster that might be slowly making its way to the bell tower of Notre Dame. Avnova took the opportunity to fly silently through the opening, disappearing up into the darkness of the cavernous stairwell.

"Emmy," Hawk prompted, "we'd better go, too." He shivered so badly now that his voice shook like an old man's. Reaching down and taking hold of the back wheels of the chair, Hawk rolled toward the door, and I sprinted to open it, as once again, we entered the darkness.

By this time, we had become something of a well-oiled machine, with Hawk tapping his wristwatch as he rolled up the ramped hallway without incident to the next level. The night wind moaned outside the old building, whistling through the cracks and crevices of dilapidated walls. With each tap of the light, I began to realize we were passing along another long, narrow corridor with a series of doors on both sides. Each had the same type of small square window at eye level, as in the hall we had just left. When we entered this hallway, a sign hanging just inside the door caught my eye before Hawk's watch light died out: Ward A.

It might have been the wind but I could have sworn I heard a voice whisper, *"Violent Ward."* Before I could look around for the source, Hawk called from up ahead.

"There's some kind of room at the end," he said, speeding up, "and there's a little more light."

I didn't blame him for making haste in this corridor. There was something about the air in here. Of course, it stank of mildew, rotted plaster, and wood, but there was something more. This smell was almost sweet—like stale gingerbread. I didn't have time to dwell on it because Hawk was almost to the end of the hallway.

Here, it widened into a circular room with floor-to-ceiling windows. As he rolled around the room tapping his light, Hawk read aloud some of the graffiti written on the walls by other uninvited guests of the abandoned structure. Most of it was just the usual stuff, like initials and names of street punks, but at the bottom of one window was printed the word Solarium on a blue tile plate.

And then, my heart did a flip-flop and my sore throat let loose a high-pitched squawk, as a voice behind me said, "No sun in the solarium today, I'm afraid."

Chapter Fourteen

She has taken a silver wand and given him strokes three, and he's started up the bravest knight that ever your eyes did see.

—Old English ballad (Anonymous)

Hawk let out a shout that caused him to pitch forward, almost flipping the chair on its side.

I spun around to see a middle-aged man holding a lantern. He was dressed in a long dark coat with ruffles at his wrists, much like the man I'd seen when I had slipped into the past. For a moment, I was afraid I *had* slipped back, until I realized Hawk had turned his chair around and was staring at the figure, wide-eyed.

Shoulder-length gray hair framed sharp, beady black eyes above a beak of a nose and downturned mouth. The mouth switched gears, turning up in a smile as the man advanced two steps toward us, as we, in turn, moved back the equal number—well, at least *I* did; Hawk rolled clear back to the wall. The man in black stepped forward again, and once more I retreated. It was like some weird dance, resembling fencing moves.

Finally, he said, "You needn't be afraid. I could not hurt you even if I wanted to—which I don't, by the by." He placed the lantern on the floor and extended his hand in a show of faith.

"I'm Edmond Halley," he said simply. "And you are?"

"Edmond Halley!" Hawk exclaimed, rolling slowly to where I stood. "Did you just say your name is Edmond Halley?"

I wondered if Hawk's hearing had been affected by the exposure to the cold water.

"I did," said the gentleman.

"You mean, like the guy who discovered the comet?" Hawk's teeth were still chattering and it came out sounding like, "Ya-a-a m-m-mean, like the g-g-g-guy who disc-c-covered the ca-ca-ca-comet?"

"I beg your pardon, young man, but I only speak the King's English." Mr. Halley's eyebrows drew together in a frown.

Since I doubted it was possible for me to get any colder, I took off my pea coat and carried it to Hawk, who cleared his throat for another attempt.

"I think he just asked you if you discovered the comet," I said over my shoulder, as I bent down and began wrapping Hawk in the soggy woolen overcoat.

"Oh, the comet," Halley sighed. "Yes and no on that. I fear there is a long tale connected to that story."

I wondered if he had made the bad pun on purpose. If so, his face showed no indication of it. Evidently, it had sailed over Hawk's head, too, because he gripped the coat up to his throat and continued.

"But you're dead! I mean ya-you, the ca-ca-comet was dis-discovered in 1682!" In frustration, Hawk wrapped his arms around himself. "That would make you over th-th-three—"

"Three-hundred fifty today," Edmond Halley said, standing straighter. "Or maybe I should say, yesterday, as it is well past midnight of November 9th."

Hawk seemed to suddenly have lost his voice—or maybe he was going into some kind of shock. And where was Dynnis? It seemed I was asking myself that question a lot in the past few hours.

Edmund Halley cleared his throat. "Well, I suppose I should ask what you children are doing in this place at this perfectly dreadful hour." His tone was conversational, but his face betrayed him. His eyes were unnaturally bright, and he kept rubbing his hands together like Wile E. Coyote right before he tries to eat the Road Runner.

"Ah, Sir Edmond," Dynnis said, coming into the circle of light thrown out by the lantern on the floor. "It has been a very long time." He crossed the room and, dropping to one knee, began lowering Jeff onto the floor beneath the bank of windows.

"Mr. Bartholomew, splendid to see you!" Halley sprung into action, rushing over to help Dynnis ease Jeff down and make him as comfortable as could be possible on the filthy tile floor. When each one stood, Halley extended his hand, which Dynnis accepted with a smile.

"What is it that brings all of you to this black place on this unearthly night?" Halley repeated.

"The Bargain." Dynnis' smile disappeared like the sun behind a storm cloud.

Sir Edmund took back his hand. He walked to the windows and turned, frowning. "You mean someone has found the lost documents? Surely they would be long gone by now. And if not, who has set events in motion that would disturb the Bargain?"

Dynnis inclined his head toward my cousins and me.

"Surely, not these children!" Halley exclaimed.

"They are direct descendants of Avnova," said Dynnis. "Sir Edmond Halley, meet Stephen, Jeffrey, and November Atwood."

"Atwood," Halley repeated, and he looked at us with new respect. "I see. And just what did you three find?"

When I hesitated, Dynnis spoke up.

"You can tell him, November. Sir Edmond can likely be of some help with our search. He was a child when the Bargain was struck, and his family was indirectly involved, although he was in England at the time."

"We think we found a map to something that was buried a long time ago," I began.

"Three Stones, Three Echoes, and Three Seals," Sir Edmond recited. He walked to where Jeff lay and knelt down, putting his hand on the unconscious boy's forehead. "And what has happened to this young man?" His soft voice held compassion.

"Elf-shot," Dynnis supplied.

Sir Edmond looked sharply at Dynnis. "Elf-shot! Where? How badly is he hit?"

"It is just a graze, but a deep one—he has fallen victim."

The last two words caused a shiver to run down my already icy spine.

"What's going to happen to my brother?" Hawk had regained control of his voice and all trace of the chatter was gone.

Sir Edmond and Dynnis exchanged a worried look.

"As I started to explain earlier," Dynnis said, "Elf-shot is an arrow-shaped stone usually made from soft yellow flint. They are flung as a dart with great force and even greater accuracy."

"In the Highlands of Scotland they are called *saighead sidhe.* The Scottish witch, Isobel Gowdie, claimed in her confession to have seen the devil directing elf-boys to make the arrows, which were then given to witches to throw at people and livestock," added Sir Edmond.

"Are you telling us *witches* were shooting those things at us in the tunnel?" Hawk asked incredulously.

"Not witches—elves."

"Elves," Hawk repeated, his voice level.

"Like those seven guys with Snow White?" Jeff was struggling to sit up, rubbing his eyes like he had just awakened from tasting the poisoned apple himself.

Hawk spun around, his face breaking into a smile. "Snow White had *dwarves,* you dweeb." He laughed as he rolled toward his brother. "Dude, are you okay?"

Jeff nodded his head as he ran his hands through his hair. "I think so," he said slowly, then looked around. "Man, what happened? How did I get here?" He tried getting to his feet, but wobbled on his knees, then sat back down.

Dynnis was instantly at Jeff's side. "Jeffrey, tell me what you remember. Did you see who shot you?"

"I was shot?" Jeff seemed surprised by Dynnis' words. Then he glanced down at his arm. "Oh, yeah. Something hit me." He touched the spot on his left arm.

"Let us have a look," Sir Edmond offered, and Jeff pushed up his sleeve. After a close examination of Jeff's arm, Sir Edmund stepped back. "There does not seem to be any wound in evidence," he said, clearly confused. "You say this boy has been shot? Elf-shot leaves a mark for some time—usually a great one."

Dynnis brought the lantern closer to make an inspection. "Nothing at all. Most unusual." He placed the lantern back on the floor, then addressed Jeff. "What is your full name?"

"Jeff Atwood," Jeff answered slowly.

"I asked for your *full* name."

"It's Jeff … um … Jeff …" He looked up at all of us standing around him in a circle and then down. "I don't know anything more than Jeff Atwood," he said to the floor tiles.

Hawk leaned forward, his voice urgent. "What's your middle name?"

When Jeff, still staring at the floor, didn't respond, Hawk prompted, "You were named after Mom's grandfather."

Jeff's face remained blank, and Hawk looked at Dynnis and Sir Edmond as if they held the answer to what might be wrong with his brother. Both men shook their heads, their somber faces showing that clearly they didn't know anymore than he did.

Sir Edmond spoke first. "I have heard it said that the term 'Elf-stroke,' from which we get the word 'stroke,' meaning a paralytic seizure, is sometimes the result of poison entering the bloodstream." He shook his head as if to contradict himself. "But that does not follow with the fact that there is no obvious wound where the young man was struck."

"Stroke," Hawk said, still staring at his brother, who sat hanging his head as if he were standing in front of the principal, or maybe the whole school board, in shame.

"You mean Jeff has had a stroke?" His haunted eyes begged either man to contradict him.

"Not in the way you think," Dynnis said. "Elf-shot, or Elf-*stroke,* if you will, refers only to a kind of paralysis caused by a blow or pass of the elf hand, which can cause a person to lose consciousness or to fall down—temporarily paralyzed."

Jeff suddenly lay down and closed his eyes. "I'm tired," he sighed.

Hawk's mouth set. "We have to get out of here—now." Rolling into the middle of the room, he shouted, "Avnova!" And before I could turn around, the giant red hawk flew into the circle of light provided by the lantern, landing neatly in front of the wheelchair.

Hawk leaned toward the enormous bird. "Help us—please." Avnova walked to where Jeff lay and rested her head on his chest. When she raised it, she opened her beak and made a warbling sound that rose from low in her throat.

Dynnis stiffened, then turned to Hawk and me and said, "Avnova will lead us to the entrance by a different route than we entered, due to the flooding in the first basement." As he began to lift Jeff onto his back, Jeff moaned and rolled onto his side.

"My head," he said, reaching up. "I can't feel my head."

Dynnis retreated as Avnova stepped forward, opened her beak, and picked Jeff up by his coat. Turning toward the door, she lifted off smoothly and flew through it, taking Jeff with her.

"Let's go!" shouted Hawk, pushing the wheels of the chair with all his might.

Dynnis and I ran to catch up with him, and I looked back over my shoulder at Sir Edmond, who still stood in the circle of light. "Godspeed!" he called after us. "I'll be waiting right here when you return!"

I waved and ran after Dynnis, Hawk, and Avnova, who was now out of sight down the black corridor.

When we return? Not on your life, pal. As I ran after the others, I decided that when we made it out, *if we made it out of this nuthouse*, I was never going back inside again—no matter what.

We were all out of breath, even Hawk, by the time we had run down the ramps and made our way through several more corridors to the ground level and out the double doors of the main building.

I couldn't believe how good the icy air felt after the damp and fetid interior of the asylum.

"Avnova has flown ahead with Jeff, but she can only take him as far as the front lawn. We must make haste!" Dynnis grabbed the handles of Hawk's chair and sprinted ahead, full throttle. I would have dearly loved to stop and catch my breath, but I knew the others would need me to help get Jeff into the house, and so I ran with a stitch in my right side growing stronger with each footfall. My breath puffed out of my mouth like steam from an overworked engine.

The temperature was below freezing now, and I could feel my clothes beginning to stiffen, making it even harder to keep going. I was losing momentum and watched as Dynnis and Hawk pulled farther and farther ahead. Finally, the pain was too much, and I stopped to catch my breath as the others rounded the last curve down the long drive to the street. Standing with my hands on my knees waiting for the sharp pain to subside, I heard the sound of crunching gravel.

"Young lady, what are you doing out this time of night?"

I turned to see Mr. Whoozi-What's in a golf cart. He had come up behind me with the headlights turned off.

I could have asked him the same thing, but decided it might not be in my best interest.

"Oh, hi," I gasped. "I was just out for a jog." I tried to straighten up but the stitch pulled me back down, so I just stood there, looking up at him as he drew beside me.

He glanced at his watch. "At three in the morning? Do your aunts allow you to run around the neighborhood at all hours, alone?"

After the night's adventure, I wasn't exactly quick-witted, so I said the first thing that came to mind. "Well, they really don't know I'm out, but I like to run"—I looked up at the nearly full moon, shining brightly now that the fog had lifted—"by the light of the moon!" I wheezed, trying to make my voice match my cheery words. "But I think I may have overdone it a bit." I smiled lamely.

Whoozi-What's got out of the cart, took hold of my arm, and led me gently to the passenger's side. "Why don't we just get you home then?" he said, as if talking to one of the asylum's inmates who'd attempted an escape.

For a moment, I thought he might turn the cart around and take me back to the administration building to be handed over to a phantom orderly. Instead, he climbed into the driver's seat and pressed his large foot on the pedal. The cart lurched forward, and we sped in silence down the rest of the drive. It was then I noticed that he was wearing a guard's uniform.

"If you'll direct me, I'll take you all the way home," he said, looking over at me.

Oh, boy. What if he sees Dynnis—or worse, Avnova carrying Jeff in her beak? I must have been on the brink of total collapse because I suddenly found it all very funny. I pointed toward Hazen Avenue. "It's just up ahead, but watch out for the gnome, the human popsicle, and especially the giant hawk with a kid in his—oops, I mean *her*—mouth." I giggled idiotically and Mr. Whoozi-What's looked at me in alarm. I surprised myself by adding, "And why were *you* at the asylum at three in the morning?"

"I'm the night watchman," he replied, putting on the brakes.

We'd reached the edge of my aunts' property. The lawn stretched quiet and empty in the moonlight. I jumped out of the electric cart and thanked Mr. Whoozi-What's.

"Well, next time you decide to take a run in the wee hours of the morning, bring a flashlight, and signal me by shining it toward the old Banner Building to the left of admin. I have a small office, and I can see the drive clearly. Two blinks and then two more will let me know who you are and that you're okay—okay?" He frowned. "But you really shouldn't be out by yourself at night."

After promising to follow his advice, I waved good-bye and watched as he rolled back the way he had come, before making my way, as quietly as possible, into the house.

I headed for my cousins' room and stuck my head in. Hawk was sitting up in the bottom bunk with only the soft glow of the night-light. Jeff was safely tucked into the upper one, and I didn't even have the energy to ask who—*or what*—had placed him there.

"He's sleeping," Hawk whispered.

"Sounds like a plan," I answered. "Good night; see you in the morning." I started for my bedroom.

"It already is morning."

"Then, good morning." I wanted nothing more on earth at that moment than some nice dry pajamas and my bed.

But an hour later, I was still on my back, wide awake. The events of the evening kept playing out, over and over, like a shadowy video across the ceiling. *The Children of Avnova,* Dynnis had called us. That implied some kind of strong connection between my cousins and me. If so, Jeff and Hawk didn't seem to be any better informed about it than I was.

I rolled onto my side and drew up my knees. I didn't want to be a Child of Avnova. In fact, I didn't even want to be in this bed, in this house, in this cold, nasty old town another minute. I didn't want to have to deal with Jeff and his strange *Elf-shot* illness, or worse yet, be responsible for Hawk's wheelchair stuff. Up until now, I'd done a pretty good job of avoiding anyone in a wheelchair. I didn't even make eye contact with them in public places. But wouldn't you know it? Fate had to plunk me down in the middle of a family—*my family,* no less—where I was forced to worry about losing someone all over again who I was beginning to grow really fond of. And that asylum—I screwed my eyes tight as a fresh image of the old relic rose behind my eyelids. I felt tears begin to seep out, and I rubbed them away roughly with the back of my hand as I flopped onto my back again.

What was the matter with me? I wasn't a coward—well, not usually. Okay, so maybe almost drowning in a decrepit old mausoleum had shaken my bones a bit. But what did it say about me that I was ready to scamper back to Phoenix like some weenie? I flipped over onto my stomach and pulled the pillow over my head. I wasn't six years old anymore, but I suddenly wished with all my heart that I had Beast, my ragged old friend with the stuffing coming out of his knees and the paint worn off his eyes. What I feared was not the old asylum, or sharp-shooting elves, or even ghosts of dead men with lanterns. I buried my face into the mattress and gritted my teeth. What I feared most was the growing knowledge that somehow, in some way, I was responsible for the four people sleeping under this roof. Something gnawed and twisted in my gut and whispered that very soon, I would be tested. And this time I had better not fail.

Chapter Fifteen

Let us in! Let us in! Who is crying above the wind's din?
Let us in! Let us in! We are pale and cold and thin.

—Olive Dove, *Let Us In*

I AWOKE TO SOMEONE SOFTLY CALLING MY name: "November," then, "Emmy, wake up!"

The urgent whisper hacked its way through the layers of sleep. Hawk had rolled his chair beside my bed.

Pushing myself onto one elbow, I squinted first at him and then the clock: 7:00 a.m. It was barely light outside.

"It's not him!" Hawk hissed.

"What?" Was I dreaming this? I certainly hoped so. But when I tried to lie back down, Hawk grew frantic.

"No! Don't go back to sleep! I'm trying to tell you, it's *not him*!"

"Hawk, what are you talking about?" I sat up and swung my legs over the edge of the bed. "*Who's* not him?" Did that even make sense? No. Nothing in my world made sense anymore.

"Jeff! It's not him!"

I was waking up now, and I blinked hard several times, trying to focus on what he was trying to tell me. "What do you mean, it's not him? Who is it then?" I asked, rubbing both hands over my face to rid myself of the last vestiges of sleep, thinking that the whole conversation was starting to sound more and more like a bad comedy routine.

"I don't know," Hawk said, shaking his head. "But just a little while ago, I woke up, and he was standing at the window, all hunched over like he was in pain, so I asked him if he was okay. And when he turned from the window, I could see his face clearly in the light and … it's somebody else!" Hawk's face was pale with fear. "November, that kid in my bedroom is not Jeff!"

I didn't know what to say. Hawk leaned forward in his chair, and with a determination that I have never seen before, he said quietly and deliberately, "I am a twin—an *identical* twin, and I have a *connection* with my brother. And I am telling you that the boy who is sitting in our bedroom right now is no one that I know. He is not Jeff."

I felt the hair raise on my arms and legs. "I believe you," I said, and I did. "But if the kid we brought home last night is not Jeff, then who is he? And more importantly, where is Jeff?"

"Hawk, I was afraid of this last night, but when you did not seem to notice it, I hoped for the best." Dynnis walked across the room and hopped up on my bed. It seemed that my room was to be the meeting place this morning.

"What are you saying?" I asked Dynnis as I got up and put on my robe.

"What Sir Edmond and I didn't say last night, because we didn't want to alarm you, is that Elf-shot is a term used to refer to disease, caused by elves or fairies, usually in livestock but sometimes in humans as well. The term comes from the fact that elves could shoot an object, visible or invisible, into a creature, causing it to fall into a deep sleep, much like a coma. In its place, a replica body, or Changeling, was left to sicken and die, while the real victim was carried away to the Elfin Hill."

"Is that what you think happened to Jeff?" I asked, and Dynnis nodded, his expression solemn.

"My brother has been taken by elves?" Hawk asked, in disbelief.

"'Twould seem so," he confirmed.

Hawk's eyes darted frantically toward the door and the hallway, then back to Dynnis and me. "So how do we get him back?" he whispered, as if the boy in the next room might, at any moment, burst in and demand his own answers.

Dynnis closed his mouth and exhaled heavily through his nose before saying, "We go back inside the asylum and into the Elfin Hill and get him." His tone was so matter-of-fact that he might have been suggesting a trip to the supermarket for mayonnaise.

I felt the bottom drop out of my stomach at the thought of going back inside that moldy old heap, even in the daylight. But the notion of Jeff, wounded and held captive somewhere deep beneath the moldering bricks by whatever strange beings had shot him, was even worse.

Hawk and I looked at each other. "When?" we asked in unison.

Dynnis looked out at the growing daylight. "I believe one of your modern acronyms for that would be ASAP." He hopped down from the bed and started for the door. "And, if I am right, Jeffrey does not have much time."

"Let's go." Hawk turned his chair around and started for the door.

"Wait!" I called, "What are we going to do about Jeff?"

Hawk stopped halfway into the hall and turned. "We're going to go get him. What else?"

"I think she means what about *him*?" Dynnis motioned to the figure now standing in the doorway.

"Hey, what's up?" Jeff, or *whatever* he was, stood scratching his head like he had just awakened.

"Who're you guys going to go get?" He started into my room and then stumbled, grabbed Hawk's chair, and just managed to stay on his feet.

I moved fast and caught him before he fell.

"Let's get you back to bed." I steered the boy, who I could now plainly see was not Jeff, as he swayed and leaned heavily on my shoulder, back to the bedroom belonging to my cousins. I noticed an odd odor coming from him as I helped him get back into his bunk. It was the same stale gingerbread smell I had noticed in the asylum.

Hawk was silent as I tucked the boy—or *Changeling*, as Dynnis had called him—into Jeff's bed, pulling the covers up to his chin. Almost immediately, he closed his eyes and fell into a deep sleep, complete with soft snoring.

Hawk still sat in the doorway, looking at the Changeling with a mixture of fear and confusion. He turned his haunted eyes to me. "How are we going to get out of this house and leave him here with Mom?"

It was a good question and one I didn't have the answer to. Aunt Marsha would realize that the boy lying in Jeff's bed was not her son as soon as she looked at him.

"Draw the blinds. Darken the room," Dynnis said. "It's a gloomy day, and since our lad here will most likely sleep, do you think it increases the chance that your aunts will leave him alone for the better part of the day. It may buy us the time we need to get Jeff back."

Hawk agreed that his mom and Aunty Gin would most likely let him sleep since it was a Saturday. "We'll need to convince them that Jeff just has a bad cold and asked to be left alone. It might work, but Mom won't let him sleep long. She'll probably try to wake him up by lunchtime."

"Then let us make haste." Dynnis helped Hawk out of the Dune Buggy and into the desk chair. "November, go get dressed—and be smart about it. I will give Hawk a hand with his clothing. You go to the kitchen and get something for us to eat along the way. We've no time to waste."

Dynnis helped Hawk take off his pajama top as I hurried to throw on some clothes and brush my teeth.

My aunts must have decided to sleep in because there was nobody in sight as I raided the fridge. One lonely banana lay in the crisper, along with two apples. I stuffed them into Hawk's backpack and grabbed three bottles of V8 and some granola bars from the basket on the table. It wasn't much of a meal, but it would have to do.

Hawk and Dynnis made their way down the hall toward the front door as I exited the kitchen. Hawk was back in his manual wheelchair that, I was glad to see, was none the worse for having survived the flooded basement of the Danvers Asylum. Without a word, we all went into the foyer, where I hastily put on a hooded, thickly lined sweatshirt, and then helped Hawk put on a dry ski jacket.

"Where do you two think you're going?" Aunt Marsha stood in the hallway just outside her bedroom. She wore faded jeans and a turtleneck pullover covered by a red and black checked flannel shirt. In the dim morning light, she resembled Paul Bunyan's little sister. She stood with her head tilted to the right, her body language saying that the explanation she so patiently waited to hear had better be a good one.

Hawk and I both froze. Dynnis stood with his hand on the doorknob.

"To the school library—we need to do research on our project for history," Hawk spoke up. "And Jeff said he didn't feel good, so he's not coming." Hawk busied himself zipping up his jacket so he didn't have to look his mother in the eye while he lied through his teeth.

"Oh? What's wrong with him?" Aunt Marsha glanced back toward the bedroom.

"Oh, it's nothing much. He just said his stomach aches, and he's feeling really, really sleepy." Hawk looked up then and smiled. "We were up kinda late last night." His smile looked unconvincing, and I watched Aunt Marsha's head tilt back and her eyes squint. Hawk saw it too and quickly added, "We're going to do the research while he sleeps and then later today, we'll go over it—when he's feeling better."

Neither Dynnis nor Aunt Marsha had moved, and now she stared at the door—right at the very spot where he stood. Her eyes strained a little more as she moved her head slightly from side to side as though trying to focus on something she could not quite see. Hawk followed her eyes to where Dynnis stood, clutching the doorknob, as if ready to do a white-rabbit exit down the hole into Wonderland.

"Is something wrong, Aunt Marsha?" I asked to break the tension that now gripped the narrow hall like a closed fist.

Raising her eyebrows and blinking her eyes, Aunt Marsha shook her head once as if to clear her mind. "No. I suppose not. But you need to eat something first." She started toward the kitchen.

"I got fruit and granola bars—oh, and V8!" I smiled, holding up the backpack as evidence of all the nutritious goodies inside.

Doubt showed clearly on my aunt's face now. "Why are you two in such a hurry to get to that school on a Saturday?" Her eyes narrowed in suspicion.

"Remind her that the school library is only open until noon," Dynnis whispered from the doorway.

"Our project is due on the eleventh, and the library is only open until noon." The strain in Hawk's voice belied his attempt to appear casual, and his mother folded her arms and pursed her lips, tilting her head back in what I realized was a classic sign that she wasn't buying it.

She regarded us for a long moment, then said, "Well, in that case, I suppose it's okay." Her voice was filled with the same reserve reflected in her eyes. "But you are going to need to take care walking to the school. The fog is thick this morning, so stay far off the road. Drivers won't be able to see you until the last minute. And come straight home afterward," she added, as we scrambled toward the door.

"Okay, we will," Hawk called back, as he rolled through the doorway. "Oh, and Mom, don't bother Jeff. He said to tell you he really wants to sleep—all day, if he can."

Aunt Marsha's voice carried from the kitchen as she made her way toward the coffee pot. "We'll see about that."

Dynnis opened the door and Hawk, pushing on the wheels as fast as he could, rolled out into the early morning mist, with me right behind him.

Aunt Marsha was right. The fog that had lifted briefly last night was back with a vengeance. Soft folds of gray swirled around, moving ahead of us like a million layers of cold, wet gauze. Looking down, I noticed that the coldest layer seemed to be at our feet. It rose and snaked around our ankles like the stuff created for stage plays and horror movies. I suddenly had the feeling that if I could run fast enough, I could break through it into the brightness of a sunny Saturday morning. Dynnis must have had the same thought because without a word, he started running and disappeared into the mist.

"Hey, wait!" I shouted, gripping the handles on the wheelchair and racing after him. It was then that I heard what sounded like a battle cry erupt from somewhere overhead.

"Hawk, let go of the wheels! I can push you faster!" I shouted over the noise that had suddenly grown out of the air. It sounded like a war was happening right above our heads. If we had been in a haunted funhouse in some amusement park, I would have thought there were speakers overhead projecting loud sounds of hand-to-hand combat for thrill seekers, but this was Danvers, Massachusetts, not Six Flags.

The clanging of metal against metal suggested broad swords in a fierce contest. This was accompanied by thuds and the sound of clubs hitting flesh, followed by loud grunts and deep, long moans. Voices shouted and horses neighed in fear and pain, blending into the racket that grew in volume until I thought, at any moment, we would be crushed by something flying or dropping down on us from the invisible, thunderous world erupting above us.

"November, what the hell is going on?" Hawk shouted, twisting his neck around to look in my face as I hunched over his shoulder, pushing us both headlong into a fog as thick as oatmeal.

Huge drops of rain, hanging in the fabric of the mist, broke free and splashed us like tiny water balloons as we ran. I blinked my eyes and shook my head to clear my vision but with little success.

"I don't know!" I shouted back. "We just have to keep going—sounds like the whole town is under attack!"

"Maybe we should turn around and go back home!" Hawk shouted in my ear as the battle grew still louder.

Not only was I having trouble seeing, but I also was running out of breath, so I didn't bother to tell him that I didn't know the way back home. If I stopped to turn around now, I could very well lead us into more problems.

Suddenly, Dynnis broke through the cloud and brought us to a stop. "November, get into the wheelchair," he directed. At my hesitation, he grew stern. "Listen to me, and do what I say, now!" he commanded. "Get into the wheelchair, and Hawk, you sit on her lap."

"What?" Hawk yelled.

I wasn't sure if Hawk didn't hear him or couldn't believe what Dynnis was asking him to do. The sounds of the battle had now escalated to the point where all I wanted to do was curl up into a ball on the ground and cover my ears.

Dynnis grabbed my arm and pulled me to the front of the Dune Buggy. "Get in!" His shout was so fierce that Hawk shifted to his left side, and I was able to slide into the wheelchair and pull him over on top of my legs.

"If anybody from school sees us, we're never going to live this down," Hawk muttered, as he slid onto my lap.

I didn't reply because I barely had time to put my arms around his middle before Dynnis grabbed the handles of the chair, and we lurched forward at a speed I didn't think possible on the ground. As the gray mist flew past and water hosed our faces, we tore over the graveled shoulder of the road like a hovercraft, though we never left the ground. Turning first this way, then that, we sailed on through the deepening fog until at last, the battle sounds began to recede, and I realized we were at the mouth of the long, private drive to the Danvers State Asylum.

Dynnis slowed the wheelchair long enough to say, "We need to make haste before the fog gets any worse. Just sit tight, and we'll be at the front entrance in a matter of moments." Then we took off again.

He was as good as his word. In what was probably less than a minute, we rolled to a stop at the entrance to the administrative building. I took the fact that we were stopped as a signal that I could let Hawk have his chair back, and Hawk must have read my mind because without a word, I slid out from under him, and he settled back into his seat with a look that told me the less said about that ride, the better.

"Let's get inside." Still holding onto the wheelchair handles, Dynnis began pushing Hawk up the ramp to the second level.

I noticed that the fog had grown darker, virtually blotting out any daylight until finally, at 9:30 in the morning, it was as dark as dusk.

"Where are we going?" Hawk had packed two flashlights, and we both held one as we made our way down the gloomy, damp corridor.

"Back to the room where we met Sir Edmond last night. He might have some idea as to what might have happened to Jeff."

I was glad that Dynnis remembered the way because all of the corridors looked exactly the same to me. "Dynnis, what is happening outside?" I swung my light toward the windows to see if anything was visible, now that we were up on the second floor.

"Yeah, and where did you go when you ran off into the fog?" Hawk added.

"I cannot be certain, but I believe what we were hearing was a battle between the Children of Nudd and the Children of Llyr," Dynnis explained as we made our way down the dark corridor. "You see, in Elfin lore it is believed that there are three families that rule the earth, air, and sea. The Children of Dôn, who guard the earth and are usually a peaceful lot; the Children of Nudd, those that rule the air with their leader, Bilé, a warrior who will stop at nothing to win; and the Children of Llyr, led by the sea god Lêr, who control the sea. There is an ongoing feud between the Children of Nudd and Llyr over who will triumph—the powers of heaven, light, and life, or the sea, darkness and death. When things become unbalanced, as they are now, the scale tips toward one or the other, and a battle usually ensues.

And as for where I went, well I heard the stampede of Nudd horses, and I went out to see how far the fog extended, hoping I could find a spot where we could ride out the storm, so to speak."

He paused to take a breath before continuing. "And I am afraid I could not find the edge of it. It appears to have swallowed up the entire town. I took a brief moment to stop in to see a good friend of mine who is somewhat of an expert on the Nudd and Llyr dispute, and he agreed that whatever is causing this fog to hold Danvers in its grip has caused the two families to start a battle for power."

"So what's going to happen?" Hawk asked. "I mean, can the whole town hear it?"

"Yes and no," answered Dynnis. "To most people, the sound of the fighting will come through as very strong thunder. Remember, we heard it the other night? But since you are the Children of Avnova, you heard the actual battle, and because of that, you were in immediate danger. Avnova, remember, is the guardian of both the forests and the rivers—land and water," he explained. "And since she is most often in the form of a creature of the air, her family members are in danger of being taken hostage by either of the warring parties."

"Do you think that's who took Jeff?" Hawk asked.

"No," Dynnis replied. "Whoever threw that Elf-shot had a different motive in mind, I think. We're almost there." He slowed to look carefully at the doors now before continuing.

"We'll have to ask Sir Edmond, but if my theory is correct, you three need to finish your task in time for the Bargain to be broken, so that the balance can be restored and things can right themselves." He stopped in front of the same shabby door we had entered last night.

"First, we need to find Jeff," Hawk said, but Dynnis ignored him and motioned for me to open the door.

Chapter Sixteen

The creaking door has a spell to riddle—I
play a tune without any fiddle.
—James Reeves, *Spells*

THE BLACK ROOM WAS UNCHANGED FROM THE previous night and completely empty, except for some old wooden crates piled in the corner. It was hard to imagine that it was mid-morning as Hawk and I swung our flashlights around the gloomy solarium.

"Sir Edmond?" Dynnis didn't need to speak very loudly for his voice to echo in the empty chamber, and instantly we saw the soft glow of Sir Edmond's lantern as he came toward us from the shadows.

"The battles have begun, I see," he said, by way of greeting. "Avnova has gone off to assess this one's magnitude."

Dynnis nodded. "And the young lad we took from here last night is, as we feared, a Changeling."

The two men regarded each other gravely.

"How can we find my brother, Sir Edmond? Can you help us?" Hawk asked, as Sir Edmond bent forward and placed his lantern on the floor. Straightening up, he indicated the backpack we had shown him last night.

"Mr. Bartholomew tells me that you have a map as well as the documents concerning the stones, seals, and echoes."

I reached for the backpack, but Hawk moved quicker and swung it off the handles, handing it over to the elderly gentleman.

Dynnis had gone into the shadows and returned carrying a long, low wooden crate that Sir Edmond accepted gratefully and used to spread out the manuscript and other papers. He leafed through them as

Hawk held the flashlight steady for him to read. After a few moments he looked up.

"Well, if I am reading this correctly it indicates that the first seal is located in the room directly below us—the library. However," he paused and stroked his chin, "that leaves us with a bit of a problem. The route that you need to access the room is in the part of the basement that flooded last night."

I heard Hawk's frustrated sigh. "Do you know of any other way to get into it?" he asked.

Sir Edmond shook his head and then said, "Wait a moment; let me look at this again." He went back to the manuscript and the other papers. "Here is what I'm looking for," he said, picking up the second page of notes. "This symbol is a map; I am sure of it now. It is a map of the interior of the hill on which this place rests." He held the paper beneath the light as the three of us gathered around.

"Look there," Sir Edmond continued. "See, there are two rings and then these elongated symbols"—his long bony finger pointed to the three symbols inside the two circles—"each with its own design, the third one ending in an X." Sir Edmond's eyes shone with excitement. "If you can get to the library, I am sure you will be on the correct path to the first of the three seals. The map also shows that there is more than one entrance to the room." He traced his index finger over the first of the three symbols again. "Here."

Sir Edmond Halley picked up the backpack and emptied its contents onto the wooden crate. The banana, apples, and granola bars all fell in a noisy jumble to the floor; the plastic bottles of V8 rolled in three different directions into the darkness. He shook once more and the heavy *thunk* of the loadstone sounded as it hit the edge of the crate, then bounced away on the cracked floor tiles.

Ignoring the food, Sir Edmund retrieved the stone. "And this is how you're going to find your way to the center of the Elfin Hill," he said.

"How's that?" asked Hawk.

"This loadstone has magnetic properties that allow its use as a compass." Sir Edmond held the irregular black stone in the palm of his left hand. "Ah, this is a rare gem indeed." He stroked the rock reverently. "Loadstone is used in my time in the making of compasses for His Majesty's ships. I was fortunate to have command of the British naval ship *Paramour* for two voyages, at which time I studied the variation between the direction that a compass needle indicated as north, and True North. The loadstone I employed at that time was of a superior grade but"—he looked again at the stone he now held—"nothing compared to this. What I could have accomplished if I'd only had one of this strength and quality."

"So you were a sea captain and not an astronomer?" Hawk asked. "But I always thought—"

"I am both," Sir Edmond replied.

"But why are you here, in this …?" I gestured at the inside of the asylum.

Dynnis said, "November, we really do not have time to go into all of that right now."

"No, it is quite all right. Mr. Bartholomew," Sir Edmond said. "I will be brief. You see, I am a traveler. Long ago, an associate of mine, Sir Isaac Newton, and I—"

"Newton!" Hawk gasped.

"Yes, I was his student and then later his partner in the study of the holistic properties of electro-magnetic energy." Sir Edmond smiled. "And just yesterday, we discussed Isaac's formula that gives proof mathematically that all magnetic attraction throughout the universe is equal."

"You're a traveler—not a ghost?" I blurted. He had began to lose me with his scientific jargon.

Sir Edmond and Dynnis both laughed aloud.

"A ghost? Oh, no—no, no," Sir Edmond chucked, then recovered himself and continued. "You see, on my eightieth birthday I discovered that the earth not only possessed two magnetic poles, but two ring poles. Ring poles are places where universal magnetic energy flows into a singular receptor, where it is renewed and then recycled back out into the universe—a type of black hole exclusively for magnetic energy, so to speak. This energy is a never-ending source of power. The ring poles can also be used as a doorway into another timeline."

"But I don't understand," Hawk interrupted. "Are you saying that one of these ring poles is right here in this asylum?"

Sir Edmond nodded his snowy head and pointed to the floor. "Down there—in the library."

"And that's how you *travel* from your time to this?" Hawk continued, and Sir Edmond nodded again.

"Why?" I asked. "What could possibly be here that would interest *you*?"

"Why, the ring pole itself," Sir Edmond replied, as if it were the most obvious thing in the world. "I have been through it many times now and each layer, or *ring*, as I said before, takes me to a different time period on earth. I have just now returned from the year 2108, where I was studying the harnessing of the seven-centimeter electro-magnetic bandwidths that circle the earth. It is a wonderful, non-exhaustive supply of energy." Sir Edmond shook his head twice. "Shame it will take the next one hundred years from this time to find a clean, safe replacement for that foul fossil fuel that is currently being pulled from the planet—and another hundred years before earth recovers from the damage." His mouth turned down in disgust.

Dynnis, who had been sitting on the floor, now rose. "I am afraid that time is not a commodity that will accommodate any more discussion. We need to locate an entrance to the library and get on with the business of finding Jeff before he becomes so mesmerized that even when—or *if*—we find him, he will still be willing to come with us."

Sir Edmond nodded, his face thoughtful. "I am not sure my idea will work, but it is worth a try, if you are not afraid of heights." He looked at Hawk. "It would mean leaving your wheelchair."

Hawk nodded without hesitation. "Anything."

"Well, Mr. Bartholomew can carry young Hawk here, and November, you will need to carry the wheelchair."

Dynnis was already busy gathering Hawk onto his back, much the same way he'd carried Jeff last night. I nodded and got busy folding the wheelchair and after gathering a few things back into the pack, I threw it over my right shoulder and lifted the chair under my left arm.

"Ready," I said.

"Then follow me and step *exactly* where I step." Sir Edmond started for the tall windows at the far side of the room. When we'd all gathered behind him, he pulled down on the ropes that opened the long wooden window at the very end. Immediately, fog swirled in like tendrils of hag hair, reaching and wrapping itself around our bodies and necks with icy fingers. In amazement, I watched as the aged scientist climbed nimbly out on the roof of the round turret. Dynnis and Hawk went next, and I followed, struggling with the wheelchair that just barely made it through the narrow opening, taking a chunk of windowsill with it. The mist was so thick that I couldn't see to the end of the roof, so I followed the Dynnis/Hawk form in front of me until they began to climb a metal ladder that disappeared into the black cloud that seemed to be covering the whole earth.

The wheelchair bit into my left hand as I hauled it with one arm, while using the other to climb the ladder. At the top, Sir Edmond gave me a hand up to a narrow ledge that appeared to go around the tower to the next set of landings obscured by the fog. It may have been a good thing that I could not look down because by now, we were on the third, maybe fourth, floor, not to mention that we were about to walk blindly on the concrete ledge of the old brick building.

Wordlessly, we began the slow journey around the face of the main tower structure of the asylum. No words were spoken, as we needed all our powers of concentration just to keep from plunging into the cloud below, and no words can do justice to the stark and utter fear that gripped me as I made my way next to Dynnis and Hawk, step by agonizing step, along an edge so narrow that I had to turn my right foot out and my left foot in. Hawk reached out and held on to the sleeve of my right arm. I assumed it was a gesture of reassurance, rather than an attempt at keeping me on the ledge.

The metal edge of the wheelchair now felt permanently embedded into my left palm, which began to go numb. Just when I thought I couldn't hold on to it any longer, I felt myself sliding through the wall. I looked frantically to my right to see if Dynnis and Hawk were sliding as well, but suddenly, I stood in front of a fireplace in a tiny cramped room. There was a small, thin woman, who looked a lot like Aunty Gin, wearing a dark red dress that brushed the ground; a dirty white scarf was tied turban-style around her head. As she swept around the hearth, she looked up, startled to see me standing there.

"No!" I said loudly. "No, not now!" I shook my head in frustration. I couldn't let myself slide now. The woman's face showed confusion.

"How be thee here?" she demanded.

"No-o-o-o!" I leaned forward with the force of the scream and almost fell off the ledge.

"November!" Dynnis called, not looking back. "Are you all right?"

Hawk still clutched my sleeve, and he pulled with all his might until I feared he'd pull himself clear off Dynnis' back.

"I'm fine," I lied.

"Only a few more feet." Sir Edmond's calm disembodied voice floated over us. "Just a few more steps."

I heard the creaking of another set of old ropes as Sir Edmond raised the window into another room. "Careful now—watch your step."

That was an understatement. We made our way gingerly over the windowsill, and Sir Edmond took the wheelchair in one hand, while holding the window up with the other as I clambered over the sill and collapsed into the room.

This room was almost a twin of the one before, but it had more windows so there was light enough to see that it had once been used as an office. There were a number of desks and some ancient, dust-coated office equipment piled with moldy manila folders and papers. The wooden floor was littered with more files, as if a whirlwind had blown through the room, tilting shelves and scattering the contents of filing cabinets.

Sir Edmond wasted no time. Taking a seat in one of the desk chairs, he placed the loadstone on top of the desk and began chipping away at it with what looked like a letter opener. He opened the desk drawer and took out a round tin container and emptied paperclips back into the drawer. As he set to work, Dynnis and I helped Hawk back into his chair, and we all took a moment to catch our breath. In no time at all, Sir Edmond finished.

"There," he announced. "This compass should direct us to the hall of seals. Let us give it a try."

Staring into the tin, he looked back up and headed to the far side of the room, where he pulled open what looked like a walk-in closet and disappeared inside. He reappeared almost instantly with a big smile on his face.

"It is as I suspected," he grinned widely. "There is a staircase in here that has direct access to the library. The loadstone is working; shall we go?" Holding out his arm like a *maître d',* he motioned us inside.

Dynnis and Hawk resumed their piggyback as Sir Edmond took the wheelchair, and we all entered the closet, descending four flights of stairs back to the bottom level of the building.

After a few twists and turns, during which time Sir Edmond showed us the functions of the loadstone, we made our way to a glass-paneled wooden door with LIBRARY stenciled on it. Sir Edmond turned the knob, and the door swung open to reveal a small antechamber, its ceiling so high it disappeared into the darkness above, and three very narrow dark-paneled doors. Each door had a brass knob surrounded by dark yellow wax that extended across the jamb, effectively sealing it shut.

I looked at Sir Edmond, who was consulting the loadstone.

"Which one do we open first?" Hawk asked, now settled in his chair.

"The stone is pointing to the right," Sir Edmond said. "I've not been this way before, but I believe this might be one of the doors to the Room of Rings.

"Then let's go," Hawk said, wheeling himself forward.

The wax seal shattered as Hawk turned the knob, and an unearthly screeching sound instantly filled the chamber, making me clamp my hands over my ears in reflex.

It was like the discordant screams of hundreds of tormented souls.

"The Shriekers!" Sir Edmond shouted. "Someone, quickly—take down what they say!"

Chapter Seventeen

They've all come to catch you and scratch you at midnight.
To fight you and bite you, you can't get away!
—Alan Temperley, *Hallowe'en: A Poem for Bedtime*

Dynnis motioned to the backpack, and I pulled the zipper and reached inside for a tablet and pencil. Just as my hands closed on the pencil, something flew down from the darkness above and grabbed my hair, pulling it as if to tear it from my scalp.

"November, drop down!" Hawk shouted as he swung his flashlight at the thing that was flapping and lifting me to my toes.

I did as I was told, and I don't know who was shrieking more, me or the thing that had me, but Dynnis somehow managed to catch the pencil that flew out of my hand as I struggled with the wildly flapping creature entangling itself in my hair.

Within moments, there were more of them—hundreds it seemed. Hawk swung like a major leaguer, making contact with the brown, hairy bodies that flew down like rabid bats from the darkness. But these were not like any bats I had ever seen before. They had tiny human faces and long bodies covered in flowing hair the color of gore. Bats have two feet but these creatures had hairless arms as well, with long-fingered hands that stretched and reached for whatever they could grab. And, I realized with horror, their mouths were forming words as they flew at us with a speed that did not seem possible, given the narrowness of the space we were in.

"Don't struggle," Sir Edmond said, suddenly next to me, as he grabbed the creature and freed it from my hair, tossing it back into the fray. He gestured toward Dynnis, who was furiously writing on the yellow tablet.

"Sit on the floor and cover your head until they are through," he continued, swinging one arm overhead to ward off any attacks on himself.

To Hawk he shouted, "Lean forward, and put your hands over your head." Hawk stopped swinging and followed Sir Edmond's orders. I did one better. I got on my knees and rolled into the tightest ball I could manage, with my forehead on the cold concrete floor and my shoulder-length hair pulled around my neck and tucked into my collar. The position made it possible for me to cover both my head and my ears. And so I remained for what seemed a very long time.

Strangely enough, while the screaming creatures flew their dive-bombing raids above me, my mind started to wander. I thought about what I had seen when I slid back into the wall of the ledge. Who were those people I saw each time I slid back? The woman who resembled Aunty Gin had not only seen me, but seemed to recognize me as well.

If ever there was a good time to slide out of a place, now would be it. I tried focusing on the last vision I'd had of that distant place. But instead of the now-familiar feeling of going into the softness of another time and place, I felt the bump of a hairy body as it scraped across the back of my hands with its sharp nails.

Then, just as suddenly as it had erupted, the shrieking stopped. I remained still for a long moment, then cautiously lowered my hands and looked up.

Hawk still hunched in his chair with his hands over his head. Dynnis still sat on the floor against the door with the broken seal, scribbling on the yellow tablet; and Sir Edmond was gone.

Very slowly, I unwound and sat up on my knees, the hall now silent except for the scratching of the pencil.

Hawk opened his eyes, took his fingers out of his ears, and raised up to a sitting position, his head tilted back toward the darkness above.

"Are they gone?"

I nodded. "I think so."

Dynnis stopped writing and got to his feet. "I think I was able to get it all," he said. "And weren't *they* something!" He tossed his head toward the ceiling. "I have only heard about them in stories from my childhood, but I never thought they were *real*." He chuckled like a little kid who had just been given proof the tooth fairy exists.

"And just who *are they*?" I asked, my annoyance plain. Maybe he thought they were just cute little fairy-tale creatures, to be enjoyed for their aerial talents, but I did not relish having my hair pulled out by the roots, never mind fearing they might tear the very eyes from my head or rupture my eardrums. Clearly, my body language showed I was less than enchanted, and Dynnis sobered.

"Yeah, and what were you writing?" Hawk added.

"They are Shriekers." He approached Hawk and handed him the tablet. "And this is what they were saying." He explained, "As I said before, I have only heard of them through legend. The Shriekers are guardians of the Elfin realm. They are what you might call the watchdogs of the gates to the underground. The elves do not like to be disturbed and so they place seals on each entrance to their tunnels. The Shriekers are put there to give directions to welcome guests."

"Some welcome," I muttered. "I'd hate to see what they do to people they don't like."

"Well, to answer that," he continued, "those visitors who are not welcome into the realm or who do not understand the Elfin code of conduct will not understand the directions the Shriekers offer and, therefore, will interpret their sounds and actions as an attack." He grinned. "Kind of a nice, neat way of keeping the riff-raff out, if you will."

"So, you are saying that those *things*"—I threw an uneasy glance upward—"were giving us *directions* and not trying to gouge our eyes out?"

"Exactly," Dynnis nodded, "and that is what I was copying." He indicated the tablet Hawk was now reading.

"The three echoes that your document speaks of came, or will yet come, from some form of those Shriekers. Because of the pitch and volume of their screams, it is impossible to hear what they say unless you listen to the echo their voices produce." He motioned to the spot where he had sat taking notes. "As I sat on the floor, I was able to concentrate on the words that came through the echo and write them down. Ingenious, isn't it?"

Hawk looked up from the tablet. "So what we have here is the first of the three echoes?"

"Yes," Dynnis answered, "and possibly the most important of the three." Before he could explain further, Sir Edmond poked his head around the door with the broken seal.

"It is as I suspected." He waved us toward him. "This is another way to the Room of Rings." He opened the door wider. "Please come inside; there is someone I would like you to meet."

Although Sir Edmond's jovial tone implied we were in for a treat, I had my doubts, and by the look Hawk threw me just before he rolled through the doorway, so did he.

"Well, Aunty Gin always says 'In for a penny, in for a pound,'" I said. And on the strength of that cliché, we followed Dynnis through the door.

***

The shaft-like hall gave way to a low-ceilinged room paneled in thick, dark wood, freckled here and there with black knots. And where the hall magnified the slightest sound, this place hummed like the inside of a huge beehive. Hawk and I looked around, trying to locate the source of the sound, but nothing in the room suggested anything more than the living quarters of the elderly man who stood beside one of two burgundy wingback chairs, upholstered in large pink cabbage roses. The room was lit by two tall oil lamps resting upon a creamy lace cover atop a low wooden table centered in the room. The table was piled high with books and long tubes that looked like they might hold maps. Several faded Persian carpets covered most of the concrete floor, lending the room a cozy feel.

I took all of this in with one glance because the *someone* Sir Edmond wanted us to meet was hurrying toward us.

"Hob, I would like to introduce my friends." Sir Edmund stepped forward. "November and Hawk Atwood and Mr. Dynnis Bartholomew, I would like you to meet Hob, the keeper of the Rings."

The slight, stooped figure approached us with a wide smile splitting his wrinkled face.

"Hello, hello," he said, taking long strides across the threadbare carpet, his words coming out *halloo, halloo.*

Although painfully thin and bent, he was surprisingly energetic. Khaki overalls and a thin white T-shirt hung from his spare frame. His pant legs flapped like loosely tied sails on a gusty day as he made his way toward us, holding out both hands in greeting. Wispy strands of gray white hair moved around his shiny skull like smoke, catching in bushy eyebrows that rose and fell as if they had a life of their own.

"It's not often we get company," he beamed, the brows coming in for a landing just above bright blue eyes. "Please, please, come in, come in." He gestured toward the rest of the room that I now realized was his living, sleeping, and eating area.

Just outside the circle of light cast by the lamps, I could make out a small bed covered with a patchwork quilt; this was next to a tall whitewashed cupboard and washstand that supported a blue and white pitcher and bowl. Against the far wall stood a tiny cookstove and an open, four-shelved wooden cabinet, crammed to overflowing with canned goods and food stuffs. Next to the shelf was a small sink, beneath which hung several wire baskets filled with potatoes and onions, among other vegetables, and fresh fruit. Almost directly across from where we stood was another six-paneled door with a gold lever for a handle. Directly in the middle was a small neatly lettered sign that warned: *Enter Slowly.*

"As caretaker of the Rings," Sir Edmond said, nodding toward the yellow tablet Hawk still held, "Hob can direct you to the right area for your purposes."

"The Rings," Dynnis repeated, "as in those rings you spoke of before, that allow you to *travel*?"

"Precisely," Sir Edmond responded. "I've been using the Rings for more than three years now, and I still wonder at their complexity."

"Is this the Room of Rings?" I asked.

"Oh, no, no," Hob replied. "This is my home." He indicated the door with the lettering. "The Room of Rings is through there."

"So that would explain the humming sound," Hawk ventured.

"Perhaps we're getting ahead of ourselves." Sir Edmond addressed Hob. "My friends and I have not had much opportunity to discuss the function, much less the origin of the Rings. Perhaps you can explain better than I how it all works."

Hob's face grew solemn and his eyes large. "I'm afraid I do not know exactly how the Rings work," he said, holding his hands palms up. "I have been caretaker of them since I was a teen, and that was not yesterday, believe me." His rusty voice caught on a chuckle, causing him to cough and then loudly clear his throat. "And in all that time I have never questioned how they worked or where they came from." His beetled brows lowered like storm clouds, then lifted as if a high pressure system had suddenly blown in. "But my mother would probably be able to give us the answer. We could ask her."

His mother! Hob had to be in his eighties, at the very least. How old was his mother? Hawk gave me a look that said he was thinking the same thing.

Quick as a blink, Hob was at the other door. "Mother?" he called softly, opening the door a crack. "Are you decent?"

A tiny voice answered. Hob opened the door just a bit wider, and a little old lady, no bigger than a six-year-old, emerged. Her pink scalp showed through her sparse white hair like strawberry frosting under coconut topping. Dressed in a floor-length flannel nightdress, she ambled into the room on arthritically gnarled bare feet and deposited herself on the wingchair, where she tucked her hands under her legs, letting them swing free.

Hob made the introductions, and his mother squinted at us through unusually large, pale, rheumy blue eyes.

"Mother, these folks are wondering about the origins of the Room of Rings," he began, in a voice much louder than he had been using. "I remember your telling me once that you learned about it in school." Hob produced a small footstool and placed it beneath the old woman's dangling feet.

"Hob! I'm not deaf, and where are your manners?" His mother's voice sounded how I imagined a chicken's voice would if it could talk. She clucked her tongue twice. "Haven't you even offered our guests so much as a beverage?" Her wizened little face could have been the model for a dried-apple doll.

Hob's eyebrows flew to his hairline along with his hands. "Oh, my goodness!" he gasped. "I *am* sorry! What am I thinking? It has been so long since we've had guests." He scurried to the shelves above the sink and began taking down plates and saucers.

"And since we have company for *tea*," his mother stressed, "you may as well go get Grandma. You know she always loves a tea party."

Now even Dynnis looked surprised. The three of us exchanged looks, and the set of Dynnis' mouth told us that we were not alone in thinking this was very odd.

Hob was just coming through the other door with two chairs and stopped dead at his mother's suggestion. "Oh, Mother, I'm not sure Granny would be up to—"

"Nonsense!" His mother waved her hand as if to brush away the protest. "Granny loves a good tea party, and we haven't had her out in months!"

Sir Edmond and Dynnis moved forward to take chairs from the elderly man, as he looked at his mother with a pained expression.

"Oh, very well," he sighed, shoulders slumping. "I'll get the rest of the chairs, and then I'll go get Granny."

Hawk wheeled himself alongside me. "How old *are* these people anyway?" he whispered.

I shook my head because Hob was making his way back into the room again with two more chairs, but it was what followed behind him that drew an involuntary gasp from me.

"Oh, wow," said Hawk.

The tiny figure making its way across the room toward the other wingchair looked like a turtle without its shell. Dressed in a gown identical to the one Hob's mother wore, the little hobgoblin, no bigger than a human infant, toddled on stubby pink feet. Her fine white hair fell in a tangled mess to the floor and dragged behind her like a badly webbed bridal veil. Rubbing her eyes as she entered the pool of lantern light, Granny looked around at all of us with huge milky blue eyes and gave a mighty yawn.

"Been dozing a bit," she said, as she climbed slowly up into the vacant wingchair and then sat, facing us. She had the voice of an infant too, high and tight.

In the meantime, Hob had busily cleared the table, and we all sat down as he dashed about the room, stoking the stove and setting out the tea.

With his mother and grandmother sitting like the Queen and the Queen Mum, I was reminded of the tea party in *Alice in Wonderland* and wondered if the Mad Hatter himself might next come through the door—or maybe *his* grandmother.

"Well, since my son is clearly lacking any social graces, *I* will make the introductions," his mother said, loudly enough to make Hob stop and turn around before hurrying back to get the steaming kettle. "I am Abella, and this is my mother, Adorabelle."

Sir Edmond introduced the rest of us and began pouring the tea for everyone, as Hob set down a plate of sandwiches and small cakes that he had somehow conjured up in that short period of time.

I was just handing a cup of tea to Hawk when Adorabelle said, "Hob, you should go get Great-Grandma. She sleeps entirely too much, and it would be such a shame for her to miss this."

Dynnis stopped with his cup halfway to his mouth, and Sir Edmond coughed, spraying the front of his coat with tea. While Sir Edmond was reaching for the cloth napkin Hob had provided at each place setting, Hob turned to his grandmother.

"No. I do not think that is a very good idea," he said firmly.

"Oh, yes! That is an excellent idea," Abella clucked. "Great-Grandma hasn't been awake in nearly a year. What better time than a party to get her blood going again!"

"And where, may I ask, is Great-Grandma?" said Sir Edmond, clearing his throat and wiping his face.

Hob, his mother, and grandmother exchanged questioning looks. "Well, the last time I saw her she was sleeping in the oven," Adorabelle said.

"What?" Hob shot out of his chair and ran toward the glowing woodstove.

"No, no, Mother, she's in the cupboard, as usual." Abella shook her head in amusement, then said to Hob, "Don't mind your Granny; you know she's feeble."

"I am not!" protested Adorabelle.

"Are, too," countered her daughter.

By now, both Sir Edmond and Dynnis were on their feet, helping to search in various parts of the room for poor Great-Grandma, and I was halfway to the stove behind Hob when I heard him mutter, "Oh, I knew this wasn't a good idea. They will be the death of me yet," as he changed direction and started toward the tall cupboard next to the washstand.

I turned and headed back to the table as Hawk pushed himself away and over to the two old ladies. Leaning forward, he said gently, "You're Tanis, aren't you." It was a statement, not a question.

Abella's eyebrows rose, and a small smile played around her mouth. "You are an impudent young man, but you are right."

Sir Edmond, Dynnis, and I returned to the table as Hob came forward carrying what at first glance looked like a pile of rags. It wasn't until he laid it in a shallow breadbasket that I realized it was a living creature. The bundle moved ever so slightly as the tiny being adjusted itself and then lay still.

"This is my great-grandmother," Hob said, slowly unwrapping the little figure that lay as if in a cocoon. "Ambrosine."

Chapter Eighteen

She took me up in her milk white hand, and she's set me down softly on her knee; She's changed me again to my own proper shape, and no more I toddle about the tree.

—Old English ballad (Anonymous)

In my wildest nightmares and in all of the creepiest movies I'd ever been to, I had never before seen anything like what Hob just brought into the room. The tiny body of his great-grandmother looked like a blob of pink baby flesh with tiny teeth and fine yellow fuzz for hair covering its body. With all the substance of a jellyfish, it lay curled in a ball. And as we watched, it hiccupped, causing it to move enough to see an eye that was, thankfully, closed. I backed away. I didn't think I could have stood it if that eye had opened.

"Fascinating," Hawk said, as he gazed at Ambrosine.

"Go ahead, son, explain to your friends what you mean by Tanis," said Adorabelle, getting to her knees and slopping her tea onto the chair cushion.

Hawk sat back. "The Tanis is half elf, half human. Because elves are immortal, that means the Tanis can never die, but because they are half human, they age like mortal humans. So even though they can't die, the Tanis does get older. In fact, after awhile they begin to go backward."

Hawk adjusted himself in his chair. "At a certain age the Tanis begins to revert backward, growing smaller and smaller until they are no more than an embryo. As they shrink, they sleep more and more until they reach a point where they are so small, they are like unborn babies and can begin growing up again, like any other newborn."

We all looked at the sleeping embryo of Ambrosine.

"You are correct young man, except about one point," Abella said. "Unlike humans who begin to decline in the second half of their first century, we Tanisians go well into our third century before we begin our decline." She raised her chin proudly. "Don't look too bad for 248, do I?"

"And I've been told I could pass for 320," Adorabelle added.

We all looked at Hob. "I believe Great-Grandma is close to 400, but happily, she will soon renew," he said, ignoring his own age.

Abella leaned forward in her seat and squinted at Hawk. "Young man, what is wrong with your legs?"

I saw him stiffen at the bluntness of her question. "I was born with damage to my spine," Hawk answered.

"No, I'm not asking why you're in a wheelchair." Abella pointed to Hawk's pant legs. "I'm wondering what that is on your legs?"

Hawk looked down, and we all saw what she meant. The hems of his jeans seemed to be glowing, and as we watched, the blue white light moved up both legs toward his knees.

"Oh, no!" Hob exclaimed. "He's starting to travel! It must be the metal in the chair!" With one quick motion, Hob grabbed the back of Hawk's wheelchair and pulled it to the far side of the room. "It's the Rings," he explained, as he smoothed the glowing creases from Hawk's pant legs as if they were flames. "The magnetic pull is great, and he has been sitting near the door for some time."

Sir Edmond spoke up then. "You are right; the hour is late, and we need to be getting on with our purpose. Hawk, what instructions did the Shriekers give?"

Hawk pulled the tablet from the backpack, where he had stowed it during the tea party. "I'm not sure I understand them." He frowned.

"Let me see," Abella said, sliding down from the chair. She took the tablet from him, walked back to the table, and placed it near the oil lamps. After fumbling around amid the books and maps on the floor, she located a minute pair of spectacles and, placing them on her nose, she began to read. After a few moments she looked up at Hob, who was returning from putting Ambrosine back in her cupboard. I had taken away the last of the tea things as she and Hawk studied the tablet.

"Ring 8," she said. "The Seer and the Joker."

Hob looked confused. "The Joker? Mother, are you *sure?*"

Abella's wrinkled little face puckered like she had just tasted vinegar. "Of course I'm sure, you fool." She plucked a tube from the pile and emptied it onto the table, where Hob helped her spread it out. "See, there." She pointed to a coordinate on what looked like a printed spider's web. "It's the only one that makes sense."

Hob went back to the cupboard, but this time, he opened one of the deep drawers and removed a wooden box, the kind used to hold recipes, and returned with it to the table.

Adorabelle had gotten down from her chair and was crawling around under the table, pretending she was a cat. Abella reached down and swatted her bottom.

"Mother, get out from there! We cannot get anything done with you fooling around. Go play—off with you!"

Adorabelle scampered, giggling, from beneath the table and stuck her tongue out at her daughter before running to the door with the gold handle. She opened it and disappeared inside.

Ignoring both of them, Hob lifted the lid on the box and removed a thick deck of cards. The figures on each one seemed to represent a place on a map and contained many numbers that looked like coordinates. But like playing cards, they were printed so that they held the same image no matter which way you held them. Hob selected two and placed them on the table in front of Abella.

Peering over the tops of her reading glasses, she inspected them closely. "You, girl." She crooked her finger, and I stepped toward her. "Here. Stand here." Abella motioned for me to stand in front of her. When I did so, she raised up on her toes and peered into my eyes. I felt like I was being probed by a laser as her dark pupils bore directly into mine.

"You are the Seer," she announced. "I knew it as soon as I set eyes on you." She took my wrist in her tiny hand, and I felt a slight electric charge run from her hand into mine. "You have been back there already, haven't you, my child?" she said as quietly as her squawky voice would allow.

How could she possibly know about my sliding incidents?

"Been to the time of the Witches, I see." Although rusty, her voice had a relaxing quality that made me want to remember anything she said.

"I don't understand." I wanted to, but images were beginning to flood into my head, and I wasn't sure if they were my memories or someone else's.

"You have the Gift," Abella continued.

"Gift?" My head felt floaty, and Abella began to waver back and forth in front of my eyes.

"You are the One." She gazed at me as if she were looking into a crystal ball, turning her head this way and that. "You are the One for whom they have been waiting for so very long."

I wanted to ask her *who* had been waiting, and for what? But my mouth would not form the words. Abella was a charmer, and I was the snake.

She broke eye contact, causing me to snap back into reality—such as it was.

Abella was all business now. Stepping around to the other side of the table, she grabbed the cards, then opened a shallow drawer in the side of the table and took out a pair of pinking shears. She proceeded to cut each card in half, diagonally, before motioning to Hawk and the others to join us at the table. When we had all gathered around, Abella gave half of the Seer card to me and half of the Joker card to Hawk. The other two halves of the jagged cards she handed to Hob.

"Now." She looked at Hawk and me standing side by side in the lamplight. "Those are your tickets back from the Rings—guard them well." Abella indicated the door through which Adorabelle had gone. "Hob will take you into the room shortly, and you will begin your journey. *Do exactly* as he instructs." She leaned her tiny body forward onto the table for emphasis.

"The Rings are very strong and extremely subtle. One wrong move, and you will end up—who knows where?" She held her hands up. "And without the correct tickets, you will not be able to return to this place." Her watery eyes regarded us solemnly. "Do you both understand this?"

Hawk started to say something, but Abella held up her hand. "Hob will explain all the details about the Rings when you walk through that door." She gestured toward the door with the gold handle. "But I need to make sure you understand the importance of the tickets I've given you. You are not to entrust them to *anyone, no matter who they are or what they say.* Is that clear?"

Hawk and I both nodded.

Abella straightened. "Very well, then. Good luck to you both." She waved her hand in a gesture of dismissal.

I took hold of the handles of the wheelchair, and we followed Hob to the door. I suddenly realized that Dynnis and Sir Edmond had not moved from the table.

"Aren't you coming?" I asked, looking over my shoulder.

"No," Dynnis answered, coming toward us.

I turned Hawk around. "What do you mean?" we asked.

"I cannot go with you. Hawk, you read the echoes. You two must go to Salem Village as it was in 1701." He took a deep breath. "You see, in order to stay the age you are now, you can only travel back in time to those years before you were born, or else you will revert to the age you were in that year. In Salem Village in 1701, I was seven years old." Dynnis' smile was bittersweet. "I am afraid that I would not be of much help to you."

"And I, too, am alive in 1701 but in a different part of the world. Therefore, I do not qualify for a ticket at this particular time," Sir Edmond put in.

"So, we go alone?" Hawk's voice was small.

Sir Edmond nodded, and Dynnis said, "Look at it this way. You will probably get to see me as a child anyway, and what a little scamper I was, too. And you can tease me about it when you come back with Jeff, all safe and sound."

He must have heard me gulp because he came to us then and took one of our hands in each of his. "You won't be alone, November. I promise." He squeezed our hands tightly. "You are bringing full circle the events that were started long in the past. You have the strength, the knowledge, and the tools needed to fulfill the promise that was made those many years ago." His crinkly old eyes gleamed with a fire I had never seen in them before.

"Go forth, Children of Avnova, and forge the remaining links in the chain that has, until now, stood unfinished. And I will be right here when you return." Dynnis stepped away then and raised his hand in a gesture of farewell as Hob opened the door.

"Godspeed, my friends," he called out, as Hawk and I passed through the doorway—and into the Room of Rings.

Chapter Nineteen

O, seventeen hundred and one, never was a year so well begun,
Backsy-forsy and inside out, the best of all years to ballad about.
—Robert Graves, *The Two Witches*

The humming we heard only as a faint background noise in Hob's living area caused the room we now entered to sound like the floor of an auto-assembly plant. And what a room it was. Tall, unadorned, whitewashed block walls disappeared into the darkness above the shiny black floor that stretched out like a soccer field in all directions.

In the middle of the cavernous space, rising as if from the very center of the earth itself, stood an enormous wall of shimmering ribbons of light. So this was the source of the sound we had heard from the other room! The steady hum in Hob's living room was now amplified by the turning of a million gears at extreme speed. Close up, the wall looked like a rainbow, except someone had taken the bow out and stretched it straight. Each subtle color spun in a circular motion, like infinitesimal slices of wheels, so fast that it was a blur. And each of the millions of paper-thin wheels, rotating at such high speed, had its own unique sound. The combined effect was like being inside a gigantic working clock. Hawk and I craned our necks as we took in the sheer size of it.

"Welcome to the Room of Rings!" Hob shouted, like the proud owner of a new resort. "Let's get you ready to go." Removing what looked like a fishing rod from a tall wooden rack bolted to the floor, he explained, "This is a push-pull rod." He held it out for our inspection. "Notice it has a blunt end and a hook beneath it. I'll being using this to help you enter and exit the Rings."

"I don't understand," I said at the same time that Hawk said, "Enter *that*?"

Hob's eyebrows flew like moths to the top of his forehead. "Oh, my! I've gone and done it again, haven't I? I always start in the middle of things! Please, please forgive me! I'll start over and try to begin at the beginning. And where is…?" He looked wildly around him, as if he couldn't quite figure out where the beginning was and hoped to spot it lying discarded in a corner.

He was so flustered I felt sorry for him and was about to suggest he stop and take a deep breath when Adorabelle came scurrying up.

"Not to worry, Hob." Her tiny voice held just the right mix of sensitivity and authority. "You go get things ready; I shall explain the process to our young travelers."

Relief replaced misery on the old elf's face, and the eyebrows settled into place, like puffy fair-weather clouds above calm seas.

"Oh wonderful, wonderful." He smiled down at his grandmother. "Excellent idea. I'll do just that—just that." He made a false start off in the direction of the Rings, spun around, and opened his mouth as if to say something, closed it, spun back around, and strode off, muttering to himself and shaking his head.

Adorabelle, too, was shaking her little turtle head. "Dear, dear Hob," she cackled. "He's always been a good boy, but he's an easy one to rattle. Well, what can one expect when he has spent his entire life in an insane asylum?" Her big swimmy eyes darkened as if an unwanted thought had just surfaced. "Years ago, when this place was in full operation, we knew some dark days, and Hob—well, he had to deal with the staff and the inmates now and then—hard, hard dark times." She waved her tiny wrinkled hand as if to brush off the bad memory and return to the here and now. "But, let's get back to business." She toddled over to a tall wooden cabinet anchored to the wall on the right side of the door. It held at least a hundred drawers of various sizes, some big enough to hold a small child, others so tiny they looked like trays in a jewelry box. The cabinet was painted cheery yellow, the drawers a dark gold. Climbing up a narrow ladder propped against the cupboard, Adorabelle opened a small drawer near the top. It was long and deep, requiring her to plunge her entire arm in to extract a narrow tube like those I had seen on the table in Hob's room. Clutching it to her tiny body, she made her way with surprising speed to the bottom of the ladder, then motioned for us to follow her to a table beneath a hanging lamp with a translucent green shade.

Climbing on a step stool, Adorabelle opened the tube and removed the stiff document, spreading it out on the table's surface.

"Gather 'round," she commanded. "Here is an overview of the Rings." She reached full length across the diagram and placed her index finger on a spot at the upper left. "This is *your point of entry.*"

"Excuse me," Hawk interrupted, "but I have a few questions before we get to the *traveling* part." He crooked his index fingers into an air quote.

Adorabelle gave him a measured look. "All right," she said, leaning back on her elbow. "What would you like to know?"

"Well, first of all, what *are* the Rings, and how do they work?"

Adorabelle gazed at the shimmering light show that was causing us to shout in order to hear each other over the din. "No one knows when, or by whom, the Rings were built. The story of their source is the basis for many legends handed down through centuries by my Elfin ancestors. What I do know for sure is *how* they work. You see, in my youth I was head science coordinator for the realm—the Elfin kingdom of Frell." She indicated the Rings. "What you are looking at is a QSEPTT. We call it the Q, for short. The letters stand for Quantum Superposition Evolving Particle Time Translator; in other words, it's a time machine. The particles that turn in the colorful wheels are light particles moving beyond the speed of light and shooting off into infinitesimal slices of the time continuum. This diagram"—she turned back and pointed to the large chart before us—"is a map showing the exact spot to enter and exit the Q, or the Rings, if you will."

"Superposition Quantum Time Translation," Hawk replied. "That area of quantum physics hasn't been developed yet. I mean, I just read an article a few months ago by Yakir Aharonov, a research scientist at the University of South Carolina. He and his team produced a paper describing how an aspect of quantum mechanics called *state superposition* can be used to transfer objects inside a closed and isolated system into the future or the past." He looked over at the noisy wall of colors. "But no one has taken them seriously enough to try to prove their theory."

Adorabelle's smile was one a modern-day pilot might bestow on Wilbur Wright's confusion as to how a jet can surpass the speed of sound. "They'll get there one day; don't you worry." She leaned over and patted Hawk's knee. "They're on the right track." She gave him a wink and turned back to the diagram. "Time is running out for us, however, and we need to get you two on your way. So listen carefully—it is vital that you understand the instructions if you are to be successful in this journey."

We both leaned in as she pointed to the point of entry on the diagram.

"You are going to do three tries—two trial runs and then the final," Adorabelle explained. "The first entry will be a very short trip into the past—maybe just an hour or so—to get you used to the feeling of traveling. It can be a bit disorienting at first. Also, you will need to test your entry and exit cards, or e-cards, and your ability to find the Point of Zero." She paused. "Are you with me so far?"

"Point of Zero?" I asked.

"Point of Zero is where you will find the necessary slot for your e-card; you know, the ones Abella gave you in the other room? Point of Zero will only be visible for thirty seconds, once you summon it. You *must* be able to locate and identify it in that time, or you will have to wait until the next renewal cycle." Her little face wrinkled up like she'd just gotten a whiff of something rotten. "And that could take several years, I'm afraid. Now, if you will give me your cards I will show you how to activate them."

Hawk and I produced the jagged-edged cards Abella had given us and held them out to Adorabelle. She recoiled as if we had offered her poison.

"*That is your first mistake!*" she shouted. "Did you not listen to Abella? Never, and I mean *never,* offer your e-card to *anyone! No matter who they are—is that clear*?" Her little face was crimson with rage. "*I said, is that clear*?" she shrieked.

Hawk and I nodded, shoving the cards in our respective pockets.

"Good." She stepped down from the stool and walked in the direction of the Rings. "Now let's get started."

I followed Hawk as he rolled behind the little hump-backed nightshirt that was Adorabelle to the far end of the Rings, where she stopped a few feet away from the whirling wheels of color. Up close, the noise was almost deafening.

Adorabelle shouted above the din. "You will go back for a short time to familiarize yourselves with the Point of Zero, then you will travel back a second time a bit farther—say, a couple of years—to make sure you've gotten the hang of it all. Then …" Adorabelle lowered her head, looking like a general preparing to tell his troops about the toughest part of the battle. "Then you will travel back more than three hundred years, to the year 1701." Her voice took on the quality of someone who has resigned herself to the task of telling someone something she knows that person does not want to hear. "I'm not sure what you will encounter there, but whatever it is, you must find the strength to complete your task." She looked hard at me. "November, you are the one who must lead them," Adorabelle said. "I know you don't fully realize what that means right now, but it will all become clear as you follow those directions." She motioned toward Hawk's backpack. "You are the girl 'in her thirteenth year,' whose arrival has been the source of many songs and stories among my people. You are The One who will set free those who have moldered in chains over the centuries."

Before I could respond to her chilling words, she brushed her hands together briskly, signaling no more talk.

"Now take out your cards and look at them."

We did as she instructed.

"Locate the star hidden in the picture; count its points, and then multiply that by two in your head." Adorabelle gave us only a few seconds before saying, "Next, I want you to add to that the number of years you have been alive. Got it? Okay. Now you should have come up with a two-digit number. For example, say it is twenty-four. Two and four make six, so six is your entry number. You will then sing the numbers of six backward to yourself like this—six, five, four, three, two, and *one*! And say the final number, *one*, aloud. Go ahead, try it," she ordered.

I scanned my card for the star—it was located in the upper left and had five points. Five times two equals ten, plus my age equals twenty-two, which added together makes four. I hummed, tunelessly, four, three, two, and then shouted, "*One*!" at the same time Hawk did.

Like a holographic image from a movie, an oval appeared in front of each of us, close enough to touch. Hawk reached out and put his hand through the one in front of him.

"An oval, like a big zero," he said. "Sweet."

I couldn't help but smile—it was cool. I looked closely at my Point of Zero. Around the outer edge were scrolls and symbols written in a language I had never seen before. In the oval's center was a raised image of a ravine with a glowing bridge spanning its distance and a slot along the bridge's edge. I put the card into the slot, pulled it back out, and the oval disappeared.

"Mind you, you have thirty seconds to activate your e-card. You will repeat the same procedure on your return trip. Remember, you need only place it in the slot, and then remove it quickly to begin your return entry." Adorabelle waved for Hob to join us—he had been standing patiently while we configured our numbers and activated the Point of Zero.

"Hob will now show you how to enter the Q." Adorabelle stepped back.

Hob held the push-pull rod and motioned for us to step forward. "One in front of the other," he instructed.

Hawk went first. Hob took the long pole and, using the blunt end, slowly pushed Hawk toward the whirling rings of color. Then, with a sudden thrust, Hawk disappeared in a burst of color that splashed out as if it were liquid.

Motioning to me, Hob grasped the pole, and I took my place in front of him. I was so close to the wheels now that I could feel the breeze from them on my face. I felt a gentle prodding and then, *whoosh*, I sailed through a mesh of colors and soft winds that sang like a million harps in heavenly harmony. But almost as quickly as it began, I was pushed out the other side into the watery sunlight that was trying to cut through the thick fog in Aunt Marsha's front yard.

Adorabelle was right. The trip was a bit disorienting, like a fun-house ride where you are suddenly pushed from pitch black to daylight. I blinked a couple of times to get my eyes focused and then saw Hawk rubbing his, looking around as if he had just awakened from a nap.

"So how was it?"

Adorabelle stood on the edge of the lawn dressed in infant-sized brown leather pants with a dark green tunic tied in the middle with a rawhide lace. Her round little body looked like a tiny stump with feet encased in soft suede moccasins, her white hair falling softly to the ground around them.

"Adorabelle!" Hawk and I both said at once.

"No need to look so surprised." She laughed at our startled expressions. "Did you think we were going to send you alone?"

"But aren't you afraid of being seen?" I asked.

Adorabelle waved her hand in dismissal. "Oh, I forgot to tell you that the trial runs are simply to get you used to traveling. Even though the Q sends you back in time, no one is aware of you." She walked up to where Hawk and I were now standing alongside the ramp into the house. "And you cannot interact or communicate with them at all. This is merely a test to see if you can handle traveling." She squinted closely at us. "There are those who cannot adjust to the continuum shift, even for short distances, but you two seem none the worse for wear."

Adorabelle stood back. "Well?" she asked, like a guest whose hosts needed to be reminded of their manners. "Aren't you going to invite me in?"

Chapter Twenty

Through breaks and through briars, o'er ditches and mires, she follows the spirit that guides now.

—Robert Herrick, *The Hag*

It was an odd experience, walking through the door to my aunts' house, and by that I mean we walked *through* the door—like ghosts; and in a way, I guess we were. Adorabelle checked her calculations and said we had traveled two hours into the past, give or take a few minutes. When we left the Room of Rings, Hawk said his digital watch read 12:37 p.m. It now showed 10:34, a little over an hour after we had originally left for the library.

Even though we had just walked through a door and were supposed to be invisible, I still felt the compulsion to creep through the front rooms, making as little noise as possible. Hawk evidently felt the same because he rolled down the hallway slowly as if trying to avoid the squeak of the manual wheelchair.

"Nice place." Adorabelle's voice sounded loud in the empty room, and Hawk and I both jumped.

The house was unusually quiet, and I suddenly realized that it wasn't the absence of my aunts; it was the absence of Hawk and Jeff and me. We couldn't hear ourselves reflected in the room. Aunty Gin said kids were the life of any house and because we were there when she said it, we were making the life sounds possible. Now, we were here but the house wasn't aware of us and, for the first time ever, I knew what a room sounded like without us.

As my mind wandered along those lines, Hawk led the way down the hall to the room he shared with Jeff. As we approached I could hear voices inside. Apparently taking Adorabelle at her word, Hawk rolled right in without slowing and stopped just short of running into Aunty Gin as she stood beside Jeff's bunk. She looked down at Aunt Marsha, who sat next to the Changeling. The gray creature lay very still on his back, beneath the covers.

"I've tried calling the doctor again," Aunty Gin said. "The phones are all out, and the cell doesn't connect either."

Aunt Marsha had her right hand on the Changeling's forehead and the other on his chest. "He just won't wake up," she said, so softly I could barely make out her words.

"Well, this is weird, even for us," Aunty Gin replied. "The batteries in all the cars along the street are dead." She walked over to the window. "And this blasted fog seems to have consumed the entire town." She turned back. "Marsha, we need to get Jeff some attention. He's far beyond my abilities."

Aunty Gin hit the top of the dresser with the flat of her hand. "Damn and blast!" she exploded. "How are we to get him help? And where are November and Hawk?" She looked helplessly at Aunt Marsha sitting on the side of the bed.

"I'm afraid it's worse than you think." Aunt Marsha's voice sent chills down my back. "This isn't Jeff."

I heard Hawk's intake of breath as Aunt Marsha turned haunted eyes toward her sister. "And I have an awful feeling that Hawk and November are gone, too."

"What do you mean, gone?" Aunty Gin stepped over to the bed and leaned down closer to the pale figure lying in the bed.

"This boy is dying ..." Aunt Marsha's voice was almost a whisper; "... but he's not my Jeffrey. In fact, I'm pretty sure he's not even human. Look here." She smoothed back the shaggy blond hair that fell over the boy's ears. Now it was Aunty Gin's turn to gasp. The tips of his ears were pointed.

"Mom!" Hawk leaned forward. "Jeff's okay! We're okay! We're going to get—"

"They can't hear you, son," Adorabelle said, placing her hand on Hawk's shoulder. "There is nothing you can do for them right now. You must stick to your path and perhaps things will work out the way you hope in the end." Adorabelle turned to me. "It's time to return. You have another trial run to complete before you can continue on your journey. Are you ready?" She motioned for me to take hold of Hawk's chair and turn him toward the door.

As I did so, I looked over at the two women sitting beside the dying Changeling and thought my heart would break for them. Just then, Aunty Gin lifted her head and looked right at me. She frowned for a split second and then a beautiful smile lit her face, and she turned back to her sister. "Don't worry," she said, leaning in and pulling the covers up around the sleeping Changeling's shoulders. "I have a feeling that November and Hawk have things well in hand."

I wished that I had Aunty Gin's faith; Adorabelle led us back into the hall and instructed us to begin activation of the Point of Zero.

***

Strangely enough, the trip back through the Rings seemed to be a bit longer than the first time. In fact, not only did I hear the delightful music and see the whole spectrum of colors, but this time I also smelled the wonderful aroma of freshly baked bread for an instant, just before something hooked onto the front of my jacket, and I was yanked out of the mesh back into the Room of Rings.

Hob undid the hook with lightning speed and reached in again, reeling Hawk in before I could catch my breath. Then he was off like a shot to the far end of the Rings, where he plunged the push-pull rod in and extracted a man who might have been dressed for a Shakespearian stage play.

Hawk tilted his head toward the oddly dressed man, who stood running his hands over his face like he had just broken the surface of deep water. "What time period do you think he's from?" Hawk said.

"1626," Adorabelle answered. "And *he's* none of your concern. You two need to start the next trial run." She instructed us to begin the countdown to the next Point of Zero, and before we knew it, Hob pushed us back into the Rings.

After having traveled to and fro, I thought I had a pretty good grip on the functioning of the Rings—I was wrong. This trip was much longer, and I found that I could move around and through the misty mesh. Not only that, but I soon discovered that the longer the trip, the more I could use my other senses. I could still hear the music, but it was different—not like harps playing but more like a well-rehearsed chamber ensemble. I could pick out flutes, oboes, and clarinets, along with stringed instruments. I could also see primary colors mixing to become new hues and forming shapes and pictures of places and people that I had never seen before—for all I knew, they could be from distant planets or galaxies. I smelled flowers, spices, and even the pungent scents of the sea. When I reached out, the mesh parted like a heavy curtain made of dry, soft talcum powder, swirling away to reveal other scenes and smells and sounds.

I'm not sure how long I wandered in the Rings, but eventually I was pushed out the other side into a brightly lit room, full of people in various stages of undress. Before I could get my bearings, Hawk bumped into me and almost sent me sprawling.

"Whoa," he said, not even trying to lower his voice this time. I had to admit the sight before us was pretty strange.

The large room was designed in a semi-circle. Bright sunlight streamed in through tall, unadorned windows above a highly polished hardwood floor. White Formica-topped tables were haphazardly placed around the room and each held a variety of arts and crafts materials, game boards, and other indoor activities. The walls, all the way around the room, displayed the results of many hours spent working on those crafts and puzzles by the people who either sat at the tables or wandered around aimlessly talking to each other—or to themselves.

Something stirred next to me, and I looked to my left. There, in a battered rocking chair, sat a middle-aged woman with limp gray hair, holding a baby doll and crooning a lullaby as she stroked its hard plastic face.

"This is the solarium where we met Sir Edmond," Hawk said suddenly, as if it had just dawned on him where we were.

"You are correct," Adorabelle said, bouncing out of the air behind us.

Hawk and I both turned and our mouths flew open. Although her voice had not changed much, she sure had. If I didn't know she was the one accompanying us on our trial runs I would have thought someone else had tagged along for the adventure.

A very tall older woman stood smiling down at us. She had salt-and-pepper hair that fell from the middle part at the top of her head, straight down to her shoulders, where it was trimmed with a blunt, even cut all the way around. Though she had some wrinkles around her eyes, her face was otherwise unlined, and her complexion smooth and pink; her eyes were the only recognizable feature. Like dark sapphires, they twinkled as Adorabelle laughed at our amazed stares.

"We've traveled back more than fifty years!" she said, by way of explaining her dramatic transformation. "Welcome to Danvers State Hospital—today is November 10th, 1951. I believe your friend the gnome told you that when you travel into the past to a time during your lifetime, you will become the age you were in that year." She twirled around like a runway model. "I was only 290 in this year, and I hadn't started to revert yet—late middle-age, you humans might call me." She stopped spinning and grew serious as she looked closely at us. "But enough of that. How are you two? Any ill effects?" Adorabelle scrutinized us for a moment before stepping back, apparently satisfied. "No? Well, then, let us have a look around. I'm afraid you've not had a really good look at this institution." She raised her arm in a sweeping gesture. "It was really quite grand in its day. And as I previously said, you are correct, Hawk; this is the solarium of the hospital. It was used as a dayroom for patients to have art therapy, get some sunshine, and socialize."

Adorabelle crossed the room, Hawk following, and I took a step to join them when I heard the woman in the rocking chair say, "My name is Annie—what's yours?"

I looked back, and she was staring right at me, as if waiting for an answer. Adorabelle and Hawk were still making their way across the large room toward the bank of windows.

"Well, don't you have a name?" Annie asked.

"Uh … my name is November," I said, glancing around to see if any of the others in the room could hear me. No one else seemed to.

Annie smiled. "November. That's a lovely name, isn't it, Deidre?" She gazed down at the doll and then back up at me with a shy smile. "Deidre thinks so, too."

I hadn't really looked beyond her shabby nightdress and lank hair, but now, I saw that Annie had beautiful brown eyes and a lovely face.

"Hi, Deidre," I said to the doll.

"Oh, I know she isn't real," Annie said, smiling down at the painted face of the baby doll, "but she reminds me of my own little girl, Deidre."

At the expression on my face, Annie hastily continued. "Oh, she didn't die or anything; Deidre is a grown woman now with her own family. It's just that I so loved it when she was little." She cuddled the doll close. "I just like to pretend that I still have her in my arms." She looked up. "Are you new here?"

Before I could answer, a heavyset nurse in a starched white uniform, a stiff little cap, and a name tag declaring in bold black letters that she was Nurse Hampton came toward us.

"Annie, it's time for your medication and your treatment." She seemed unaware of me, and I took a few steps back.

"Oh, don't go, November!" Annie held out her hand to me and looked at the nurse. "Please let me have a little more time with November," she pleaded, pointing to me.

The nurse pursed her lips. "Now, Annie, it's only the beginning of November. You still have several weeks before it's gone. Now let's get you back to your room. You can bring Deidre, and she can have a treatment, too." The nurse took Annie's outstretched arm and helped her to her feet.

Without resistance, Annie let the nurse lead her toward the double doors just to our left. She looked back as she walked next to Nurse Hampton. "Good-bye, November. Please remember me—Annie from Nova Scotia, number 125."

I stood waving even after the door had closed behind her.

"I'm afraid we need to return at once." Adorabelle's voice broke into my thoughts, and I turned to see her and Hawk beside me. "It doesn't happen often, but sometimes someone can see one of us. That is extremely dangerous during the trial runs. I've no time to explain now; just begin your countdown to Point of Zero, and I'm afraid that since the protocol has been breached, you will have less than ten seconds to activate your cards. Do it now! Or we're looking at thirty-seven years until you get another try."

Her words no sooner left her lips than Hawk activated his Point of Zero and disappeared. But although mine appeared, it would not accept my card. I tried a second time, pulling it out as fast as I could, but nothing happened. I tried a third time—still nothing.

"Let me have it," Adorabelle said in a tight voice. She tried it once, and it was then I noticed the small counter at the bottom of the outside frame. It was counting down and had reached 4 … 3 …

In desperation, I grabbed the card from Adorabelle's long fingers and plunged it in and out, just as the counter reached 1, and Adorabelle and I were launched into the Q.

Chapter Twenty-one

I have walked a great while over the snow, and I am neither tall nor strong. My clothes are wet, and my teeth are set, and the way was hard and long.

—Mary Coleridge, *The Witch*

IT WAS LIKE BEING SUCKED INSIDE A tornado. I flew off my feet and went head over heels through the blackest night I had ever experienced. I screamed so hard, I thought my lungs would burst, and then I heard someone else screaming, too.

"Hawk!" I shrieked, trying to be heard over the roar of the gale that held me, spinning helplessly, like a rag doll. "Hawk, *answer* me!" I reached out my hands, trying to find the source of the other screams. Anything or *anyone* would have been preferable to falling endlessly through this void of howling darkness. The screaming continued; either they could not hear me or were too hysterical to stop. It didn't take me long to realize it was not Hawk. The screams were too high pitched.

"Adorabelle!" I called once and then again, louder, trying desperately to make myself heard above the raging storm. Please let it be her—please let it be *someone.*

Abruptly, the screaming stopped and a deep, raspy voice said, "Reach out your hands!"

It was oddly familiar, but I couldn't quite place it. I stretched my body long, like skydivers do on television, and began shouting Adorabelle's name over and over, hoping the cacophony surrounding my free fall was the cause of her voice sounding so strange.

But the thing in the raging blackness that grabbed my arms was not Adorabelle. Its twisting grip burned as it turned me over and over, first in a tumble, then end over end until I thought I was going to throw up. Clamping my mouth tight, I tried not to scream, but the sheer pain and terror was such that I couldn't hold it together. I struggled frantically to free my arms from the singeing grip, even though I knew it was futile.

The thing held me like a white-hot vise. And I knew it had no intention of letting me go.

I have never been able to tolerate being confined or restrained, so my fear turned into anger, then rage. As I struggled, I opened my mouth and let loose a sound I would never have believed could possibly have come from me. It ascended from the very bottom of my being, while a part of me stood detached, watching the sound swirl away, echoing over and over as its light multiplied through the darkness. My captor suddenly unleashed a low, tortured wail as the echo of my soul erupted and spread ever outward, pushing the darkness away until it was gone.

Now free, my spinning gradually slowed, finally stopping altogether when my feet touched something solid, allowing me to stand. The howling winds became soft breezes as the sound traveled outward now, lighting my surroundings until I felt the warmth of the sun reach through the fog and wrap itself around my freezing body.

"November." The voice was gentle and musical, and I looked around me to find its source. "You have found your core—your strength. Do you realize what you have just done? You have defeated the Dark One. And each time you do, you will grow stronger."

"Adorabelle?" I called into the swirling mist, now infused with sunlight.

"Your guide will join you soon enough." The hypnotic voice filled the air so completely that the now-puffy white mist shivered with the vibration of it. "You will need to draw upon that strength all too soon, my child," the voice continued, and then I recognized it.

"Grandma Bran?" I called into the mist. It couldn't be. My father's mother had died four years ago.

"Yes, sweetheart, it's me," she said, as she walked out of the cloud to engulf me in an embrace I thought I would never feel again—an embrace that warmed me through to that "core" she'd mentioned. She stepped back and smiled; the last time I saw her was in the hospital, with tubes and monitors, looking old, frail, and finished with living. Now she glowed—literally—*glowed* with health.

"Am I dead?" I asked, suddenly afraid.

Grandma Bran laughed softly. "No, darling, you are far from dead." Her crinkly, pale blue eyes regarded me for a moment and then grew serious. "But you should know by now that you have a serious task ahead."

"What do you mean, a serious task?" I asked, suddenly frustrated by all the mystery. "Everybody keeps saying vague things like, 'You're the one we've been expecting,' and 'You must lead the others.' What others? And what task? I don't understand any of this!"

"Now, listen." My grandmother's voice was the one she used when she was about to tell me something serious. "You have a job to do." She raised her hand to stop my interruption. "Your family—my family, the Atwoods, are very special people. I know no one has ever told you about this part of your heritage; your mother forbade us to speak of it because she doesn't believe it herself." She paused as if trying to decide how to begin. "The Atwoods go back to the old Celtic tribes in Ireland and Scotland. We are the direct descendants of the goddess Avnova."

"I know," I interrupted, and she held up her hand again, cutting me off.

"No, you don't," she said, "not everything. You see, as Children of Avnova, we have been given certain abilities and responsibilities. It is our—*your*—obligation to see to it that those of the dark realm do not destroy all that the goddess has helped to create." She looked at me hard, then. "Every once in a while there is a child meant to do a great task—a *hard job*, to put it plainly." At the stressed words my grandmother's soft white curls bounced, reflecting the sunlight beaming down upon us. "When you were born, the Council of Avnova convened to discuss whether you were the one the legend spoke of. All the signs were there—the month, day, and year of your birth add up to the number eight. You were eight pounds, eight ounces, and seventeen inches long which, if you add the one and the seven together, makes eight. But the telling thing was that your thumbs and big toes were fused together. In essence, you were born with eight fingers and eight toes."

I looked down at my hands and thought about how I had always had scars on the tops of both my thumbs and big toes.

"Of course, the surgeons took care of that problem, but not before word spread among our community—thus, the call for the convening of the council. It was decided that if you were *The Prediction*, then the time was near for so great a task that its like has not been seen since the Burning Times—the time of the Salem witch trials, when folks like us were seen as evil and dangerous and not fit to live."

I was starting to get it. "Folks like us."

"Magical folk," she continued. "We are the guardians of the magic arts, which we take an oath to use only to help and protect those that do not have our abilities."

"You mean witches?" I asked incredulously.

"Some call us that. Others call us healers, wise people, seers, and gifted. At any rate," she continued, "I now know that you are the girl, decided upon by another council long ago, who is destined to break a covenant entered into by greedy men, desperate to rise above their stations in life." Grandma Bran smiled sadly. "It won't be easy, honey, but it is something you must do."

"I don't feel like the *chosen one*." I shrugged in despair. "What if I can't do it—what if I fail?"

My grandmother's face grew stern. "You will face a great enemy, November—a strong and angry foe who will not give up easily." She stepped back and regarded me solemnly. "He is the guardian of darkness. It was he who had hold of you just now, and he has much at stake. You fought him off. You have the strength, Em," she said. "Don't be afraid of it, but also know that each time you strike him, he will return stronger as well. You have reached down inside yourself to find your strength, and you now know how to do it. Guard that strength well; you'll need it on the rest of your journey." She backed away from me then.

"Grandma, don't go," I said, although I knew it was useless.

"I'm afraid I must." Her gentle smile made me want to grab her and hold tight, but she was already fading. "But I am never very far. Each time you think of me, I will be with you, not more than a whisper away." The fog thickened, engulfing her so that only her voice lingered on the last two words.

Then I fell through the mist, landing on my knees on the hard maple floor of the Putnam Middle School gymnasium.

Pain shot through both legs, and I wondered if I had broken my kneecaps, but the sounds around me didn't give me much time to speculate about my injuries. I had landed smack-dab in the middle of a rally or giant campout.

The bleachers on either side of the room were packed with people bundled in winter coats and hats or blankets, as if they awaited the football game starting lineup on the field, rather than sitting inside a school building. The entire place was crammed to the rafters.

But this was no school pep rally. Most of the town was there, along with a good portion of their belongings. As I got to my feet, I noticed sleeping bags and coolers, telescopic chairs, cookstoves, lanterns, and other camping gear near groups of families with small children and even some dogs and cats on leashes or in crates.

I turned full circle and took in the scope of the refugees. Backpacks, suitcases, and laptops sitting on agitated knees filled the bleachers. One little boy rolled a Frisbee in front of me and ran to fetch it. As I stepped back to avoid a collision, someone grabbed my arms. After my recent experience in the Rings, I jumped and cried out as fingers pressed into the seared flesh of my lower arms.

"It's just me," Adorabelle said. She let go and then came around in front of me. She was tiny once again, and her big eyes held mine for an instant before she took my right hand and pushed up my sleeve. Her eyes widened, and I followed her gaze to the band of burned flesh encircling my arm like a bracelet. She shoved up the other sleeve, revealing the same blackened ring on that arm as well.

"No wonder you cried out when I touched you, child." Adorabelle's voice held the softness that only white-hot anger can produce.

"What's going on?" I asked. "What are we doing here—and where's Hawk?"

Adorabelle pointed to Mr. Barbatos, the seventh-grade science teacher, attempting to set up the microphone at the far end of the room. "I heard him tell someone he's going to make an announcement to the crowd concerning what's been happening in Danvers." She took my hand and led me carefully through the crowd and into the corridor outside the gym.

"Of course you know they can't see us," she continued, "but there's something you don't know. When we launched through the POZ—Point of Zero—we were a teeny bit late. That is quite serious. It can cause all sorts of problems." Adorabelle's eyes registered concern, and she ran her fingers through her cotton-candy hair. "Because we missed the launch by a fraction of a second, it affected the damping coefficient."

I tried to follow what she was saying, but she was so agitated that she was literally walking in circles.

Without warning, she turned on her heels and began scurrying down the hall, motioning for me to follow. We entered the first classroom we came to, and Adorabelle grabbed a chair and pushed it up against the chalkboard. Climbing up, she took a piece of chalk and scribbled on the board, while explaining the strange symbols she made in much the same manner a professor might explain chemical theory.

"You see, the damping coefficient of a process can go one of three ways. It can be $\xi = 1$, critically damped, or $\xi \geq 1$, which is over-damped, or $\xi \leq 1$, which is under-damped." She stopped to see if I was following her and, after reading my expression, turned back to the board and erased the squiggles with her stubby fingers.

"What it all means," she said, getting down from the chair and walking toward the windows, "is that rather than go in a straight line back to where we began, we became critically damped." Adorabelle turned and held up her hands. "We overshot our target."

"What do you mean?" I did not like the sound of this.

"We're two days in the future. Today is November 12th."

"November 12th! You mean we missed—"

Adorabelle nodded. "Exactly. It's one day after Hollantide."

"But *the Bargain* ..." I began.

Adorabelle inclined her head in the general direction of the gym. "By the looks of things in there, the Bargain has been sealed."

"And Jeff? Hawk?"

"Don't know." Her huge eyes blinked rapidly.

Suddenly we heard the microphone come to life and reverberate through the classroom wall.

"Will everyone give me their attention—attention, *please*!" Mr. Barbatos' voice held a tone I had never heard before.

"We had best get back in there and see what he has to say," Adorabelle suggested, heading toward the door.

Mr. Barbatos and Mr. Roth stood at the far end of the gymnasium on a raised platform. Roth wore a heavy crimson cape that fell from his massive shoulders to the floor. His dead-black eyes seemed to take in the entire crowd without having to blink.

In contrast, Mr. Barbatos was dressed in a brown woolen suit that clearly had seen better days. His wild brick red hair flew in all directions, like the flame on a match. He raised the microphone to his mouth. "I would like to begin by saying that my companion and I understand your fears and anxiety about recent events in Danvers and I—*we*—want to explain what has occurred and what is yet to be expected."

"We want to know what's happened to our homes!" a man shouted from the crowd.

"Yeah, what's causing all the explosions?"

"Where's the fire department?"

"What's happened to the power?"

"Why have we all been herded in here?"

The voices overlapped, people got to their feet, and the crowd seemed on the verge of action, if not downright violence.

"Everyone, please stay in your seats!" Mr. Barbatos shouted into the mike, but people were getting up and pushing their way to the lower rows. The crowd on the floor began to move in a wave of humanity that caused some chairs and lanterns to be knocked over.

Mr. Roth stepped forward. "*Sit down.*" Although he did not raise his voice, and Mr. Barbatos still held the microphone, the words reverberated through the room like a thunderclap. Amazingly, everyone did as he said, and the room grew quiet.

Mr. Roth stepped to the edge of the platform, raising both arms as if to encompass the entire audience. "What everyone here *needs* to know is that what you call *your town—your Danvers*—is no more." He lowered his head but not his arms, and his eyes seemed to simmer from within. "You have been *herded* here, because you are the remaining descendants of the Children of Avnova, and as such, you are to be returned to Salem Village—intact. The Bargain struck in the winter of 1700 had a minor flaw."

"What *bargain*?" a familiar voice called out, and I watched Mr. Whoozi-What's step forward from the lower bleachers. "And what do you mean, we are the descendants of some children of … whatever!" He threw his arm into the air on the last word, dismissing it.

"Be seated," Mr. Roth said, without moving a facial muscle or raising his voice an octave.

Mr. Whoozi-What's didn't move a muscle either, except to clench his already tightly held jaw even tighter before saying, "You aren't in charge here! We demand answers as to what is happening in this town. Our homes have been blown off their foundations and we've been rounded up in the middle of the night like so much cattle and, yes, *herded* like them, into this school. And I, for one, have had just about enough! Now, either you give us some straight talk or we'll find someone who will!"

Mr. Roth's only movement was to raise his chin during Mr. Whoozi-What's' speech and, on the last word, splay the fingers on his left hand in Mr. Whoozi-What's' direction. Like a bolt of lightning, a powerful charge shot from his fingertips across the room, directly into Mr. Whoozi-What's' chest, knocking him to the floor.

I screamed the only name I knew him by, but it didn't much matter because even if I could have been heard, I would have been drowned out by another voice that belonged to the woman who fell on her knees beside him.

The rest of the crowd stood as if frozen in time. Mouths open or hands covering them, arms around children who whimpered into their bodies, they did nothing to tend to the fallen man who now lay on the floor of the school gym.

I started toward where the woman knelt, running her hands over his shirt in an effort to put out the flames.

"Daniel! Daniel!" she called to his limp form.

But suddenly the POZ blocked my way. I turned to Adorabelle. "I didn't count down!" I shouted at her, over the woman's keening. "Why is the POZ here?"

Adorabelle shook her head. "It's the damping. It's correcting itself." She waved at me frantically. "Put in your card. Quickly!"

"But …" I waved my arm in the direction of Mr. Whoozi-What's.

Chapter Twenty-two

Who goes there with its shadow on the wall passing
with a sigh and a shiver through the mirror?
—Robert Fisher, *Hallowe'en Fright*

ADORABELLE GRABBED MY HAND, YANKING ME BACKWARD forcefully, as I started for Mr. Whoozi-What's. I wondered at her strength until I realized I was not the only thing going backward. As I stumbled, trying to keep my balance, I noticed everyone around me was going in the opposite direction. It was as if I was in the middle of a movie that someone had slammed in reverse.

"Hold on!" Adorabelle shouted, clutching my hand even tighter. "The coefficient has corrected!"

I watched Mr. Whoozi-What's shoot up from the floor, the electrical charge bouncing back from his body, just as we were launched into the fog.

I don't think I blinked twice before Hob yanked us out into the Room of Rings. It was Adorabelle's hand that kept me from tumbling into Hawk's lap.

He raised his arms in preparation for the expected collision.

"Hawk! You're here!" I said, and he lowered them and frowned.

"What are you talking about? And what happened to your hair?"

My hands flew to my head and what I felt made me gasp. Looking wildly around for something that would show my reflection, I spotted a door marked ***Necessity*** not too far from where we had first entered the Room of Rings. Without a word, I dashed toward it, slamming the door shut behind me.

The dull glow from a hanging gaslight provided just enough light to show I had entered a restroom of sorts. The long narrow room disappeared into shadows at the opposite end, but I could make out a washstand with an old-fashioned pitcher and bowl against the right wall. The toilet next to it was nothing more than a crude wooden seat built into a box, like the ones I had seen in pictures of outhouses. But I was only interested in the large oval mirror hanging on the wall opposite the washstand. The intricate dark frame was made from twisted pieces of wood, like hundreds of gnarled fingers, entwined in a ghoulish braid. The mirror itself was tarnished and silvery, with tiny cracks, like wrinkles on an old weathered face. Stepping forward, I stifled a scream at the image that gazed back at me from its depths, until I realized it was my own reflection. I looked like someone had taken my waist-length hair and brushed it all straight up in the air; but what had caused me to gasp was the single white feather now growing from my hairline.

"Something wrong?" The soft voice had the effect of a shout on my frazzled nerves, causing me to squeal and jump back. I hadn't noticed the woman seated in the shadows. She was just to the right of the mirror, beside a narrow table containing small towels, lotions, and other toiletry items, and was dressed completely in black—long skirt covering her feet, a turtleneck to her chin. Straight black hair accentuated her pale, grim face.

Snow White in mourning.

"I'm s-sorry," I stuttered. "I didn't see you there."

Thin, bloodless lips turned up in a parody of a smile. "Has the mirror troubled you, dear? Is there anything I can help you with?"

Her cat-like voice, a combination meow and purr turned into words, was at once creepy and compelling.

"Uh, well … no—I mean …" I stammered, trying to smooth my hair back down where it belonged, while backing toward the door.

"You are not going to leave without a consultation, are you?" The woman raised a bony hand and pointed toward the mirror.

"Consultation?"

"Why, yes." A spark in the black eye sockets flared momentarily. "Have you not come to talk to *The Looking Glass*?"

At my hesitation, she continued.

"Just remember, you must speak a truth in order to be rewarded with a *necessity*—but beware that if you speak a falsehood, you will be *consumed* at the most critical moment of your life."

"I … don't think I really need to …" Never taking my eyes from the gaunt figure, I retreated until I could feel the doorknob at my back. Reaching behind me, I grasped it, intending to make my escape.

"If you choose not to consult The Looking Glass of All Mysteries, you will be making a grave mistake." The woman held out both skeletal hands in appeal.

The Looking Glass of All Mysteries? The Vellum had said something about finding a looking glass. I cast back in my memory for the exact wording. And then, as if someone had suddenly switched on a recording, I heard Hawk reading, "*Go beneath the stones of Hathorne on the Eve of Hollantide and find The Looking Glass of All Mysteries; for under its seal lies the door to eternity.*"

"Is that not why you are here?" The woman's voice had fallen to a near growl, and her chin rose as if I had just done something terribly offensive.

"Of course," I said, as if I had intended to talk to that mirror since first opening the door. "Of course it is." I strode back to the looking glass with as much confidence as my shaky knees would allow and stood in front of it. The girl that stared back at me looked anything but self-assured.

"Tell it a truth, dear." The woman growled as she shifted in her seat like it was becoming too warm.

I looked into the glass and my mind went completely blank. A truth? What was she talking about? What truth did I have that this looking glass needed to hear? And what was "truth" anyway. "One man's truth is another man's fantasy," my dad used to say.

"*Then say it.*" The woman's face shifted suddenly and swiveled toward me, her eyes glowing as if lit by flames from within. Her lips parted in a snarl, revealing sharp, carnivorous teeth.

I turned back to the mirror. Say what? I looked for some sign from the depths of the looking glass, but all I saw was the distant reflection of the gas lamp behind my terrified face.

"*Say the truth—say it* now." She was up on all fours on the chair, her long hair hanging down, catching the foam that her panting produced, as she glared at me.

Suddenly, I saw my dad's face in the mirror. "Say the quote, November; the one you just remembered—quickly!"

"Dad!" His face dissolved; the mirror once again reflecting my own.

The woman let out a howl that raised the hair on every inch of my body.

"One man's truth is another man's fantasy!" I shouted so hard at the mirror that a few specks of spit flew from my mouth onto its surface. With a loud crack, the looking glass exploded, splintering into a thousand tiny fragments. I threw my hands in front of my face but not before I saw what looked like a panther leap from the chair the woman had occupied only moments before, and disappear into the darkness.

Shards of mirrored glass flew in all directions as I dropped into a crouch, burying my face in my knees and covering my head with my arms. Moments after the explosion, I heard the door open, and Adorabelle rushed into the room with Hawk right behind her.

"What happened?" The wheels of Hawk's chair made crunching noises as he rolled over the broken glass. "Are you okay?"

I nodded as Adorabelle inspected me for cuts and shrapnel.

"I think so," I managed, as she helped me to my feet. I pointed to where the looking glass used to be. All that remained was the twisted frame that now lay on the floor, broken into three pieces.

"That was The Looking Glass of All Mysteries," I said, as Hawk rolled over to where it lay. He studied it and the wall briefly.

"*Under its seal lies the door to eternity*," he recited softly. "There's an outline of a door here." His eyes shone. "This may be the way to the place where they've taken Jeff." Without another word, he began pushing on the wall with all his might. Adorabelle and I joined him, and together we pushed, kicked, and I even tried the old shoulder-shove routine, but the door would not budge. Then again, it was not exactly a normal door. There was no knob or apparatus with which to open it, nor did it seem to have hinges. It was simply a rectangle cut into the heavy wooden wall, and it was either not cut all the way through or had never been opened.

As we stopped for a breath, Hob appeared in the doorway of the restroom.

"I'm afraid you must be on your way—time is not on your side." He looked worriedly at his pocket watch and then shook his head in dismay.

"Hob, what do you know about a door in this room?" Adorabelle asked, frustration clear in her voice.

"I don't know of any door … oh, dear," Hob said, as he entered the room and saw the broken mirror on the floor. "What has happened in here?"

"The mirror had a door behind it. We think it might be a way inside the Hill of Hathorne," Hawk said, but Hob shook his head.

"There is no time! No time at all! You must hurry if you are to meet your deadline! This is the Eve of Hollantide, and you've only a small number of hours left to finish your journey!" He stepped forward to take the handles of Hawk's chair.

"No!" Hawk backed away. "I'm not going anywhere." He turned to me. "Keep kicking, November. Better yet, go get something we can use to pry it open. The clues said this was the door to eternity. It has to lead us to where they've taken my brother, and I'm not leaving until I get it open!"

"Hawk," I said, as gently as I could, "I don't think this door will lead us to Jeff. The woman I spoke to before the mirror exploded didn't say anything about its being a passageway or a tunnel into the hill. Maybe we better do as Hob says … I mean, tomorrow is Hollantide and when I was in the gymnasium, I saw …" I knew I was beginning to babble but I was trying desperately to get through to Hawk, who was visibly shutting off any attempts at reason.

"*No*!" Hawk pulled back even further. "I don't give a tinker's damn about what these people say! We have to *finish!* My *brother* is running out of time, and right now he's the only thing that matters!" Hawk planted his feet firmly in the footholds of the chair, with his arms on its wheels, and dug in.

Adorabelle's raised eyebrows said plainly, "It's out of my hands," and Hob's eyebrows hopped up and down like caterpillars on a hot plate.

Clearly, it was up to me to do something but for the life of me, I didn't know what. Maybe I had not told the mirror the right *truth*, or maybe we could not open the door because I was responsible for breaking the mirror. Maybe Hawk was right, and we should keep trying. On the other hand, if Hob was right, we were wasting precious time that we would need to finish our quest, ultimately leading us to

Jeff, not to mention saving Mr. Whoozi-What's and half the people of Danvers.

"Hawk, I think you know which way is the right one, as do you, November."

I spun around to see Dynnis standing in the restroom door holding what looked like a bundle of rags. He came farther into the room and stood in front of Hawk. Without another word, he placed the bundle in Hawk's lap and indicated the hidden door.

"That is not the door you seek," he said, leaning down and picking up the broken pieces of the mirror frame. One by one, he turned them over and then laid them back on the floor, stopping at the very last one.

"Aha, just as I suspected. This is what you were supposed to find." He handed the twisted wooden piece to me.

The design of the gold coin embedded in the back of it looked familiar. I held the frame piece out to Hawk, forcing him to take his hand from the wheel of the chair in order to accept it, as he balanced the bundle Dynnis had dropped in his lap with the other.

"It is the sigil of Astaroth; his seal," Dynnis said, as if reading my mind. "And I believe it is most likely the second of the three seals that you seek. However, right now you two need to finish what you have started, and you'll need a powerful guardian to guide you." He nodded at the rags in Hawk's lap.

Hawk's guarded look told me he was not entirely convinced as he handed the frame piece back to Dynnis and looked down at the small bundle.

"What is this?"

"Not what—*who*," Dynnis replied. "You are about to enter a world, the likes of which you have never seen before, and for that, you will need someone who knows the lay of the land—someone who has lived in that time period."

"And just who would that be?" Hawk asked, raising his chin as if in defiance.

Dynnis met his gaze evenly. "Ambrosine."

***

Looking back on it now, I think that had it not been for the shock of finding Hob's great-great-grandmother in his lap, Hawk would not have gone willingly into the Rings. But Dynnis saw an opportunity to move things along and so, with blind faith in his motives, I grabbed the handles of the wheelchair and hurried Hawk and Ambrosine out of the Necessity room and down to the far end of the Rings. Hob ran ahead, punching buttons and setting dials along the way, and before Hawk could regain his powers of speech and I my breath, he grabbed the push-pull and shoved us three-hundred-plus years into the past.

Actually, Hob shoved *me,* as I was holding onto the handles of Hawk's chair like they were my lifeline. I realized, as we began our movement into the colorful mist, that my teeth were clenched and the muscles in both shoulders were so tight it caused them to be up around my ears. But this trip did not plunge me into terror. In fact, it seemed to be much like the second one we had taken. The rainbow fog swirled in time to a beautiful melody that seemed to come from everywhere at once.

As I pushed the chair forward, I began to relax somewhat but not enough to cause me to loosen my grip on its handles. It was not lost on me that although I was convinced I had to protect my wheelchair-bound cousin from harm, it was me who found comfort from the proximity of the chair.

I realized, too, that unlike the other trips, I could see things through the hazy veils. As we progressed I caught glimpses of trees growing through buildings, then the buildings were gone altogether, and a thick forest stood in its place. I began to realize that what I was seeing was time going in reverse. Not like my experience in the Putnam gym but faster, as if with each step, we took giant leaps back in time.

I leaned over Hawk's shoulder to point out a scene playing out on my right, when his back stiffened and his left hand reached back to cover mine on the handle.

"November!" He sounded as if he couldn't breathe. "Look—the rags … they're … it's moving!"

I leaned in farther and saw the bundle shift, then fall away, revealing an extremely old lady, who began to grow larger and noticeably younger as we moved along.

"What am I supposed to do with her?" Hawk cried.

I watched in amazement as we continued to move forward. The ancient woman's sparse white hair began to thicken and darken into a deep reddish brown, while her withered limbs strengthened and straightened, gaining muscle tone as the deep wrinkles in her face smoothed into a creamy complexion. Within mere moments, she had quadrupled in size. The woman, now larger than Hawk himself, lay with her head resting on his chest. Hawk sat frozen, both hands in the air, so as not to touch her any more than he already was. Suddenly, she drew in a trembling, deep breath, tilted back her head, and opened her eyes.

"Holy crap!" I heard Hawk gasp.

Ambrosine stared at him for a moment, then leaped from his lap.

The rags that had been her wrapping now fell around her body as a tunic or loose dress. The deep blue fabric was a rough cotton material, hand-sewn and dyed.

"Good heavens!" Ambrosine said, as she took in her surroundings and then the two of us. "Am I renewing?"

She looked around her in confusion, and I was reminded of how Rip Van Winkle must have felt after being asleep for twenty years. I wondered how many years Ambrosine had been in the cupboard, *renewing.*

Since Hawk seemed incapable of speech at the moment, I answered her as best I could.

"We're in the Rings."

After a moment's hesitation, I saw understanding register on Ambrosine's face.

"Of course," she said, looking around her now with recognition. "We're going into the past. And who might you children be?"

I opened my mouth to make introductions but Hawk seemed to have regained both his senses and his bad temper.

"My name's Hawk and this is my cousin, November, and we already know you're Ambrosine—great-great-great-something or other to that guy Hob back there." He made a dismissive gesture behind him. "And we can get to know each other later, but now we *need* to get going. There's a lot we have to do, and there isn't much time!" He grabbed the wheels and plunged forward, pulling the handles of the wheelchair out of my hands.

I was so surprised by his rudeness that all I could do was smile at Ambrosine.

"Guess we'd better follow," she said with a shrug, and we broke into a trot to catch up with the wheelchair and its agitated occupant, just before it disappeared into the fog.

I had no sooner taken hold of the handles again, with Ambrosine stepping lively at our side, than the mists cleared, and we found ourselves on a dirt track at the edge of a wood. I couldn't really call it a forest because the trees were nothing more than tall saplings, with tangled underbrush and vines so dense beneath them that they made a hedge of leafy green alongside the rutted cart track.

Bright sunshine filtered down through the broad leaves, and as the music of the misty fog faded, I realized the woods were full of birds who, at the moment, were singing the glories of a fine summer morning.

"Oh!" Ambrosine breathed out the word as if she had just beheld a priceless jewel. "Salem Village." She turned toward me, beaming. "I grew up here, you know."

She took the lead, picking up speed as we made our way out of the woods, following the track downhill through a meadow of high grass toward a primitive log house with a small rough-hewn outbuilding or barn. Though she was clearly middle-aged, Ambrosine moved like a child returning home after a long time away. Bare feet skipping along in the dust, her spirits were so high that I would not have been surprised to hear her start singing.

Suddenly, she stopped in her tracks and spun around, looking at Hawk like he'd just turned into Jack the Ripper.

He and I both skidded to a halt. "What?" we both said at once.

Ambrosine frowned. "What year is this?"

"I'm not sure," I began. "We were supposed to go back to—"

"Turn around." Ambrosine's tone allowed for no resistance. "Quickly. Back into the woods!" She roughly elbowed me away from the wheelchair, grabbed the handles, and practically ran back into the trees with a startled Hawk, who shouted, "If you'll wait a minute, I'll check!"

Once in the shelter of the woods, Ambrosine slowed to a walk and then finally stopped. "Summon the POZ." The little girl had completely disappeared, and Ambrosine was all business now.

"But we just got here!" Hawk complained.

"Do it," she directed him and waved me away when I asked if I should count down mine as well.

When Hawk's POZ hovered in front of him, she reached out and tapped a small button in the top right corner. Immediately, a date appeared, wavering like a flame: *August 2, 1701.*

Ambrosine blew on it, and it disappeared like smoke. She punched another button and the POZ dissolved as well. Standing back with a satisfied smile she said, "Well, well. 1701—and August 2nd, at that." Her smile broadened into a huge grin. "Today is my birthday! I am forty-two—*again*!" She threw back her head and laughed like it was the funniest thing she had ever heard.

When she finally gained control of herself, Hawk said sourly, "Happy birthday, but what's that got to do with why we're back in the woods again?"

Ambrosine's face sobered, and she pointed to Hawk's wheelchair. "That," she said. "That contraption did not exist in this time." She began looking around her while simultaneously scratching her head.

"Well, it's not like I can do much about it," Hawk grumped. "I was born without the use of my legs." He watched Ambrosine as she walked in a circle, muttering to herself, then added, "So, what do you suggest? Throw my chair in the weeds and carry me everywhere? I mean, what did they do in the 1700s with kids like me?"

I studied Hawk's movements while he spoke. I had never seen him so agitated—so prickly. He squirmed around in his seat as if—all at once I knew what I had to do. "Ambrosine, why don't you go ahead," I said, causing her to turn and look at me suspiciously. "I'll stay with Hawk until you have a look around—get the *lay of the land*." After all, Dynnis had said she was supposed to be our guide.

Ambrosine chewed her lip, glanced toward the meadow, and then back at us. "Perhaps you are right," she said at last. "But you will need to move off the path in case someone should come along." She pointed to one of the larger trees, not too far into the undergrowth. "I believe I saw a deer path over there that will most likely lead you to a spot near that oak. I'll go as far as the road and have a look around." She assumed a stern look. "But do not try to go anywhere on your own, not until I return and we decide on the best way for you to travel in this time."

"Fine, fine. Let's get on with it, then." Hawk made a shooing motion with his hands at Ambrosine as she turned and headed off down the path.

"Let's go, November," he commanded, and I wasted no time steering the wheelchair down the deer path to the oak tree that Ambrosine had suggested.

The tree's broad branches and wide solid leaves provided a welcome shady spot on what was quickly becoming a very warm day. By the sun's angle, I judged it was past noon and would most likely get hotter as the day progressed.

Nature had also supplied a nice flat rock next to the tree trunk, and I sat down gratefully next to Hawk, who slumped silently, a look of sheer misery on his face.

He wasn't alone in his misery. I had a good idea what was wrong with him, and I really didn't want to have to deal with it. But I immediately felt ashamed of myself. After all, I was all he had, and I wasn't about to let him down now.

Taking a deep breath to summon up the courage to speak, I leaned forward. "Hawk, would you mind if I asked you something kind of personal?"

"What do you mean?" He looked at me suspiciously.

I really didn't know any delicate way to phrase my question so, after several lame attempts at forming the words with my lips, I just came out with it.

"Do you have to go to the bathroom?"

Silence.

Hawk sat gripping the arms of his chair as if wishing that at any moment he could fall through the earth and land in the magma. And I realized he had tears in his eyes.

"Well, if it's so bad that it's starting to roll up and out of your eyes, you'd better do something about it." I clamped my mouth shut along with my eyes, horrified by what I had just said. Then I heard him snort, and I opened them to see him half crying and laughing at the same time.

"Don't make me laugh November—*please*!" he wailed, shaking his head. "You're right. I have to go so bad, my eyeballs are floating!" He looked at me with haunted eyes. "But Jeff is the only one who knows how to help me—and that's when there is a bathroom around." He looked around at the forest. "I've never been in this situation before. And I've always had Jeff, or at the very least, my mom."

"And now you only have me." I finished what he was unwilling to say. I looked down at the ground, trying to put myself in his place, trying to imagine what it must be like to have to ask someone you hardly know to help with such a personal thing. "Look, Hawk, I know I'm not your first choice, but my dad used to say that sometimes you need to *just trust*, and if you tell me what Jeff usually does, I'll try my best to do it right—and I swear on his Quicksilver skateboard that I will never tell anyone." I looked around at our surroundings. "Not that they'd believe me anyway." I got up and stood in front of him and held out my hand. "What do you say ... *just trust*?"

Without a word, Hawk nodded, and we both learned that day that trust is the stuff used to build family.

Chapter Twenty-three

In the wood there burns a fire, and in the fire there melts a stone,
within the stone a ring of iron. Within the ring there lies an O,
within the O there looks an eye, in the eye there swims a sea.

—Kathleen Raine, *Spell of Creation*

By nightfall, Ambrosine still had not returned. Hawk and I had long since emptied the backpack of its V8 and granola bars. The afternoon had grown so hot, it had driven the insect life out of hiding, keeping us busy for most of it, swatting and trying to keep the hungry mosquitoes and nasty stinging flies at bay.

As the scorching sun slowly set, taking most of the bugs with it, I leaned against the tree trunk and scratched my ankles where the bloodsuckers had feasted on the white flesh above my socks.

Hawk sat tapping at his laptop. He had been at it for some time and every time I tried to ask what he was doing, he would hold up a finger and then go back to it.

Sighing, I flopped back against the tree and gazed up at the darkening sky. "I wonder where Ambrosine is. Shouldn't she be back by now?"

Hawk's response was a shake of his head as his fingers flew over the keyboard.

I went back to watching the twilight transform the royal blue of afternoon into the navy velvet of evening. The air was warm and filled with sound. Crickets gently announced the night's arrival, and off in the distance, a mournful bird called to its mate.

I closed my eyes and listened. Doves cooed in the treetops and the soft scratching sound of a rabbit or ground squirrel rustled in the underbrush. A light breeze moved through the trees making the *sssshing* sound of a librarian warning chatty visitors.

I didn't realize I was asleep until a voice said:

"*What!*"

I bolted upright—instantly wide awake. Hawk's hands were suspended above the keyboard of the laptop, his eyes focused on the bushes at the edge of the light being cast by the notebook. I could just see the outline of a person standing stock-still in the shadows.

Hopping to my feet, I said, "Ambrosine? Is that—?" Before I could finish my question, the figure strode out of the shadows.

"Who art thou, and what is this trickery?" a tall boy in his early teens demanded.

Dark wavy hair fell to the collar of a homespun shirt that was at least a size too small, judging by the way it stretched tightly across his broad shoulders and chest. He paused for a moment, taking in the notebook on Hawk's lap and apparently our appearance, and then his eyes widened when he looked at me.

I felt the air around me electrify, as with dry lightning, and I knew he felt it too. I don't know how long we might have stood there, but Hawk interrupted by closing the laptop.

"What is your name?" Hawk asked the frozen figure, standing not more than six feet in front of us.

As if suddenly realizing that Hawk was still there, the boy turned toward him, and the world returned to normal.

"What art thou?" He took a step back as if Hawk might at any moment spring at him with a snare.

"And that … that which sounds alive … yet lights the night?" His nostrils twitched, like an animal encountering a strange species—afraid, yet curious.

Hawk spoke slowly. "My name is Hawk." He lifted the computer from his lap, and I watched our visitor retreat another step. "I am in a *wheelchair*." Hawk nodded to each of the wheels. "I can't walk, so these wheels are how I travel." Hawk spoke as though talking to a very young child. "And this is my cousin, November. And your name?" he prompted.

There was a lengthy pause as the boy turned his attention back to me with a bemused look.

"Thomas Parris," he said, at last seeming to come to the conclusion that although the situation in which he found himself was strange, it wasn't dangerous. "Thou art *November* and thou art *Hawk*? A month and a winged bird; and thou sayest ye are the same as I?" Thomas shook his head slowly, like he was having trouble focusing his eyes—or maybe believing them. He pointed toward the computer on Hawk's lap. "This is no bird I have yet seen. Verily, this bird I knoweth not."

Hawk made a sound between a snort and a chuckle, bringing an even stranger look to the boy's face. He nodded to the notebook. "This is a *computer*—a machine that I use to help me write things." His amusement now under control, Hawk looked soberly back at Thomas. "And my real name is not Hawk. That is just a name my family uses. My proper name is Stephen … Stephen Atwood." He leaned forward, extending his hand. "My cousin and I have traveled from a far-off place, and you are the first person we have met in Salem Village. How do you do?"

The sheer normalcy of Hawk's tone seemed to melt Thomas' icy shell, and I watched his face go from fear and curiosity to acceptance, almost instantaneously. He stepped forward then and accepted Hawk's outstretched hand, than turned expectant eyes to me.

"My name really is November, just like the month, and … I really am a girl," I finished lamely. Those big brown eyes suddenly made my tongue feel too big for my mouth.

Thomas hesitated only momentarily before raising his chin. "I have read of the customs of many foreign lands, and it would explain your strange appearance and tongue."

I looked sharply at him before I realized he meant my *language* and wasn't referring to my malfunctioning tongue.

***

Grandma Bran always said *there's nothing new under the sun*. And I suppose she was right, because even though Hawk and I were more than three centuries in the past, talking to Thomas was no different than talking to any other teen. Except for a few *thees* and *thous*, I might have been speaking to any student at Putnam Middle School.

During the course of our conversation, Hawk told Thomas that we were from more than a *distant land*—we were from a distant time as well. That did take some explaining, but once the initial shock wore off, Thomas was like I imagined Hawk and I would be, if we had encountered someone from a distant planet, light-years beyond our development. He was curious and full of questions, especially about the technology that had brought us to that spot.

Thomas sat down on a stump in the circle of light cast by the laptop.

"So the Rings of which ye speak maketh ye to ascend to the heavens? And they are a type of tunnel through time?" He rose and stood before Hawk. "And the box with the light … doth it light thy way? Is that to help ye travel as well?"

"You mean the laptop?" Hawk tapped a few keys and motioned for Thomas to step behind him so he could watch the computer in action. When the familiar Windows tune flowed out of the speakers, Thomas' mouth fell open, and the blue white light from the LCD screen cast his head against the shadows, making it appear to float just behind Hawk's shoulder, like a charcoal drawing of circles—round head, round eyes, round *O* for a mouth.

"Mercy." He exhaled the word in reverence. "It maketh music … and such colors! Surely 'tis the product of great magic!" Thomas leaned toward the wide screen as if he couldn't get enough of the wondrous images being presented.

"Wait 'til I show you some of my games." Hawk started punching buttons. "You won't believe *Monsters and Mayhem.*"

I stepped forward, interrupting the budding male-bonding session. "You know, Thomas, we have some questions we would like to ask you."

Both boys looked up as if they had forgotten I was there. Thomas stepped away from the computer and joined me on the decomposing log at the side of the path, as Hawk shut down the laptop and stowed it in the backpack so as to save its battery. The loss of the monitor's glow plunged us into darkness, and it took a few minutes for our eyes to adjust to the pale light cast by the moon and stars. In this century, there was no competition from electrically lighted homes and towns to interfere with the glow from the heavens, and so the night sky seemed lit by the flames of trillions upon trillions of tiny candles, making a much brighter canopy than I had ever seen before.

"First off, let me start by saying that since we showed you our box with a light, it is only fair that you tell us what is in the one you dropped back there." I nodded toward the general area where Thomas had first appeared in the shadows.

He glanced back toward the deer path and then looked at me. I raised my eyebrows, and he met my gaze squarely. Then, seeming to come to a decision, he stood up and motioned for me to follow him into the shadows. A moment later, Thomas and I stood in front of a wooden box that looked a lot like the one my cousins and I had unearthed only days before. But it wasn't the one we had found under the tree roots in Mr. Whoozi-What's' yard. This box was bigger and much heavier.

"Thou art correct," he said, picking it up from the ground. "Thou hast entrusted me with thy truth and shared some of the wonders of the world to come. The least I can do is take thee into my confidence in this matter."

Together, we returned to the clearing. Thomas set it on the ground with a solid thud. I leaned forward, and Hawk wheeled in closer as Thomas lifted the lid. The box was almost a cube, measuring at least a foot in all dimensions. Because of its depth, it was hard to see what was inside, especially in the dark. I was about to suggest that Hawk boot up the laptop again when I saw him reach around and grab the backpack. Instead of opening it, he unzipped a small pouch on the side and extracted a thin black flashlight, no longer than a pencil. He switched it on, causing Thomas to laugh with surprise.

"Behold, the wonders of it!" he exclaimed. "By what name is this called? What doest thou call this torch?"

"It's a flashlight," Hawk said.

"Flash. Light." Thomas repeated the word several times as if it were a new flavor to be savored on the tongue. As Hawk aimed the beam into the box, Thomas removed a large vellum document that had been folded several times so it would fit inside. Training the light upon it, Hawk read the words aloud:

"Signed this eighth day of January in the year of our Lord, seventeen hundred, before those gathered in the interest of THE COUNCIL."

I looked at Thomas' troubled face as he lowered the paper, preventing Hawk from reading further.

"'Tis a terrible document," he said, placing it on the ground beside the box.

"What's it for?" asked Hawk.

"I knoweth not with certainty." Thomas shook his head. "I secreted myself in the cloakroom of the church on the night the Council fellowshipped with the stranger and his man." Thomas looked away then, as if reliving the experience. "The men of the Council are all goodmen. The stranger and his man were not goodmen—their clothes spake it."

"Their clothes told you they weren't good men?" I asked.

"November, I think what Thomas is saying is that the councilmen were all just working people. The term *goodman,* in the seventeenth century, was a respectful way to address common people, like our Mr. or Mrs., rather than doctor or reverend or something like that."

"'Tis truth," Thomas nodded. "My father be Reverend Samuel Parris, and my mother be Mistress Reverend Samuel Parris … but Thomas Benit and his wife be Goodman Benit and Goodwife—or "Goody"—Benit."

"So you're saying that the men on the council were just ordinary farmers or townspeople?" I asked Thomas.

"Aye," he nodded again. "Verily, I secreted in the cloakroom to know the reason why the councilmen would call to order a meeting at late night as all others of the town slept."

"And why weren't you sleeping?" asked Hawk.

Thomas looked sheepish for a minute, then said, "I wouldst watch the heavens. I doth note the constellations and the patterns of the stars. My father forbids such interests, but my mother consents to have me look at his many books with navigation charts that use the movement of the night heavens to direct coordinates on sailing ships."

"And did you discover what the meeting was about?" Hawk prompted.

"'Twas much I did not understand." Thomas shook his head as he took several more papers from the box. "'Twas the devilry of the red-haired stranger that did maketh me to dare creep behind the gathering table and remove this box after the meeting ended."

He had our rapt attention now as he lifted the last paper from the box and spread it out on the ground under the flashlight's beam.

"He did maketh each member of council draw blood with a sharp quill and then sign his name and the name of his wife and all of their children in his own blood at the bottom of the document—verily, two more times he did maketh them sign so that there were three documents the same."

Hawk and I hovered over the signatures that appeared on the thick crisp paper like old brown inkblots. Many of the names were not legible but one name stood out—*George Corwin*—in letters that were as blood red as if they had just been penned. I touched the first letter with my index finger to see if it was still wet and the entire document suddenly caught fire.

We all jumped back as flames sprang almost to the tree tops. Thomas cried out, pointing to the center of the flames, where a long, narrow face hung suspended, staring straight at me. I could feel the heat searing my face as the disembodied figure opened its mouth.

"You will fail, girl. You have not purity of soul, nor will, nor spirit, nor the strength needed to avoid—*THIS!*"

The flames seemed to fall in on themselves and then, with the suddenness of a gas explosion, they burst outward with such force that Hawk, Thomas, and I were blown off the path and far back into the underbrush.

For a moment, all was silence as I lay stunned on what felt like a thick bed of pine needles, their strong scent filling the air with spicy fragrance. I touched my face to see if I was badly burned. But I didn't feel any blisters, and there was no pain. It was dark—really dark—and I knew a moment of panic when I realized that I couldn't see anything. I scrambled to my knees, pushing away the branches over my head with my hands in order to look up at the night sky. After a heart-stopping moment when I still could not see my hand in front of my face, I spotted a slender crescent moon, low in the sky, and a few twinkling stars. Then I heard Hawk calling my name.

"Over here!" I shouted. "Are you all right?"

"Thy cousin is well. Remain as thou art—I shall come to thee," Thomas' deep voice responded.

I was still on my knees, and I spotted the flashlight in the distance flickering through the shrubbery as Hawk crunched his way down what looked like a path forged with a blowtorch. Thomas reached me first and helped me to my feet, but before I could take a step, my foot caught on a root, and I fell forward against his ample chest. “Steady there, little Doe.” Thomas’ strong muscular arms held me, and I wondered if it was more than the heat from the blast that was making my face feel so warm.

“What did you call me?”

“When I came upon thee curled up beneath the oak, I thought ye were a sleeping doe.” His voice was low and soft now. “’Tis what ye put me in mind of still.”

Doe. The shout from the darkened closet—his voice—“*Run, Doe.*”

I smiled. I could just make out his features in the moonlight. “I like it.”

Without ceremony, Hawk flashed the light on us, causing me to step back from Thomas self-consciously.

Hawk raised his eyebrows, then squinted. “Well, there’s a little redness on both of your faces,” he said as he sat back with a knowing smile, “but no apparent burns.” Then he directed the beam over the rest of me. “No, wait.” He rolled in for a closer inspection and as he moved the light over my upper body, I heard Thomas gasp.

“What is it?” I looked down at my shirt.

The front of my T-shirt was the only thing that appeared to have sustained a burn from the explosion. The pocket looked like it had been placed under a hot branding iron, and the result was the melting of the cotton fabric into what was now becoming a familiar symbol:

"November, we can't stay here," Hawk said. "Not only are you in danger, but I don't think Ambrosine is going to come back anytime soon." He consulted his watch. "It's already been more than eight hours, and we can't wait any longer. I say we count down and go back now, before something else happens. Besides, when I was consulting some of my notes on the laptop, I discovered something we missed." He looked up at the night sky, then back at me. "The Leonid constellation is in a different place in this year than it is in our time. I'm not sure what that means, but I think I might be able to figure it out if I can have some time to work on it. So let's go back—*now.*"

"Go back?" Thomas said. "But I have not yet shown thee the remaining contents of the box. I think it be important that November see everything, after what devilry hath just occurred."

Hawk looked as if he was about to argue the point, so I said, "I think Thomas is right. Whatever just happened is a sign that we're getting close—I am getting close. And even if I'm scared, and you can bet your boots that I *am that*, think about Jeff. We have to do this, Hawk, and there's not much time left." I looked around me at the shifting shadows that made up the woods. "I don't know where Ambrosine is, but I do know that we can't go back—not until we have a look around, at least."

Hawk lowered the flashlight to the scorched path and then around to the underbrush beneath the trees. "And just how do you propose I get around to 'having a look,' as you say?"

I knew the sarcasm was a tool to cover up his frustration at not having the freedom to travel around the village as he did when he was home.

"Well, thou couldst travel in our pony cart," Thomas suggested. "Or perhaps we could hide thee in the woodshed whilst November 'looks 'round.'"

The loud snort made me turn my head to see if Hawk had moved behind me and was mocking Thomas' last statement. He hadn't moved but was turned in his seat staring at what, or perhaps I should say *who,* was coming toward us.

Turning around fully, I watched a dark-robed figure approach us down the charred path. It carried a large raven on one shoulder, while leading a massive black horse, whose only marking was a silver crescent moon on its broad forehead. Hawk had turned off the flashlight but it didn't matter, because the trio gave off a glow of iridescent light as they moved.

As though mesmerized, we watched them approach until the figure in the robe tugged at the horse's lead and brought it to a stop. The raven, shifting from foot to foot, squawked "*Wither thou goest … I shall see*" three times in rapid succession.

"Be quiet, Justice!" a familiar voice said, as the figure threw back the hood.

"Ambrosine!" Hawk and I both said to the smiling face that emerged in the moonlight.

"'Tis Goody Tinsel!" Thomas exclaimed. "Me thought thou wast dead!"

"Hello, children!" Ambrosine greeted us heartily. She held the huge stamping horse in place with a tight rein, as the raven hopped around, adjusting to the new folds of the cape.

"As you can see, Thomas, I am far from dead. And Hawk, as to how you are going to travel …" Ambrosine smiled up at the straining horse and then back at my cousin, who looked as though he had just been offered a job as head bronco-buster at the rodeo—and maybe he had, at that.

"Are you suggesting I *ride* him?" he asked in a small voice.

"*Her*," Ambrosine corrected. She led the horse closer to the wheelchair, as Hawk shrank back into his seat.

"This is Candlelight, and she will take you anywhere you want to go. Put out your hand," she commanded.

Hawk swallowed once, then hesitatingly did as she said. Ambrosine dropped the lead line into it. I held my breath, expecting the massive animal to jerk Hawk right into the air. Instead, the horse leaned her tremendous head down almost to the ground and bent one knee until she was practically kneeling.

Hawk looked at Ambrosine.

"Well, what are you waiting for? Grab her mane, and let's get on with it," she said.

Hawk took a handful of the horse's flowing mane and suddenly he was sitting on her back, lead line still in his hand, blinking in surprise.

"Whoa!" he breathed.

"'Whoa' means stop," stated Ambrosine. "Say 'travel' if you want her to go, and f-l-y if you need to get somewhere in a hurry. I spell the last word because she will do just that with very little prompting, and I don't think you're ready for it yet." She turned to Thomas then. "I know that you only know me as Goody Tinsel, Thomas, but my given name is Ambrosine, and I much prefer that. And since you've already met Miss November and young Hawk here, you know that there are more things in heaven and earth than can be explained—but this is neither the time nor place to go into all of that. Besides, I also happen to know that you are much brighter than your peers *and* that you have been studying the constellations, so you should know that we are in the house of Gemini within the Leonid constellation this night. However, unlike in the century that November and Hawk come from, this constellation holds a much deeper meaning. Tonight Venus, Saturn, and the moon will form a triangle near the constellation of Gemini, just before dawn. Mercury will rise one-quarter degree away from Regulus in Leo, just before midnight. If we time it right, these two can be at the apex of Gemini in time to enter Hathorne Hill."

The import of what she was saying sunk in, and Hawk leaned forward, making Candlelight sidestep. "Do you think that's where we'll find Jeff?" he said, grabbing a handful of mane to steady himself.

"It is my best guess." Ambrosine replied, then brushed her hands together briskly. "But we have many hours before that occurs, and there is much to be done." She looked over at Thomas. "Fetch the box and go home; your family will be missing you by now." Thomas looked like he was about to protest but, as he opened his mouth, Ambrosine interjected, "Go now; tell Tituba—and only her—what you have experienced here this night. She will know what to do."

Thomas retrieved the box, then stood a moment as if reluctant to leave. Finally, with a nod to Hawk and me, he turned and started off down the path.

Reaching up to her shoulder, Ambrosine took the raven onto her hand. "Away to Hathorne House, my pet, and bring me news of its inhabitants," she instructed. Her gentle tone had the effect of a crisp command upon the bird. Justice stood straight, spreading his wings wide as Ambrosine tossed him into the air. As he dissolved into the inky blackness, a flapping sound was the only evidence he had ever been there.

Taking hold of the horse's lead line, Ambrosine pointed to the wheelchair. "We will need to move that somewhere safe, yet accessible. There is a shed behind my cottage. We will go there first." Ambrosine motioned for me to manage the wheelchair and, with a wave like a wagon-train leader, she led the way out of the shelter of the trees toward Salem Village.

Chapter Twenty-four

A one-eyed crow hops to the door; fat spiders crowd the pane,
And dark herbs scattered on the floor,
waft fragrance down the lane ...
—Laura Benet, *The Witch's House*

THE CLIP CLOP OF CANDLELIGHT'S HOOVES WAS loud against the hard-packed earth as we started down the road leading out of the woods. I glanced up at the thin moon, then at the few homes I could see sitting far back behind rough-hewn fences, each shuttered and slumbering under the starry sky. I wondered what time it was. As if in answer, my stomach growled to let me know it was well past dinnertime.

Ambrosine walked ahead, leading the big black horse, with Hawk hunched over its neck, holding tightly to the mane. He had not spoken since Ambrosine suggested putting the laptop and the wheelchair in the shed at her cottage, but I knew it was a great leap of faith on his part to leave them behind and entrust his well-being to a living, breathing animal with a mind of its own. As I looked up at him, I realized that this was probably the first time in his life that he was without some kind of technological gadget to assist him. He gave me a tremulous smile.

We had been walking for some time when Ambrosine suddenly steered the horse off the road and onto a path that wound through an open meadow of tall grass that rippled in the warm night breeze, like waves across a lake. Almost immediately, I spotted a thatched roof above white walls that seemed to catch the light from the stars and reflect it back.

Ambrosine's cottage.

A single candle burned in one window, giving the impression that the tiny house was winking at us. The structure was surrounded by a low rock wall, and as we reached the entrance to the narrow courtyard, Ambrosine brought the horse to a stop.

"The Croft." She said the name in a tone one usually reserves for a loved one. "Welcome to my home. It has been so very long since I have lived here and yet …" She turned her head away from the small house that looked very much like a giant wild mushroom growing in the moonlight. "It is as though I have never left."

It was the first time since we met her that I saw Ambrosine really smile, and it struck me that she was a very beautiful woman. Long, thick, deep red hair, the color of a maple leaf in autumn, complemented eyes that reminded me of the amethyst necklace Frank gave my mother on her birthday. Luminous skin and berry-ripe lips, now parted to show strong white teeth, as she let go of the horse and stepped to the stone wall.

"Hello, Charles!" she called out.

I wondered if she was speaking to someone in the shadows when she reached down and plucked a large black snake from the top of the wall, holding him high into the air, as if he were a small child to be fawned over.

I heard Hawk gasp and Candlelight took a step forward. Her reaction was likely the result of my leaping backward so fast that I accidentally smacked her on the rump in order to keep from falling on my own backside, as my feet got tangled up with the wheelchair.

"You need not be afraid of King Charles." Ambrosine's infectious laugh was musical. She lowered the snake and stroked his shiny black skin. "He's a lamb, really, and a fabulous mouser! Piewacket can't hold a candle to him!"

Candlelight snorted at the comment, and although my laugh came out a bit strained, Hawk's was genuine.

"Sweet!" he said, leaning dangerously forward over the horse's shoulder. "He looks like a black racer."

"I believe you are right, Hawk," Ambrosine said, as she stepped toward him, cuddling the snake that had to be at least five feet long. "Although his type is usually not fond of humans, King Charles is an exception. Here, get acquainted while we walk around to the shed." She placed the smooth-scaled reptile in Hawk's outstretched arms, picked up the horse's lead line, and started around the back of the house.

"He *is* a black racer," Hawk affirmed, tracing the patterns around King Charles' triangular head. "I've never seen one outside of a zoo before."

While my cousin exclaimed over King Charles' many attributes, Ambrosine led Candlelight into a lean-to attached to the back of the cottage. I pushed the wheelchair into an empty corner beside a haystack.

"Why is his name King Charles?" I asked, as I rejoined the group. Ambrosine motioned for Hawk to hand the snake to me. Drawing in a deep breath, I held out my arms and accepted the surprising weight of the creature that felt like one big rippling muscle as I lowered him to the ground. As befitting his royal name, King Charles raised his head high and moved slowly away, disappearing into the shadows of the make-shift barn.

"Actually, it is King Charles II," Ambrosine said, as she picked up a brush from the grain sack where she had seated Hawk and began brushing the glossy hair of Candlelight's broad back. "And as to why? Well, look up Charles II of England in the library when you get home. I think when you've done a bit of reading about him, you will be able to answer your own question." Replacing the brush, she scooped Hawk up like he was a rag doll. "Now, let us go inside and have something to eat while we wait."

The inside of The Croft was as inviting as the outside promised it would be. After depositing Hawk on a quilt-covered seat beside the rock fireplace, Ambrosine set about building a fire and boiling water in a large black kettle suspended on a hook above the flames.

I sat on a three-legged stool next to the hearth and took in the cottage. It was one large room. A narrow handmade ladder in the middle was the only means of reaching the loft that extended halfway across the cottage. The low ceiling beneath it was hung with bunches of drying herbs and wire baskets of onions and potatoes.

Beneath the window with the candle, a long wooden bench held the weight of glass containers of all shapes and sizes. These ranged from small corked jars containing what appeared to be ointments and salves to mid-sized cloth-covered ones filled with stewed tomatoes, corn relish, and jellied fruits. The gallon-sized ones contained various ground herbs and spices and several varieties of dried beans. In addition to the glass jars, there were at least a half-dozen crockery bowls, several with wooden spoons sticking out and one with a mortar and pestle. I was reminded of a picture I had once seen of an old apothecary shop.

Behind Hawk's seat on the opposite side of the room was a single rope-bed covered with a hand-stitched quilt. A tall pole that surely must have been Justice's perch, stood at the foot of it. The floor was rough oak, scrubbed to a smooth patina, with a multi-colored rag rug in the center.

Hawk and Ambrosine quietly discussed the merits of black-racer snakes and King Charles, in particular, as she set out plates with thick slices of dark brown bread and a crock of creamy butter, to go along with heavy mugs of fragrant English black tea. Between the candle on the sill and the firelight, the little cottage took on the feeling of a snug ship, adrift at sea on a black night. It gave me the sense that as long as we were within its walls, nothing could harm us. *Enchanted*—that was The Croft.

I smiled at my thoughts as I reached out to accept the saucer containing the buttered bread Ambrosine offered. As I looked over Hawk's shoulder, my breath caught in my throat, causing me to choke, and the heavy plate dropped to the floor with a clatter. There, in the shadows of the far corner, just below the rafters, two orange eyes glowed like embers.

Hawk twisted around to see, and Ambrosine followed my stare, then began to chuckle.

"Easy, child. I am afraid I have been remiss in introducing another of The Croft's inhabitants." She rose and walked to a tall dresser in the darkest corner of the room. We watched as she took something down, then made her way back to where we sat.

"This is Piewacket," she said, stepping into the circles of light provided by the now-dwindling candle and low firelight. In her arms was the largest calico cat I had ever seen. It had to weigh twenty-five pounds if it weighed an ounce. The orange eyes that had seemed demonic a moment ago now regarded Hawk and me with sleepy indifference.

"Pie, say hello to Hawk and November; there's a good girl," Ambrosine instructed the cat, as she leaned down and dropped the rotund creature onto its feet. Piewacket blinked at us and then opened her mouth, but whether or not she had the power of speech, we were not to know because at that precise moment, a knock came at the door, causing both Hawk and me to jump.

Ambrosine's laugh sounded like a musical scale being played on a harp as she strode to the door. "My, my, you two are a bundle of nerves tonight!" she sang, as she opened it. "Please come in."

Thomas stepped into the room, followed by a woman with her hair tucked into a blue gingham turban and wearing a long gray dress, covered by an equally long white apron. She appeared to be a servant.

As they stepped into the puddle of light, my eyes widened, and Hawk's expression mirrored mine. "Aunty Gin?" we both said at once.

The woman seemed confused, too, but for a different reason. Her eyes narrowed as she took in my face, causing me to get up from the stool and move back under her scrutiny.

"Ye be bewitched, girl?" She had a thick accent that sounded like the islanders I had met on vacation with my parents in the Caribbean. I had also heard the same speech cadence in New Orleans. As soon as she opened her mouth, however, I knew that as much as this woman looked and sounded like Aunty Gin, she wasn't. Before I could respond, Ambrosine interjected.

"May I introduce my young friends, Mistress November and Master Hawk. November and Hawk, I present Tituba, the Parris children's governess."

Thomas had already settled himself on the raised hearth beside Hawk and had begun stroking the cat, whose purrs of contentment resounded from the walls; Tituba and I sat down beside him.

While Ambrosine sliced more bread and filled additional tea cups, Tituba leaned toward me, her dark eyes seeming to take in every detail of my face.

"Ye resemble young Dorcas … but older." She shook her head as if in wonder and then stared at Hawk.

"And young master—he familiar, too, but ye garments be strange." She leaned back then, with a look of dawning realization. "Ye be the ones me be seeing in me night dreams," she whispered, as if to herself. "Young master in a chair with wheels and young maiden of light!" She extended her hand, palm up, and at my hesitation nodded for me to take it. As my palm met hers, the entire cottage filled with blinding light—the same light I had seen when I was lost in the raging storm inside the Rings. But now, rather than moving away, it surrounded us, filling the room with an intensity so powerful I could taste, feel, and hear it all at once. Then Tituba let go, and the light disappeared with a crack like a thunderbolt.

"Whoa, what just happened?" Hawk sat blinking as if he had just been caught by a camera flash.

Tituba sat back, a knowing smile on her lips.

"'Tis white magick," she nodded toward me, "and thou hast great power."

"Yes, she does, and she will need every bit of it tonight." Ambrosine set the tea and bread plates before her new guests. "Tonight is the eve of Hollantide in Hawk and November's time. It is also the night of the Leonid constellation and the apex of the hour when the Bargain will come full circle." Ambrosine took her seat in front the fire, rounding out our little group.

"I have asked Thomas to bring you here tonight, Tituba, because we haven't much time. You see, before November can complete the task that lies ahead of her, she and Master Hawk must first find his brother, who was struck with Elf-shot and taken by the Sprites." She leaned toward Tituba. "I know that you have some knowledge of these beings and have helped others rescue their kin. Pray, help us find Master Hawk's twin brother, Jeff. Anything you can do will be more than a kindness."

"Is it true? Can you help us find my brother?" Hawk put in, looking at Tituba.

Tituba folded her hands in her lap and leaned back. "Me not know. young master," she said slowly, "and me make no promise, but first, prithee, did the Sprites leave a Changeling in thy brother's place?"

"Yes," Hawk and I answered.

Tituba nodded once. "Then 'tis the Spell of Replacement that must be performed on this Hollantide Eve, in the midst of the warm season."

"Tell us what to do—please." Hawk looked around him. "We need to write this down, November—if only I had my laptop."

Tituba gave him an odd look, and I saw Thomas restrain a smile. Then she continued. "The spell needs must be performed on the Eve of Hollantide, during the time of the Wild Hunt, when a host of spirits rides through the night searching out to capture human souls." Tituba's face became foreboding. "*Mother Holle, Freya, Odin, Herodias, Herta* ... all ride this night and if thee hear them coming, for they make a ponderous noise, fall flat on thy face and pray they not notice thee."

Thomas' and Hawk's faces were riveted on Tituba's.

"Thou must first go to the crossroads betwixt the church and the cemetery. By the by, the Wild Hunt should swoop past. Stand quietly and respectfully, without fear, as they pass. The last hunter should give thee a coin, which will always return to thee no matter how thou hast spent it or given it away."

A soft tapping sounded. Ambrosine went to the door, and Justice the raven flew into the room, coming to rest on the perch at the foot of the small bed. Ambrosine motioned for Tituba to resume as she took the bird from its perch and walked back out into the night.

"Thou must carry parsley in thy pocket," Tituba continued. "It be sacred to Hunt leaders and be thy password to safety."

I looked at the jars of herbs and hoped there was some parsley in one of them as Tituba continued.

"When the Wild Hunt be passed, thou needs must go at once to the graves and must call on thy brother 'til the Sprites bring him forth." Tituba looked first at Hawk and then at me. "This gonna take great will and patience but must be done. The Spell of Replacement cannot be cast 'less both the Changeling and the Taken One be in the same place."

"But how will we get the Changeling there?" asked Hawk.

Tituba thought for a moment. "Me know not the way of this. Me only done Replacement once and the Changeling be present." Her high, smooth forehead wrinkled in dismay.

"Please continue," I urged. I had taken a look at my watch as she spoke—9:26.

"To perform Replacement Spell, ye must break an egg in two, empty it, and boil Rose of Jericho water or Indigo water in the two halves. When all the water be boiled away, deliver the shells to the Taken One; thee must do this in the presence of the Changeling. It is the boiling of the water 'til it be vapor that will cause Changeling to laugh." Tituba paused to sip her tea before continuing. "In order for the Spell of Replacement to work, Changeling *must* laugh."

Ambrosine came back into the cottage then, carrying the raven. "It is time," she said.

***

The night air had cooled considerably as we stood just outside the stone wall of The Croft. Tituba and Thomas stepped to one side, while Ambrosine lifted Hawk onto Candlelight's back and handed him the lead line. I carried the backpack with all the herbs, special water, and egg shells wrapped in soft cloth. With charcoal from the fireplace, Ambrosine had drawn a crude map to the crossroads and Hathorne Hill on a piece of flour sack. Justice hopped from foot to foot on her shoulder, as she stood holding the horse.

"I cannot come with you," she had informed us back at the cottage. "This is a path you both must travel alone."

Now Ambrosine patted Candlelight's nose, quietly giving instructions the horse appeared to understand.

Hawk did not seem confident. He shifted and fidgeted and squirmed, and finally, he said, "I don't think I can ride this horse."

Ambrosine stopped talking to Candlelight and looked up at him. "Of course you can," she said.

"But what if she spooks? I mean, it's not like I can get down and just walk, or stop her if she runs away with me, or bucks me off, or … whatever." He ran his hand through his hair in agitation.

"Candlelight is not going to do any of those things, Hawk." Ambrosine's voice was that of a patient riding instructor. "And I am afraid she is your only way into the Elfin realm."

Stepping around from in front of the horse, she put her hands together like a stirrup. "November, let me give you a leg up."

"Me?" I squeaked. "You mean, I'm going to ride, too?"

"'Tis the only way to get to the fairyland," Tituba said. "By the hooves of a midnight horse."

I placed my left knee in Ambrosine's laced hands, and she lifted me as if I were made of cotton onto the patient animal's back.

I adjusted myself behind Hawk as he said, "But how will we know our way back? I mean back to where we came from?" He looked down at Ambrosine. "Will the POZ work while we're riding Candlelight?"

Justice began hopping faster, back and forth, then let loose an ear-splitting squawk before announcing:

> *"How many miles to Babylon?*
> *Three score and ten.*
> *Can I get there by Candlelight?*
> *Aye, and back again.*
> *If her feet are nimble and light,*
> *You will get there by Candlelight."*

Ambrosine smiled. "Does that answer your question?"

Before Hawk could respond, Thomas stepped forward. Reaching up, he pulled from around his neck a thin piece of leather with a talisman attached to it. It was an elongated, smooth black stone, anchored by hardened clay at one end and fastened to a thin piece of metal attached to the leather. He held it out to me, and something like moth wings fluttered deep in my stomach as I leaned down so he could place it over my head and around my neck. I looked up and felt his warm breath on my face, turning the fluttering into a stampede.

"'Tis a thunderstone," he said softly. "Placed around thy neck, it ensures the wearer will return safely to the giver." He paused, then stepped back. "It may also be used to open any door or pathway."

By now, Hawk had turned around and was openly taking in the exchange between Thomas and me. But I didn't care. I touched the stone talisman, still warm from Thomas' touch.

"I *will* return," I said, and saw him nod, his lips turning up in a gentle smile.

"I shall await thee, my Doe."

Thomas looked up at Hawk then. "Travel well, friend." He held up a fist, which I was surprised to see Hawk match with his own. I wondered when Hawk had had time to teach him that twenty-first century handshake.

"Time to be off," Ambrosine said, and Thomas and Tituba stepped back. "Remember your commands," she called, as Candlelight carried us down the path toward the road. "They are all you need, and Candlelight will do the rest."

I looked back one more time, but they were gone. The Croft stood outlined against the dark sky, with its single candle as the only point of light in a black sea.

The big horse seemed to know where she was going and plodded along the roadway at an even pace. The wind had picked up, and I wanted to reach into the backpack and pull out my sweatshirt, but I didn't dare let go of Hawk, for fear of falling as the horse picked its way around the stones and ruts in the road, swaying this way and that. Hawk repeated the steps involved in the Replacement Spell as if it were a mantra. As I brushed the hair out of my eyes for the umpteenth time, I felt Hawk's back stiffen.

"What's that sound?" he said, over his shoulder.

I listened, and then I heard it too, off in the distance—the sound of heavy hooves pounding toward us. Because the wind was so strong, it was hard to tell which direction they were coming from, but it was clear they were coming this way—and fast.

Candlelight heard it, too, and picked up the pace. Hawk leaned forward over her neck, grabbing two handfuls of black mane. I followed suit, grabbing Hawk round the middle as the great horse broke first into a canter, then a gallop, and finally a flat-out run. The night seemed to come alive with sound as we hurtled down the dusty road. My hair stung my face as it flew wildly around my head.

"They're getting closer!" Hawk shouted, the wind snatching his words away.

I could barely hear him because another sound had arisen along with the gale-force winds. A long bugling, like a mournful blast from a bagpipe or the sound made by the horn of a fox hunt, repeated over and over through the darkness. "The Wild Hunt!" I shouted in Hawk's ear. "But we're not at the crossroads!" I screamed.

Another blast from the bugle echoed through the trees, over and over, as did the pounding of the hooves that I now knew were directly behind us—and gaining.

I thought back to what Tituba had said: *Fall on your face or stand without fear.*

Neither option was readily available to Hawk right now. We needed to get to the crossroads with enough time for him to get down off the horse, so that I could face the riders alone. I dared a look behind me and was sorry I did, because what pursued us down that empty road was like nothing I had ever seen before. At least a half-dozen riders in black hooded cloaks whipped their steeds until streams of white foam flew from their red mouths. It had been only a glimpse but it was enough to make me squeeze my eyes shut and bury my face in Hawk's shirt, as I tried to erase the image of the Wild Hunt riders. Skeletal white faces and fleshless arms protruding from beneath flying robes, they mercilessly beat their steeds to gain ground on their prey. We needed to go faster—we needed to *fly*.

Chapter Twenty-five

Now I'm furnished for the flight, now I go, now I fly
... my sweet spirit and I, oh, what a dainty pleasure
it is to ride the air, when the moon shines fair.

—Thomas Middleton, *A Witch's Song*

"CANDLELIGHT, FLY ... *FLY*!" I SHOUTED OVER Hawk's shoulder, and he joined me in shouting the command. I felt the mighty horse bunch her hind legs, springing into the air as if from a launch pad. It was impossible not to cry out as I felt Candlelight leave the ground. I don't know what I was expecting when I shouted the word, but it certainly wasn't what happened next. Instead of the leap of a fast horse that digs in just before launching into a mad dash, Candlelight actually lifted off the ground and rose into the air. And before either Hawk or I could make another sound, we were above the trees.

"Whooo-hooo!" Hawk shouted to the heavens, as we tore through the windy night sky. He tilted his head back in pure, ecstatic glee, causing his hair to stand straight up in the breeze. I had to laugh aloud, even though I was scared witless at how high we were and the fact that the wind was now even stronger.

But Candlelight calmly flew, defying all known laws of gravity with the same assurance she had shown when we first headed down the dirt road.

"I hope she knows where she's going!" I shouted in Hawk's ear.

"Don't worry; she does," he answered.

I wasn't so sure I shared Hawk's unquestioning faith, but I saw no point in pressing the issue. After the first few moments of panic, I began to settle down and enjoy the flight. I saw, as we soared over silhouettes of farmsteads and fields dotted with haystacks, that we were heading west. The map Ambrosine gave us had shown the crossroads as being about two miles west of The Croft.

While in flight, Candlelight tucked her front feet up under her body, but after a while, I became aware of her pulling them forward, like the landing gear of a plane, just before setting down. We began to descend, and just when I thought we were going to land in the middle of a grove of tall, willowy trees, we shot forward into a clearing, where two narrow roads intersected.

We had long since left the Wild Hunt party behind us, and as Candlelight came to a soft landing in the middle of the two roads, there was neither sign nor sound of them.

"That was truly awesome," Hawk said, leaning forward and patting Candlelight's neck. The horse nickered in response and shook her massive head as if it was really no big deal.

Then we heard the bugle echoing in the distance. Hopping down, I led the horse to the ditch at the side of the road, where she leaned down to help Hawk dismount. When he was on the ground, Hawk instructed Candlelight to go into the woods and, after a momentary hesitation, the horse did as she was told. But the sound of her retreating hooves was drowned out by the pounding of approaching ones.

"Hawk, lie down on your face and don't look up, no matter what!" I shouted.

He sat looking at me so long that I thought he hadn't heard me, but just as I was opening my mouth to repeat myself, he said, "November, you can't show fear," and I realized it must be written all over my face. I swallowed, and then I remembered what Tituba had said: *Stand quietly and respectfully, without fear, as they pass.* It was a tall order, but I nodded to show him I understood.

"Get down and stay there!" I shouted, fiercely.

Hawk grinned. "That's it! That's the look!" and he flopped forward into the mud, covering his head with his hands.

I could feel the road vibrating beneath the soles of my feet as the Wild Hunt bore down on us. The wind carried a smell like seared meat and burning flesh as the bugling repeated again and again, echoing throughout the land. "*Three echoes*," the document had said; this was the second set.

Shivering, though the night was warm, I tried to imagine that I was somewhere—*anywhere*—else, as the first of the riders came into view. Locking my knees, I stood at attention, staring straight ahead so that I only had a peripheral look at them until they were directly in front of me.

The first rider came to a stop and looked down. The stench that wafted out from beneath the flapping black robe was overpowering. I swallowed hard in order to keep the bile from rising up into my throat. Within seconds, the others had gathered, and they lined up next to each other. Then, as if in some kind of weird drill formation, they began to exchange places so that each passed in front of me at least once. I continued to stare straight ahead at a point of light. I was not sure if it was a star or a candle in a distant window, but I kept my eyes fixed on it and tried very hard not to blink. The drill went on and on as the riders took turns stopping and staring at me, and I was reminded of the time my parents and I went to London and stood before the Queen's Guards at Buckingham Palace. People tried to make eye contact with the high-helmeted men who stood at rigid attention, ignoring the tourists, who tried everything to get the guards to respond to them—they told jokes, played the fool, and even kissed them, all without success.

Now, the tallest and leanest of the unholy group rode his horse right alongside me and leaned down. His putrid breath blew in my face like the stench from a crematory furnace.

"Hold out your hand." His voice was the sound of dry leaves falling from a dead tree.

I extended my left hand and felt something drop onto my palm. Without lowering my head, I glanced down and saw a shiny black body with eight legs and a red spot on its back—a black widow spider. Of all the things in the world horrific enough to stop my heart, this was the worst.

In pictures in my science book and on class field trips to the zoo, I had always stared in morbid fascination at one of the most deadly spiders on the planet and shuddered at the thought of ever having to actually touch one.

Now, I stood looking down at the biggest specimen I had ever seen, as it slowly began making its way across my palm toward my arm. I was going to scream. I wanted to throw my hands in the air and fling the horrible creature into the bushes, into the ditch, into oblivion. I could feel the scream rising up from my toes as the spider stopped at my wrist and put its furry head down, touching the base of my thumb—and then, as I pulled in a huge breath to let loose a howl that would rouse the entire village, I heard my grandmother's voice.

"Draw on your strength, Emmy; it's there. Reach down, grab it, and hold on tight."

The scream froze in my throat, and the spider stopped moving.

"Close your hand," the dry voice ordered.

I plumbed the depths of my supposed core of strength, as I gritted my teeth and complied. I bit my bottom lip in anticipation of the painful bite, but instead, as I curled my fingers over the sleek figure eight, I felt the insect flatten and lie still.

The rider pulled his horse back, and another, smaller hooded figure maneuvered a snorting, foaming horse in front of me.

"Well, what say you for this prize?" This voice was like a rusty hinge.

I heard Tituba's voice: "*Stand respectfully.*"

Still holding my left hand closed and with eyes straight ahead, I drew myself up to my full height and raised my right hand to my temple in a military salute.

"Thank you," I managed, through clenched teeth.

I know I must have flinched, but I would like to think it was only slightly, as the hooded figure burst forth with a cackle so fetid and so loud and shrill that it caused all the leaves to fall from the trees by the side of the road. Before its echo had died, the other riders turned their steeds like a flock of starlings and galloped off into the night.

The silence that fell after they disappeared into the darkness was so complete, I thought for a minute that I had been struck deaf by the witch's shrieking laugh. Then Hawk's voice from the ditch made me realize I was still holding my breath. I let it out with a sigh that bent me in two and emptied my lungs.

"November? November, are you okay?"

Thankfully gulping a new lungful of gloriously clean, sweet-smelling air, I opened my left hand, fully prepared to find a dead spider embedded in my palm. But the black widow was gone; and in its place was a gold coin about the size of a quarter.

I turned and headed toward Hawk. "I'm fine … now. And look," I said, dropping to my shaky knees in the dirt beside the murky ditch. I held out the coin to Hawk, who sat looking up at me, his face covered with mud. He wrinkled his dirty nose as he lifted it from my hand.

"No offense, but you stink." He tapped his watch and in the few seconds of light it provided, he took a close look at the coin. I was about to remind him that he wouldn't exactly smell like a rose either, if he had been in the company of those ghouls, when he said, "This is the same kind of coin that was in the box we found under Mr. Whoozi-What's tree—Charles II. It even has the elephant with a castle on its back like the other one." He looked up. "Charles II. Charles the Second—like Ambrosine's snake. Do you think it's a coincidence?"

"I don't think anything is a coincidence anymore," I said, plopping down and crossing my legs. I trembled at the thought of the black widow. "And I'm not so sure I can take another round like that again."

Hawk sat back, just looking at me for a moment. "How bad was it? I mean, I could hear the horses, and the awful smell made me want to puke, but that scream—that was something straight out of the fiery furnace."

Candlelight came trotting out of the woods and now stood with her head down, as if telling us that it was time to go. Hawk gave back the coin, and I pushed it into the small change pocket of my jeans. Reaching down, I gave him a hand out of the muddy ditch and onto the horse. Then, as I stood trying to figure out a way to leap up on the giant animal myself, Hawk held out his hand to me, and I paused only momentarily before taking it. I was amazed at the strength in his arm as he pulled me up and onto the horse's back, and when we were both safely astride, he gave Candlelight the command to travel to Hathorne Hill.

I stole a look at my watch as we cantered down the road. There was just enough moonlight to see that it read 11:00. One hour until midnight on the eve of Hollantide, and we still did not have a clue about where Jeff was, much less this Bargain we kept hearing about.

I must have sighed, because Hawk said suddenly, "November, you better pull yourself together because the landscape is changing. Look at these hills; I'm sure we're not far from Hathorne Hill now."

And he was right. I could see the shadows of rolling hills in the distance.

I looked at the clouds scudding across the sky, causing the moon to pop in and out as if playing a game of hide-and-seek, when Hawk said, "I know where we are—this is Gallows Hill."

Candlelight halted, blowing and looking around as if she expected something to jump up out of the ground at any moment. "Are you sure?"

"I've lived in this area all my life and …" He paused a moment to swivel around, looking in all directions before turning back to me. "Yes. I'm positive. It's Gallows Hill. That tree"—he pointed to a tall oak that stood alone near the top of the rise—"that's where they hung the witches. And over there"—he pointed past the tree to where the hill sloped steeply downward into a ravine—"is where they threw the bodies and just buried them in a mass grave. Everybody who grew up around here has heard that story."

As the words left Hawk's mouth, Candlelight jerked back.

"Whoa," Hawk said, but not in response to the horse's movements.

I spun around to see what he and Candlelight were both staring at. There in the watery moonlight, silhouetted against the blue black sky, was the outline of a body swinging from a noose attached to a stout branch of the tall oak. Before either of us could react, the scene shifted and the body became two.

Candlelight whinnied in fear and began to prance, causing Hawk to lean forward and hold onto her mane in order not to fall.

"She knows something is wrong," I said, stating the obvious.

"No kidding," Hawk commented. "We can't just stand here. I think we should move on."

We had only gone a couple of yards when I felt the ground begin to shift, and Candlelight snorted loudly, pulling to the right, causing Hawk to nearly slide from his place on her back.

"Easy, girl, easy. November, I think this is the Convergence that Ambrosine told us about," Hawk said.

Suddenly, the air began to shift. The wind, which had been steadily rising, started to get colder. It was like someone had just opened the door to the deep freeze, letting loose an icy blast over the land. Within moments, we could see our breath, as frost began to spread over the ground. What few trees there were lost their leaves and stood bare and bent in the frigid night air.

Then we heard it—a great tearing noise, as though the earth was cracking open like the fragile eggs I had placed in the backpack. And with it came an enormous rushing sound like the flapping of a million winged creatures. The ground shook so hard that I was forced from the back of the horse. The earth quaked, but instead of the ground cracking and swallowing us whole, it erupted. With a giant heave, a great fissure opened up, pushing forth something huge and bruised that soared to a terrific height.

I tried to keep what little wits I still had as I struggled to keep my balance. The eruption was tremendous. The monolith that emerged generated an enormous sound, like a giant being roused from a long slumber. But this was no flesh-and-blood entity; it was made of bricks and mortar that looked like they had been soaked in centuries of blood.

With a loud groan like a gargantuan ship straining at her moorings, the monstrous structure finally came to a halt and stood, stretching high above us into the night clouds. I threw my head back, looking up at the spires, turrets, and balustrades above the tall Gothic windows. It all looked eerily familiar ... and then I realized why—we were standing in front of the administration building of the Danvers Insane Asylum.

"It's Danvers!" Hawk cried, his eyes widening. "Holy—what is *that*?" The whispered words became ice crystals as they fell from his mouth onto the horse's back.

Candlelight gave a low whinny as we watched a cloud of mist form close to the ground in front of the building. It seemed to be lit from within and suddenly, like a curtain being drawn apart on a backlit stage, the two figures emerged. One of them was carrying a smaller version of itself—a child perhaps. The taller of the two waved the mist away and then, spotting us, headed in our direction.

"November? Is that you?" called an uncertain but wonderfully familiar voice.

"Mom!" Hawk answered, as my two aunts made their way out of the icy fog to where we stood.

Aunt Marsha carried the near lifeless Changeling, with eyes like black holes in its ashen face.

"How—?" I began. Aunty Gin stepped forward and grabbed me in a fierce hug as her sister smiled up at her son.

"A security guard who works at the asylum came to the house a little while ago and told us you had gone inside," Aunt Marsha said, tilting her head toward the towering structure.

"We knew at once what that meant," Aunty Gin continued. "All the things that have been happening around Danvers—the fires, explosions—we shouldn't have missed the signs."

Aunty Gin took Candlelight's lead line out of my hand and began guiding the horse away from the building. We all walked in silence until we were far enough down the hill so as not to be in the shadow of the asylum.

Candlelight knelt, and I helped Hawk down, as Aunty Gin spread out a blanket from the backpack on which to lay the Changeling.

The night air was freezing cold but very still. The clouds had blown away, leaving stars sparkling like shards of ice. Even with our sweatshirts on, Hawk and I still shivered—whether from the cold or recent events, I wasn't quite sure.

"But how did you manage to find us?" Hawk asked.

Aunt Marsha sat next to her son, holding his hand as if she would never let it go. "One of the things we have never discussed with you and your brother is the extent of our abilities," she said softly. She looked over at Aunty Gin, who smiled and nodded as if giving her the go-ahead to explain. "Our family goes back to an ancient time—the time of the Celts and the Picts—times of powerful magic and even more powerful creatures. Throughout the millennia we have inherited, by blood, the responsibility for helping those who do not possess our abilities." Aunt Marsha paused before continuing. "Ever since we were children, my mother would urge us"—she made an inclusive gesture toward Aunty Gin and herself—"to keep our powers sharp by practice, and silent by design. That was the way she said it." Aunt Marsha leaned forward, putting her elbows on her knees.

"But what about you, Aunty Gin? You're not an Atwood by birth," Hawk said.

"I come with my own set of tricks." She smiled. "I've no idea about my birth family's past, but I do know one thing; I have always had a recurring dream in which I am living long ago in a small house on a low hill. I must be a servant, because I am in charge of three children who are not my own—a boy and two little girls." She paused as if the memory were bittersweet. "I am also very much in demand by the villagers for my potions and herbal remedies. The wife of the richest man in town came to me once for an elixir to cure his baldness!" She laughed.

"The children you cared for—do you remember their names?" I asked.

"The girls were Abigail and Betsy, and the boy's name was Thomas."

Hawk and I exchanged glances.

"Aunty Gin recognized the signs of the Convergence, in conjunction with the time of the sealing of the Bargain, and convinced me that you three were in trouble," Aunt Marsha added.

"She didn't even realize it was the eve of Hollantide," Aunty Gin chuckled, shaking her head.

As if in response to the last three words, the front doors of the asylum slammed open and a band of small, thin figures dressed in tight leggings and tunics began to file out, playing high, sweet music on flutes and piccolos. They had tiny, pointed faces and sharp bright eyes that darted furtively back and forth as they emerged from within the blackness of the forbidding asylum, as if leading a parade. Tall hats rode low on their brows, just above peaked ears. Black curl-toed shoes with large brass buckles marched toward where we all stood—all except Hawk, who had slid forward and now sat next to the Changeling on the blanket.

There were at least a dozen of them, and as they drew nearer, they divided and began to encircle us.

"Don't look at them—don't make eye contact!" Aunty Gin said, ducking her head. "They're Sprites. They will mesmerize you, and steal away your willpower."

"Just like the document said." Hawk quoted: "*Such are the subtle wiles of them that they steal and draw away the minds of anyone they seize.*"

They were all around us now, and we sat with our heads bowed like devout parishioners at an unholy picnic. The music was subtle and drawing, each note sounded a plea to rise and join in the merrymaking.

It made me drowsy, and I began daydreaming about bright sunny fields of clover and bees carrying sweet nectar to their hives, buzzing softly around my head, urging me to come and taste their fine honey. One touched my lower lip, leaving a dab of it for me to sample. It was the most divine thing I'd ever tasted, and I wanted more—had to have more. I rose to follow the swarm when something grabbed my leg. The buzzing grew faint then, and I knew the bees were leaving. I had to go with them—had to have more honey—couldn't resist. But no matter how I kicked and tried to free my leg, it was held fast. Then someone shoved something dry and tart into my mouth.

"Chew!" urged Aunt Marsha. "Chew it up girl—*now!* I'll not lose another child."

The taste was awful, like munching on old hay. I shook my head, and the fog that had held me spellbound began to clear. "Yuck! What was that?" I asked, as I swallowed the last of the dry flakes. I would have given anything at that moment for a Coke. I looked up then and saw the Sprites marching away, back into the shadows of the building.

"Parsley," Aunty Gin said. "It has properties that counteract any bewitchment potion."

"I was bewitched?" I looked around me.

"Oh, yeah," said Hawk. "You were kicking and trying to get loose to follow the Sprites, but Aunty Gin tackled you and held you down." He chuckled at the picture we must have made, tussling around on the blanket. "I told Aunty Gin about that dried parsley in your pocket, so she held onto you while Mom got it and shoved it into your mouth."

I looked at Aunt Marsha and Aunty Gin. "Thanks … I guess," I said, spitting out a stem.

Hawk looked at his mother. "I still don't understand. How did you get here? I mean, we're hundreds of years in the past, and we had to go through tunnels and rings, and we have this thing called a POZ, and—"

"Hollantide," Aunt Marsha said, as if the word itself were explanation enough. "On the eve of Hollantide, like the eve of All Hallow's, the veil between worlds thins, allowing those of the spirit world to enter."

"Yes, and now we need to get on with the business of finding Jeff before it is too late," Aunty Gin said, rising. "November, fetch the horse." She took the backpack and began putting the stuff back into it. "We can't perform the spell here. I can see that now."

I set off to fetch Candlelight, who was busy munching grass just a short distance away. After Hawk climbed on, Candlelight allowed Aunt Marsha to put the Changeling in front of him. Hawk looked none too pleased at having to steady the pasty figure, which hung over the horse's neck like a drape. Though clearly wasting away, the pale creature still possessed enough strength to hold onto the horse's mane.

"So where are we going?" Hawk asked Aunty Gin as she began leading the horse from the roadway. "We need to go into Hathorne Hill," he added.

"And you will," Aunty Gin replied. "But first, we need to find your brother, and for that, we must go behind the building and into the woods."

"You've got to be kidding me," I said. "After what just walked off back there? I don't think so."

"Maybe she's right, Ginny," Aunt Marsha said. "I mean, doesn't it make more sense to do as Hawk says and keep to the road?"

Aunty Gin's mouth set. "We need to go to the woods," she repeated, taking a firmer hold on the lead line.

"How do you know?" Hawk insisted.

"Because of that," she said, pointing to the peak of the monolith.

We watched as the giant hawk, Avnova, spread her massive wings and swooped down smoothly toward the darkened tree line.

Chapter Twenty-six

Come, witches, come, on your hithering brooms!
The moorland is dark and still.

Over church and the churchyard tombs
to the Oak wood under the hill.

Come through the mist and wandering
cloud, Fly with the crescent moon.

Come where the witches and warlocks crowd, Come soon … soon!

—Clive Sansom, *The Witches' Call*

I NOTICED MY AUNTS PULLING THEIR COATS closer around them as we stepped into the cold night wind, leaving the building behind. In front of us, a large overgrown field stretched into the distance, the once-lush grass now frostbitten and shriveled. In the milky moonlight I could see that we were on top of a hill that stretched for many acres before sloping down on the other side.

Candlelight headed straight for the middle at a brisk walk, causing Hawk and the Changeling to grasp her mane and hang on, as the rest of us broke into a jog in order to keep up. We had not gone far when the toe of my sneaker struck something hard that threw me forward. I just managed to put out my hands in time to catch my fall. As I got to my knees, I saw what had tripped me.

Embedded in the earth was a round stone about the size of a small dinner plate. The number 125 was carved into its face. Candlelight and her passengers, along with my aunts, had gone on, unaware that I had fallen behind. I got to my feet, took a few steps, and saw another marker, and then another—each with a different number. Not all were round; some were square, others, short cylinders rising just above the grass, and one was shaped like a crude Celtic cross. I knew I had to catch up to the group as they made their way across the field toward the woods but, in the gloom, I was afraid I would trip over more of the strange stones that were placed in rows, like grave markers. I cupped my hands to call out to the others, then let them drop to my sides instead. With sudden clarity, I knew that *that* was exactly what these were—grave markers.

"November!" The soft voice had the effect of a shout, making me spin around and cry out in alarm. I had seen this woman once before, who now stood near me with her long white gown flowing around her in the twilight. She had been holding a baby doll, then, too.

"Annie?" I said.

"It's me." She smiled. "And Deidre's here, too." She held up the tattered doll. "Have you come back to visit us?" Annie's face had the look of one whose hopes were so often dashed that she dared not believe.

Then it hit me—125. Annie's last words to me were, "*Please remember me; Annie from Nova Scotia, number 125.*" I looked down at the stone marker next to where Annie stood.

"Is that where you are buried?" I asked as gently as I knew how to ask such a thing.

She nodded, still smiling. "You did remember. You came back to visit us."

I didn't know what to say, so I phrased my response in the form of a question; "Are all these numbers the graves of patients who have died?"

Annie nodded as she looked around her.

"But why are there no names on them? I mean, surely the families would insist …"

Annie shook her head, her smile bittersweet. "Most of us had no families—at least, not any that would claim us." She began to walk among the rows and rows of markers that literally blanketed the field. If they had all been tall white crosses, it would have resembled Arlington.

Despite knowing I needed to catch up with the others, who had now disappeared down the other side of the hill, I continued to walk along beside Annie like we were old friends, taking a stroll through the park in the moonlight.

The grave markers were all unique—no two alike. Although some were similar in size or color, each had a different look, as if its recipient had, even beyond death, tried to put his own special touch to the anonymity of the assigned number. So many—it was overwhelming.

"But how did the hospital keep track of who was buried where?" I cried, after we'd walked through several rows.

"Well, I'm sure they tried to keep track at first," Annie said, as she drifted over the stones, reaching down to gently touch this one and that, "but after awhile, it just didn't seem to matter anymore." She looked back at me with sorrowful eyes. "I'm afraid that to the rest of the world, we died when we entered Danvers Asylum, and since we were nothing but a number after that, it only made sense to the administrators that that would be the only thing we would need to remind the world we had ever been in it."

Maybe I had not lived long enough to understand the rationale behind that kind of thinking, and I hoped I never would. "How many graves are there? Do you know?" I turned, but Annie was gone.

The wind had risen to a brisk gale, and I pulled the hood of the sweatshirt up to block it. I needed to find the others—and quick. Surely they had noticed I was not with them by now. I started running, but as I reached the slope, I heard a sound that stopped me in my tracks: voices, in unison, starting low and then rising on the wind.

The music swirled around me as if I were standing in the middle of a tabernacle, listening to an elaborate funeral hymn. I felt every hair on my body stand on end as the lament swelled, its cadence rising and falling. The hood blocked my peripheral vision, and it took an extra shot of willpower to turn around.

I had heard the phrase "face the music" before, but this lent it a whole new meaning. I swallowed hard as I took in the sight now before me. Like Annie, who had been standing beside marker 125, someone now stood next to each of the grave markers. The spectral figures were all sizes and ages, some wearing the formal clothing they were buried in, others dressed in pajamas and hospital gowns. With open mouths, they sang as one, the most mournful melody I had ever heard. They stood, hundreds of them, as far as I could see, ethereal and wavering in the moonlight, each one looking with dark, hollow eyes, their arms outstretched, as if beseeching me to hear their pleas. As the chorus grew in volume, the song became a slow chant:

Save us! Please save us! We've waited so long,
We're tired, so tired,
What have we done wrong?

I know I should have been scared out of my mind at this point, but the sad, imploring words had the opposite effect. Why had these souls not moved on? What was keeping them here?

The Bargain!

The two words echoed in my ears as if they had been spoken aloud, and I knew with the same certainty I had had upon finding the grave markers that these souls were bound up in it somehow.

"I'll try!" I shouted, as loud and with as much confidence as I could muster. "I'll *really* try to help you." And I would. But if this was an example of what was at stake with the Bargain, then the stakes were higher than I ever imagined—and how was I supposed to keep the promise I had just made?

"November, we've found the entrance to the Elfin realm!" Hawk's shout made me turn around in time to see him come over the crest of the hill. He rode alone and with astonishing skill, considering the horse was at a full run. They drew to a skidding stop just short of where I stood. The singing had ceased as soon as Hawk had cried out, like someone flipping a switch. I glanced back. The field lay silent and empty, the night wind bending the tall grass covering the graves.

"What happened to you?" Hawk called, as I walked toward him. "We reached the bottom of the hill and you weren't there, and then we heard you shout, so I came back to see what was keeping you. Oh, and you'll never guess what we've found down there. It's really too cool!" Hawk's eagerness to share his news saved me from having to explain what had just occurred, providing I could have.

"Entrance to the Elfin realm?" I repeated. "You mean we might be close to Jeff?"

Hawk nodded his head, a goofy grin splitting his face. "Aunty Gin thinks so. We just have to figure out how to get inside. Come on; let's go!"

Giving me a hand up onto Candlelight, he spun the horse around like a rodeo cowboy, and we took off down the hill at a gallop. My aunts stood at the bottom, Aunt Marsha holding the Changeling, who clung to her like an oversized infant. Aunty Gin's eyes were shining with excitement.

"I believe we've found a way into the hill." She pointed to some small boulders piled against the side of the rise. "Just through there is an opening, and not too far inside is a wooden door. The problem is that it appears to be locked."

She led us to a crevice between two boulders, much like the entrance to a cave. It was just wide enough for Candlelight to pass through and, just as Aunty Gin had said, the path led to a door. Round and made from thick planks of wood, it had darkened with age and dampness until now it was almost black. A heavy latch stood in place of a doorknob, with a large keyhole beneath it. Two matching wrought-iron hinges held the door fast on the opposite side.

Aunty Gin gave the handle several attempts and then jiggled it in frustration. "See? It won't open."

"Why don't you try knocking?" Aunt Marsha suggested.

Both of my aunts and I tried pounding on the door, and even Candlelight hit it with her hoof several times, resulting in two deep indentations in the wood. Hawk sat astride the horse, holding the flashlight, while we looked around for signs of a hiding place for a key.

"Well, there must be some way for us to open it," Aunty Gin said, running her hands through her windblown hair until it stuck up like a rooster's comb.

We stood in silence, at a loss for what to do next, when all at once I noticed a small shadow flit from behind the boulder. It was in the peripheral of the flashlight beam. No one else seemed to notice so, as the other three discussed possible ways around the sturdy latch, I stepped to Candlelight's side. It could be Sprites again, in which case I needed to be careful of my approach. I made my way slowly past the horse and stood still, just inside the opening. And there it was again—but this time, I caught sight of a tiny red sleeve. Like a cat lying in wait for just the right moment, I pounced as the tiny figure emerged a third time from a crack between the boulders, catching onto his sleeve.

He squealed like a mouse caught by its tail as he wriggled and twisted, trying to break free. Grabbing him tighter under the armpits, I lifted the squirming little fellow and carried him to my two aunts, who stood with their mouths open in mid-conversation. Hawk trained the flashlight on me and my hostage.

"Let me go!" The pint-sized figure's face was red with fury.

"It's a gnome," said Hawk, "like Dynnis!"

The little gnome suddenly stopped struggling and looked up at the boy sitting atop the gigantic horse.

"How doest thou know my name?" he demanded, pulling free from my grasp and spinning to look at me in surprise as I repeated his name.

"I've not laid eyes on thee before," he said, backing up as if about to make a dash for it.

"Wait," I said, standing perfectly still and raising my hand to my aunts and cousin to follow suit. "No, you haven't met us … yet." I watched Dynnis' eyes narrow at the last word. "But you will, a long time from now. And you and I will become very close friends. My name is November." I lowered my hand and extended it toward the child-gnome that was Dynnis. I dropped down into a half-squat in order to be at eye level with him and, as I did so, I saw a spark of recognition flash in his eyes.

"November." He said the name as if it were a memory from a distant dream, and his eyes grew far away for a moment, as if visualizing that distant time and place. "Doth ring true," he said at last, stepping toward me. "Thou hast a pure soul. I see it in thine eyes. I believe we will be friends." His smile reached his twinkling eyes, causing his tiny face to split into a delightful dimple in each cheek.

"How old are you, Dynnis?" I asked.

"I shall be eight years of age on the vernal equinox," he answered proudly and then looked around him at the others. "Why art thou in this accursed place? This is the door to the Land of the Elves. There are great consequences for disturbing those who live within."

"My brother is in there," Hawk answered. "We believe he was taken by the elves."

Dynnis took another step forward in order to get a better look at the gray child lying limply in Aunt Marsha's arms. "'Tis a Changeling, is it not?"

She nodded, "Yes, this is the Changeling left in place of my son." She leaned toward Dynnis. "Do you know how to open that door? Do you know anyway to get to the Land of the Elves?"

Dynnis shook his head slowly. "Without the golden key, it is impossible to open any door to the realm. The only other thing that can open an Elfin door is a thunderstone, and they are very rare indeed."

I touched the talisman Thomas had given me.

"Of course!" Hawk shouted, causing Dynnis to jump. "The thunderstone! Thomas said it could be used to open any door."

I pulled the oblong stone suspended from the leather necklace from my neck and handed it to Aunty Gin, who turned to Dynnis.

"Do you know how this works?" she asked him.

Dynnis looked at the stone and then at the door. "I believe thou needs must hold the thunderstone against the keyhole, and it will become the instrument needed to unlock the door," he answered.

Aunty Gin followed Dynnis' suggestion, and we watched as the black stone, pressed against the keyhole, transformed itself into a golden skeleton key. After glancing back at us in triumph, Aunty Gin turned the key, and the door swung open, revealing an entryway that looked like an invitation to a tropical resort.

Exotic birds warbled and sang out as we passed through. Dynnis stopped at the threshold as the others passed.

"Aren't you coming?" I asked, as he held back.

"No. 'Tis not advisable for gnomes to venture into the company of elves, and especially not on the eve of Hollantide." He looked over his shoulder as if suddenly aware of the lateness of the hour. "I must be on to home now," he said, "or I will surely catch it from my mother." He started back toward the opening in the rocks and then turned one last time, concern showing on his tiny face. "Take care, November of the future. 'Tis a treacherous path thee and thy friends undertake to travel this night."

"I will, Dynnis. Good-bye, and thank you—'til we meet again." I raised my hand in farewell, and Dynnis did the same.

"'Til we meet again," he said, and then, quick as a thought, he was gone.

Chapter Twenty-seven

Hey-ho for Hallowe'en! and the witches to be seen. Some black, and some green, Hay-ho for Hallowe'en! Hay-ho for Hallowe'en!

—Anonymous

I HURRIED TO CATCH UP WITH THE others, not wanting to run the risk of losing sight of them again. As I walked behind Candlelight, I gazed in wonder at the fantastic landscape. It was as though we were walking through a rainforest. Tall trees laced together overhead, creating a canopy of green that allowed light to filter through, but from what source, it wasn't clear. Birds of all shapes, sizes, and colors swooped and flitted between enormous leaves and vines that hung weighted down by huge flowers in a variety of vibrant colors and hues.

Impossibly large insects resembling dragonflies and colorful mayflies fluttered among the tall verdant ferns growing beside the smooth dirt path. The entire forest was alive with sound and color. Hawk laughed as a vivid pink butterfly the size of a seagull landed on his shoulder and, just as quickly, took off again. Candlelight swished her tail at the swarms of white moths that darted here and there along the path as we traveled.

I broke into a trot and skipped in front of Hawk and the horse to join my aunts. The Changeling rode in front of Hawk again and seemed unaffected by its surroundings. It became apparent very soon after entering the door that we were descending. The path wound down, round and round, as if its builder had used a corkscrew for a blueprint. If it had not been for the forest on either side of us, I'm sure it would have made us all dizzy.

At last, we rounded a bend and came to another door with a semi-transparent panel of glass in the center and bold blue letters announcing that we were about to enter "The Halle."

Without bothering to knock, Aunty Gin grasped the crystal knob, pushing the door open. She stuck her head around it before venturing any farther. But she needn't have worried about being quiet, because the noise that burst forth from open door was enough to send her reeling backward. My aunt had barely enough time to regain her footing when the door was yanked out of her hands and flung wide."Oh, who do we see upon our stoop this Hollantide Eve? Enter, enter, fine guests and join in the merriment—*so do!*" A round woman, dressed in a long blue silk gown overlaid by an intricately woven silver necklace, stood just inside the doorway holding a pewter goblet in one hand and the doorknob with the other. She couldn't have been more than four feet tall and yet her bearing made her seem much larger. She assessed us with smoky eyes set in a smooth, round face, her blood red lips stretched wide to reveal snowy white teeth. Tilting her head back, she appraised Aunty Gin, who was the first to enter.

"Ah, thou art not in festive attire! Wherefore? Wherefore?" The woman did not pause to let my aunt get a word in before letting go of the door and extending a half-curtsy, while using the goblet as a directional signal.

"'Tis no matter. All are welcome on Hollantide. Come in, come in, and join the festivities—*Halle! And Halle!*

Like a band of gypsies, we filed into a cavernous hall that was alive with celebration. The ceiling soared at least two stories above our heads, and the room, the length of a football field, was crowded with gaily dressed people of all shapes and sizes. It was clear we had arrived in the middle of the Elfin festival of Hollantide.

There were pipers, twirlers, and jesters who juggled knives and colorful sticks. Serving wenches, carrying large pitchers of a strong-smelling dark liquid, skipped among the groups of revelers making sure no goblet was empty. Large carcasses of roasting meat turned on spits over open fires, near endless tables laden with fruit, vegetables, pastries, and assorted finger foods. Most of the partiers were dressed in evening attire, and nearly all had elaborate masks, either on their faces or held on sticks. They paused as we followed our hostess, and those with uncovered faces quickly held up their masks as we passed by. We were almost halfway across the room when the lady in blue stopped and turned.

"Oh, I am so remiss. Please forgive me." She bowed her head as if in shame and then grinned at us like a naughty child. "I have not introduced myself. I am Donella!" she shouted, as the pipers surrounded us, forming a circle by dancing side-by-side.

Aunty Gin began to speak, but Donella held up her hand.

"We know thee, Virginia Atwood. We have known of thee these many years."

My aunt's chin lifted. "Is that so?" she answered. "Then you should also know why we are here."

Donella's smile turned feral, and she inclined her head, causing the frizzy black curls piled high upon it to fall forward, like a horse's forelock. "Indeed, please follow me." Donella spun around, pushing roughly through the manic pipers, who fell back as the rest of our procession passed.

The festival continued uninterrupted as we made our way across the room, but I sensed an underlying tension—a false merriment belying a menace that threatened, at any moment, to erupt into bedlam—or worse.

I had just sidestepped a merrymaker, who leaped at my face, the smooth sharp beak of his black feathered mask coming dangerously close to my left eye, when I realized we were being led into a dark, low-ceilinged room that smelled of sweat and pipe tobacco. In fact, the ceiling was so low, it caused Candlelight to stand with her head lowered.

Four faces turned toward us as we filed in. Two men and a woman, in the same turquoise blue as Donella, sat at a long wooden table laden with the remains of a feast. Upon closer inspection, I saw a human skull placed dead center inside a ring of tall white candles, next to a rolled-up manuscript.

The man, seated in a high-backed ebony chair at the head of the table, spoke first.

"And thou wouldst be the Atwood clan, then?" His voice was surprisingly high-pitched, considering he was the size of a professional wrestler. Like Donella, his chest supported a massive necklace of linked sterling, hung with dozens of silvery dime-sized coins that twinkled in the candlelight.

"We welcome thee to our table. I am Alfrid, Hermetical Magistrate." He spread his arms to include the man and the other woman. "Chief Consul Noll and his sister, Livia." Noll and Livia inclined their heads in turn at Alfrid's introduction.

"I'll get right to the point," Aunt Marsha said, stepping next to Aunty Gin.

"Please, please do sit down." Alfrid indicated the five empty chairs at the end of the table nearest where we stood. "Prithee, partake of this fine feast."

"I'm afraid we haven't time for that." Aunt Marsha's tone left no room for argument.

Inclining his head ever so slightly, Alfrid deferred.

"We're here for my son, Jeffery Atwood. Are you holding him?" she asked bluntly.

"Holding?" Alfrid smiled, cocking an eyebrow as he repeated my aunt's word and looking at the others seated around him. "I fear thou hast been misinformed, milady—we *hold* no one." The others chuckled as if their leader had just made a very clever joke.

Aunt Marsha inhaled deeply, then pointed to the Changeling sitting astride Candlelight's back. "Do you expect me to believe that this … *this thing* is my son?" She drew herself up, causing her voice to deepen and bounce off the walls of the stuffy room.

"We expect nothing of thee, my dear woman." Noll smirked and the other three joined his lazy laughter.

Aunt Marsha had balled her hands into fists as if preparing to tear the place apart, when Aunty Gin grabbed her arm and pointed across the room.

A figure rose from a chair set in shadows beside the glowing fireplace and walked into the pool of light cast by the ring of candles.

"Jeff!" Hawk called to the boy who was dressed in the same style and color as the other occupants of the room, but who now stood rubbing his eyes, as if having just awakened from a long sleep.

The boy in blue, wearing a crown of silver leaves upon his dark blond head, squinted up at the horse and its rider with nothing more than casual curiosity.

"And just how doest thou know my name?" he asked.

Chapter Twenty-eight

The wind got up with the morning, the fog blew off with the rain. When the Witch of the North saw the Egg-shell, and the little Blue Devil again. Did you swim? She said. Did you sink? She said, and the little Blue Devil replied; 'For myself I swam, but I think, he said, there's somebody sinking outside.

—Rudyard Kipling, *The Egg-shell*

"Why don't we all sit down, after all?" Aunty Gin said, interrupting the exchange between Hawk and Jeff. She threw her sister the same look I'd seen that day in Mr. Whoozi-What's' yard—the one that said "*Go along with me on this.*"

With the exception of Hawk and the Changeling, everyone seated themselves at the table, even Jeff, who chose the chair next to Donella.

"Splendid, splendid!" boomed Alfrid; then he turned to Livia: "Please fetch the pipers, and our guests shall enjoy a merry feast indeed."

The bared teeth Alfrid flashed at the rest of us suggested carnivorous anticipation more than merriment, but as Livia hurried out of the room to carry out the magistrate's request, she accidentally hit Candlelight's back end with the door, causing the big horse to jump, throwing the Changeling forward over its shoulder. The limp figure flopped in the middle of the table, tipping goblets, flipping plates, and causing a large bowl filled with pomegranates to spill its contents which, in turn, rolled to all ends of the table like billiard balls.

Donella caught the tumbling skull before it hit her lap, as Noll made a grab for the candles.

Like a discarded scarecrow, the Changeling laid sprawled, its arms and legs thrown in all directions. I thought for a minute that it was dead until it brought everyone to a standstill by emitting one of the most dreadful sounds I had ever heard. Something between a moan and a death rattle, the bone-chilling reverberation seemed to emanate from the very core of the pale, withered creature. No zombie movie, no matter how scary and gruesome, had ever come close to the jarring effect that ghastly noise had on every nerve in my body.

I watched in horror as the Changeling moved first his arms, then his legs, into a semblance of some kind of order. With each move the groans got louder and more horrific, as he forced his bones back into their sockets. It was like watching someone set their own broken joints.

The horrific spell of the spectacle was broken by the slamming open of the door as a band of merry elves filed in, blowing loudly on wooden flutes and brightly painted pipes. Others strummed intricately stringed lyres, as they danced and spun around the table.

They were followed by a half-dozen or so jugglers in green jester hats, who leaped and hopped as they tossed large colorful batons above their heads. It was pandemonium in a small room, and I realized as I looked around that Aunty Gin was nowhere in sight.

Then I spotted her across the room, hunched over the hearth. She appeared to be cooking something. Hawk was having a tough time keeping Candlelight from spooking as the jugglers exchanged their batons through the air over and around her head. Aunt Marsha and Donella struggled to help the Changeling into a sitting position, despite his dreadful noises, and Alfrid and Noll were shouting at Livia to have the festive elves leave the room at once.

Making my way to the fireplace, I crouched down beside Aunty Gin.

"November, get me the backpack," she ordered.

Hawk's navy backpack lay on a pile of logs.

"Better yet, reach into it, and get me the vial of Indigo water," she instructed as I lifted the bag toward her.

"You're doing the Replacement Spell now?" I asked, in amazement.

"I haven't much choice. In order to break the bewitchment spell binding Jeff, we need to make the Changeling laugh—and quickly."

She took the small glass container and placed it gently on the brick hearth. Next, she broke an egg in two, emptied its contents into the fire, then quickly filled it with the liquid from the vial. Placing each half-shell carefully upon a flat cast-iron pan on a long pole, she held them over the fire. Glancing over at me she said, "Make sure Marsha has the Changeling, as well as Jeff, facing this way."

Without a word, I rose and started back toward the table. By now, Alfrid and Noll had managed to get most of the entertainment out of the room, with the exception of a few jugglers, who seemed to delight in terrorizing Candlelight and ticking off Hawk who, at the moment, was threatening to let the agitated horse run them over. I skipped around Candlelight's shifting hooves and managed to get back across the room without mishap, despite strewn dinnerware, rolling food, and the danger of being struck by a stray baton.

Livia and Donella were busy pushing the rest of the jugglers out the door as I reached the table. The Changeling sat, hunched like a misshapen lump of clay, staring straight ahead at the flames, now high and bright in the fireplace. Jeff, still sitting in the same chair, stared unblinkingly into the fire, as if completely unaware of the upheaval surrounding him.

As the door closed behind the last of the merrymakers, I heard Donella announce, "'Tis almost Hollantide. We must prepare!"

Then three things happened all at once. A loud pop like a firecracker exploded in the fireplace, blowing a small cloud of ashes into the room. Behind it, large bubbles flowed out and over the hearth, as if it had suddenly become a fountain full of detergent. And the Changeling started laughing.

Great gulping belly laughs spilled over the gray lips of the miserable creature as he sat in the middle of the mess atop the banquet table. I don't know which was worse—his terrible moans and groans or this hellish laughter. I put my hands over my ears to block the sound of it and felt a hand on my arm.

"November, we gotta get outta here!" Jeff said, looking around at the room as if seeing it for the first time.

Aunty Gin appeared at his side. Calling her sister's name, she threw the backpack to Aunt Marsha who caught it in midair.

"Follow me!" Jeff shouted as he ran toward the fireplace.

Alfrid and the others, who had been staring in awe at the Changeling, now realized our intentions and went into action.

I wondered why Jeff was leading us toward the side of the room away from the door, and the idea crossed my mind that he was still *one of them,* when he picked up speed and ran full tilt into the brick wall next to the fireplace opening. With hands placed palms out in front of his chest, he pushed on what I soon realized was a door in the floor-to-ceiling brickwork. I had my doubts about Candlelight's ability to fit through the narrow opening, but she pushed past me like a streak of light, disappearing into its depths, with Hawk hanging on for dear life, as my aunts and I brought up the rear.

Aunt Marsha was the last one through the opening but not before Noll grabbed onto her long coat. I heard her gasp as she was pulled backward into the room. Before I could react, however, Aunty Gin, who was directly behind me, spun around and threw the remaining contents of the Indigo water directly into the elf's face.

Noll howled in pain as he threw his hands to his eyes, releasing his hold on Aunt Marsha. Without a word, she slammed the door on the screaming Elfin Consul, and the three of us took off up the steep path. We weren't too far behind the others, and it would not have mattered anyway, because we could hear Candlelight's hooves as the heavy animal made her way, as fast as her shod feet could carry her, up the hard-packed slope.

Luckily, we only needed to ascend a short distance before we came to a door that resembled the one we had entered from the cave. It, too, was round and darkened with age and at first, I thought we had come full circle, until I noticed the latch. Instead of the hole requiring a skeleton key, this one called for the type used with a modern-day deadbolt.

Jeff gave three quick raps and then stood back. Two raps came in answer. Jeff knocked three more times and then kicked the door once before retreating, like the first time. After a moment, the door slowly swung inward, and a thin, stooped elf, wearing a crumpled tall hat and a badly stained leather vest, stepped through. Black tights beneath tattered leather leggings and moth-eaten suede slippers completed his outfit.

"An' jus' where're ye be goin' on this Hollantide Eve, young master?" The elf addressed his question to Jeff while taking in the rest of us. "An' who be thy companions?"

"I'll be needin' to get these mortals to the village afore midnight." Jeff fell into the rhythm of the Elfin speech so easily, I had to blink to make sure he had not become bewitched again, but I saw him throw a wink at Aunty Gin as the elf stood back to appraise the situation.

"Mortals, hm-m-m?" He stood for a moment stroking the wispy hairs on his chin as his face split into a toothless grin.

"Well, ye be knowin' a price must be paid in order to allow mortals to be leavin' the Elfin Mound." He may have been old and bent, but the elf's sharp beady eyes were alive with something timeless. Greed.

"Well ..." Jeff looked back at us, and I saw my aunts exchange a worried look. "Look," Jeff began, "we don't exactly have any—"

"Will this do?" I stepped toward the grubby little figure. The elf put out his hand, and I dropped the gold coin I had received from the witches of the Wild Hunt into his leathery palm.

A look of pure joy filled his wizened face, to be replaced almost immediately by suspicion. Peering closely at the coin, he put it to his mouth and bit down hard with his side teeth, while at the same time, lifting up on the other edge. Then the old elf held it up in order to behold its splendor. The strength of his jaw had put a crease down the side of the gold guinea, running right through Charles II's nose.

"'Tis twenty-four karat, a rare and fine guinea indeed," he cackled as he turned back to us. "Thou doest satisfy the toll—ye may go." Closing his fist tightly around his ransom, the elf waved his other hand in a gesture of dismissal and, before he could stow the precious guinea in one of the many pockets in his filthy vest, we were out the door and into the night.

We hastily made our way toward the open field. Hawk brought Candlelight to a stop at the top of the rise, and we all stood for a moment, looking at the scene before us.

The crescent moon, hanging low over the rooftop of the brooding old asylum, looked as if someone had plucked it from the night sky and placed it on the slate tiles, wedging it between the tall chimneys for safekeeping.

"Look at the sky," said Jeff.

"The Leonid constellation has moved." Hawk leaned backward to take in the glowing configuration of stars hovering just above our heads. "*When the Moon of Storms is risen to lead you out of your bed,*" he quoted, "*lying 'neath the Hill of Hathorne...*" He consulted his watch. "Eleven forty-five—only fifteen minutes until—"

"Hollantide," a familiar voice said, as two figures made their way up the slope and into view. One had a large bird on its shoulder—the other was pushing Hawk's wheelchair.

"Ambrosine!" Hawk cried, at the same time I said Thomas' name.

After the introductions, Ambrosine said, "I'm glad to see you were successful in your rescue efforts." The warm smile with which she favored Jeff faded as she looked at Aunty Gin and Aunt Marsha. "But I fear you two must get back inside the asylum—and quickly." She nodded toward the towering building in the distance. "The Leonid constellation is at its zenith, and the Convergent Shift is starting to thin."

We all looked where she pointed and watched as the asylum began to waver in the moonlight like a mirage.

"You must go now!" Ambrosine waved her arms like she was shooing chickens. "Go! *Run*, or you will spend the rest of your lives here!"

My aunts should have lifted their coats and run like the wind toward the building that was dissolving before our eyes. Instead, they both took the time to grab us in a hug, murmuring chants of protection in our ears before taking off toward the asylum.

"Mom, run faster!" Hawk shouted.

"*Go! Go!*" Jeff hopped up and down, and I held my hand over my mouth as we watched the two sisters run for all their worth toward the watery walls of the disappearing asylum. And suddenly it was gone—and my aunts were not.

Aunt Marsha's startled "*Oh!*" carried to where we stood, frozen in horror.

"Oh, my," Ambrosine sighed, as the two women turned and started back. Hawk urged Candlelight forward, and we all followed, meeting Aunt Marsha and Aunty Gin halfway.

Justice the raven circled Ambrosine's head as she trotted toward my aunts and touched down on her left shoulder as she came to a halt. Running a hand through her hair, as if the gesture might solve the problem of what to do next, Ambrosine muttered to herself. "Let me think. There *must* be a way. It seems to me that I remember helping my grandmother set a spell in place that—"

"What about our POZ cards?" Hawk interrupted, causing Ambrosine to stop pacing.

"What are POZ cards?" asked Jeff.

Ambrosine either didn't hear the question or chose to ignore it, as she stopped pacing and looked up at Hawk. "You understand the consequences of that." Her voice was flat.

My aunts did not hear her last statement because Aunty Gin was saying something to Aunt Marsha, as the latter shook her head in disagreement.

"Adorabelle told us never to let the Point of Zero cards out of our hands," I whispered. I saw Hawk stiffen.

"I remember the warning, November," he said. "And I'll understand if you don't want to give up your card. But that leaves me with the problem of who to give mine to—my mother or Aunty Gin?"

It was clear that nothing was going to change his mind. I thought about Adorabelle and how she had been so intense about never letting the POZ cards leave our possession, and now the full impact of why she was so insistent hit home. Without our Point of Zero cards, we had no way home—we would be the ones to spend the rest of our lives here.

As if I had voiced my thoughts aloud, Hawk said, "Jeff doesn't have one." His eyes clearly conveyed his meaning: *we're young; we'll adjust.*

My eyes went to Jeff's confused face. Hawk was right. I nodded in agreement. My aunts stopped talking and looked over at us.

"You had best decide quickly," Ambrosine said out of the side of her mouth, as the two women started toward us.

"Okay," I said, shrugging. "I mean, we can't very well send only one of them home."

"Will somebody *please* tell me what you all are talking about?" Jeff insisted.

Ambrosine held up her finger to forestall his questions. As Aunty Gin and Aunt Marsha joined us, she said, "Listen closely; I've no time to repeat this. There is one other way for you to go back, and *this time, do not delay*!" The aunts each started to protest during the explanation of the process of the Point of Zero, but Ambrosine's voice was tight with urgency. "The children will be fine—the cards are not essential to this mission, but they are *your* last hope!"

Even before she finished, though her instructions were concise, the air had thickened and the ground began to quake in the same manner as when the asylum had risen up.

"Count down!" Ambrosine shouted the order above the din made by the cracking earth. "*Now!*"

I heard Jeff say, "What the—?" as the Point of Zeros appeared in front of my aunts and, even though Ambrosine urged them again to insert their cards, both of the dear ladies looked back one last time, as if to burn our faces into their memories.

"We love you—*go!*" we shouted.

They disappeared into thin air just as the ground split under the eruption of another building that zoomed up as if it had been launched from the bowels of Hades.

The wind generated by the rise of this monstrosity was like a concussive blast from a volcano. Hot, heavy, and stinking of rotten eggs, I watched it lift Thomas up from the ground, tossing him through the air. The raven shot off into the night as Ambrosine stumbled, arms flying in all directions, as she tried to keep her balance. I saw Candlelight rear up on two legs, just before I was thrown off my feet and down, hard, onto my back in the damp grass. Jeff, standing next to me, was knocked down as well but was instantly up and running.

"Hawk!" he cried, racing to the still form that lay not more than ten feet away.

I was on one knee when I felt a hand beneath my elbow.

"Are ye well?"

I nodded as Thomas helped me to my feet. "I think so." The arm he had around my shoulder made me feel warm and safe, and I wanted very badly at that moment to lean back and feel him put both of them around me for a good long time.

Ambrosine called to us then. She had captured Candlelight and now held the wild-eyed horse's lead rope to keep her from darting into the dark, as Thomas and I ran to where Jeff knelt beside his brother.

"I'm okay," Hawk said, as I dropped into the dirt next to them. "Just a bit winded is all." With his brother's help, he managed to get himself to his elbows and then to a sitting position.

"Guess I need riding lessons," he grinned, rubbing his elbow and wincing slightly.

"Rodeo lessons might be more like it." I was so relieved that he wasn't badly hurt that I began to giggle, which in turn caused first Hawk, then Jeff, and finally Thomas to join in.

"Get a load of that house!" Jeff said, and we all craned our necks to take in the building that now stood in place of the Danvers Asylum. "And wasn't that some kind of stinking wind!" He wrinkled his nose. "Okay, so who let one go?" We all looked at each other, and then burst out laughing all over again.

Ambrosine approached, leading the horse, the expression on her face telling us the party was over.

"Hawk, you need to get into your wheelchair," she said, motioning for Jeff to fetch it.

"I'm not hurt—I can still ride," Hawk said, but Ambrosine shook her head.

"It's not that. I need to take Candlelight back to The Croft. It is nearly the turning of the hour."

Jeff pushed the chair to where we stood and with Thomas' help, they lifted Hawk back into its seat. I picked up the backpack and stowed it on the handlebars. The act was so routine, so mundane and familiar that, for a moment, I thought everything might turn out okay—then Ambrosine spoke.

"I have been here before." She indicated the skeletal house rising two stories above us.

"'Tis the home of Judge Hathorne." Thomas spoke the name as if it were a curse.

Ambrosine's eyebrows drew together. "This is where the Bargain was struck all those centuries ago, and here is where it will come full circle, unless"—she turned to me—"unless you can prevent it."

I felt my stomach tighten.

"You need to be strong, November." Reaching out with her free hand, Ambrosine clasped my shoulder. "You must break the Bargain, child."

"But I don't know how." As I said the words, I saw a momentary spark in the endless depths of her eyes. "Do *you*?" I was suddenly sure she did.

"It is not my place to instruct The Prediction," she answered.

The Prediction—my grandmother had called me that.

"And I don't know everything that will happen here this night. Most of it is dependant on your actions," Ambrosine continued, "but I do know the legend says that in order to break the Bargain, The Predicted One must weigh the purity of her soul against one feather from the wing of Avnova. If the soul of The Prediction should prove heavier by even so much as a sigh, the Bargain will stand."

I wanted to ask more—needed to know more—but the stillness of the night was abruptly broken by the sound of heavy horses being ridden at breakneck speed toward us.

"I must get Candlelight to safety." Ambrosine gripped the lead rope, turning the horse away from the building.

"Why? What's happening?" Jeff cried.

"The Dredmares are coming," she answered. "They belong to the Badb Sisters"—she pronounced the word as *Bave*—"a trinity of witches, in this case three hags: Morrigna, Nemain, and Morrigan. They are the harbingers of True Death—the death of the soul. It is Badb's Cauldron that will decide the fate of that soul or, as in this case, many souls. If the Bargain is not broken, the cauldron will boil, and those souls that are hanging in the balance will be lost to the Dark Lord—Astaroth." Ambrosine's voice dropped as she pronounced the name.

"You have, of course, heard of the people who were put to death in Salem Village for the sin of witchcraft." It was a statement, not a question, yet Jeff, Hawk, and I nodded. Thomas' face registered disgust. The events Ambrosine spoke of had occurred during his lifetime, and he was acquainted with all those involved.

"Those were innocent souls—nineteen blameless people put to death by horrible means because of the greed and ambition of a few." Ambrosine raised her head, indicating the village. "Those farmers and their wives and children were not witches. But there *were* black-magick witches in Salem Village when the Bargain was struck. Oh, yes, there were witches—dark, evil, baneful things, who presided over the signing of the unholy document. And they are coming back now to help usher in the hour of reckoning." She paused as if wanting to say more and fearing that if she did, she wouldn't have time to get the horse safely away.

"Wait!" I said, as she turned to go. "What do you mean, the Dark Lord, Astaroth? Is that who is responsible for the Bargain? Is he the one I must face—and *defeat?*"

Ambrosine's grave face gave way to a huge sigh, her shoulders sagging, as if she were being forced into revealing things she had been warned against.

"Yes, and no," she said. "Yes, you are going to face him—and soon—but you will not have to defeat him. In fact, that is essentially impossible, since Astaroth is evil itself. I do not want to frighten you, child. That is why you have not been told the facts of the Bargain before now. You are The Predicted One; your only duty lies in the purity of your soul and your willingness to share it. Nothing more needs rest on your young shoulders. 'Tis a large enough burden as it is."

Hoofbeats sounded just beyond the rise as Ambrosine pulled herself onto Candlelight's back.

"Dredmares are toxic," she said. "Their poison can infect a normal horse, causing it to become one of them. I cannot risk having Candlelight exposed to their corruption.

She looked over at Thomas. "Are you coming?" she asked.

Thomas looked at me. "Do ye wish me to go?"

I couldn't seem to get my tongue to work, so I just shook my head.

"Then I shall remain," Thomas said to Ambrosine, and I saw Jeff and Hawk exchange looks.

With a knowing nod, Ambrosine found her balance and turned the horse toward the road. Looking back over her shoulder, she called out, "Be strong, Children of Avnova—*blessed be!*" Then she urged Candlelight into a canter and disappeared into the darkness, as three riders came over the crest of the hill.

***

They rode horses as white as alabaster, giant beasts with eyes of night and ebony fire burning from within finely boned faces. From their flared nostrils, snow and ice blew, catching in manes that seemed to be made of dark wind and falling stars as they thundered toward us. But it was the riders that made me draw in my breath. Three dark-cloaked figures sat astride each charging steed, urging them to greater speed by beating them with long crops. Hunched over, their heads, covered by deep hoods, they looked like the crows they were named for, as they bounced in their saddles over the rough terrain. The Badb Sisters were a spectral sight in the moonlight, but it was their shrieks that forced the hair to stand up on the back of my neck.

"November, this is crazy; let's get the heck out of here!" Jeff yelled, grabbing the handles of Hawk's chair. But before I could answer, Hawk spoke up.

"No. Tituba said we needed the power of three—three Children of Avnova, and as long as we're together, we can and *will* beat this Bargain." He looked at me; "You can't do this alone, you know—and you won't have to."

The smile I'd intended to make me look brave betrayed me with the tremble of my lower lip. And seeing as how I couldn't trust my voice not to do the same, I just nodded. Jeff stepped from behind the chair, then, to stand beside his brother, and Thomas took my hand. Together, the four of us now presented a united front to the three specters bearing down upon us.

Chapter Twenty-nine

The storm will arise, and trouble the skies; this night,
and more for the wonder. The ghost from the tomb
affrighted shall come; called out by the clap of thunder.

—Robert Herrick, *The Hag*

SURPRISINGLY, AS IF WE WERE INVISIBLE, THE riders tore past us. They pulled their mounts to a dead stop not two feet from the steps of the building. Shards of sharp ice flew up from the hooves as they skidded and dug into the frozen dirt. The phantom horses stood blowing and stamping impatiently, as their riders quickly dismounted and began removing things from oversized saddlebags. Without a word, the four of us moved closer to the trio of ghouls, who looked like they were about to embark on a gruesome picnic as they set to work, placing their wares on the scrubby winter grass in front of Hathorne House.

The tallest and thinnest of the three figures carried a long wooden staff topped by a dark blue stone that glowed, as if lit from within. While the others continued to empty the saddlebags, the tall one pointed the stone toward the ground and began walking in an arc, causing the stone's glow to intensify with each step. After a few moments, the gaunt figure came to a stop.

Lifting the staff upright and throwing her hood back, she looked around her in satisfaction at the circle that now glowed eerily white in the moonlight, as another of the group entered the ring and placed a small table in the center. The tall woman made her way back to the horses as the third figure entered the circle, approached the table, and threw an iridescent green cloth over it. Next, she placed a silver bowl, a black candle in a silver candlestick, and a small silver bell with a wooden handle. Striking a long match against the heel of her shoe, the hag leaned across the table and lit the candle. The sudden flare of the wick as it caught the flame highlighted her leathery face and toothless mouth as she cackled in glee.

While working, each one threw off her hood, allowing long flowing hair to shimmer like liquid obsidian over stooped shoulders and down sloped backs. Short bursts of excited chatter and quiet cackles were the only exchange between the unearthly creatures as they toiled, and even though we had moved near enough to have been noticed, still the sisters didn't seem aware of us.

"Garnets and bloodstones," the smallest one said, as she opened a silky-black drawstring bag. The stones looked like drops of blood in the candlelight as they clattered into the bowl.

"The Tower Tarot card, three apples, and the Book," chirped the round one, placing each item in a row next to the candle.

"It will take all of us to bring the cauldron," the tall one said, joining her sisters, and without another word, they marched to the side of the house and returned, struggling under the weight of a black pot big enough to boil a pig. This they placed just outside the circle. The smallest witch ran back once more into the shadows of the building. She emerged with a scythe at least twice her size and, with the aid of the other two, managed to hammer it into the frozen earth like a flagpole.

Dusting off her hands, as if to signal all was in place, the smallest sister looked off in the distance, as if scanning the dark horizon for signs of impending visitors.

I chose that moment to look closer at the cauldron and noticed there was some kind of insignia inscribed on the side of it. I squinted to make out what it was, when Hawk whispered, "It's a scald crow. Ambrosine said it was the crest of the Badb Sisters."

"Kindling," the tall one ordered, and the other two hopped to, scurrying about, placing twigs and small branches beneath the cauldron. As the last piece was thrown on the pile, the deep resonant peal of a very large bell sounded off in the distance. Its solemn repetition, carried on the stiff breeze, seemed to rise rather than diminish as it traveled. On the twelfth toll, the inside of Hathorne House lit up like someone had suddenly ignited a thousand candles in each of the rooms. We watched as the ornate oak door flew open as if blown by a strong draft. Six men, dressed in long, tightly fitted black coats and matching trousers, exited the building single file and made their way down the steps. Without a word, they marched to where the hags stood like sentinels beside the circle. Stepping inside the glowing ring, each man chose a spot at the table so that in the end, they stood facing each other, three on each side. Two of them wore long white wigs that curled down and around their shoulders. The younger and less portly of the two reached down and plucked up the book, opened it, and, holding it in one hand, began to chant.

> *"Peace mounts to the heavens,*
> *The heavens descend to earth,*
> *Earth lies under the heavens,*
> *Everyone is strong; victory to the strong!"*

His bold tenor voice rang out in the frigid night, as if picking up where the sonorous bell had left off. The other men made various assenting noises and the tallest, whose dark suit hung so loosely on his frame that it made him look like a stick figure, grasped the silver bell on the table and rang it three times.

"Here, here, Reverend Mather!" His voice was high-pitched and strangled, like a rooster trying to clear its throat. "Gentlemen, we are gathered here for one final meeting—the one of greatest import." He stepped around the table, his long, horsy teeth gleaming in the moonlight. "This is the night that we have awaited for more than three hundred years, the night when we will seal the pact that was made on this very spot." He looked around at his brethren. "I trust all has gone as you hoped during that time?"

"Well, let us put it in this way, Samuel; it has been a long time since we have worn these blasted wigs and worried about the correct usage of thee and thou," the heavyset man in the longest wig barked, causing the others to burst into loud laughter. "And I think we can all agree that, thus far, the terms of the deal have proven to be much more than even we could have imagined those many years ago."

The knowing laughter and calls of "Hear! Hear!" from the others around the table caused the man addressed as Samuel to raise his hand for quiet. When everyone had settled, he continued.

"So am I correct in assuming that all are in agreement as to the necessity of completing the terms of the contract?" His eyes glowed as he looked at each gentleman individually as, to a man, they all nodded their agreement.

I don't know if it was a reflection from the candlelight or something else that burned in the speaker's eyes as he swiveled his head to look around the table, but for a moment, as his head swung around toward where I stood, a panorama of people suffering was reflected from his eyes. It wasn't until I felt Thomas' hand on my arm that I realized I must have uttered a sound, as well as taken a few steps toward the gathering in the circle. I turned my head as Thomas leaned in and whispered in my ear.

"'Tis my father—the Reverend Samuel Parris." He gestured toward the man who now turned back toward his companions, taking the stark images with him.

Samuel Parris turned his attention to the table. "Then let us begin."

Lifting the bowl with the gems, he selected one and held it up to the others, like a magician might before making it disappear into thin air. Then, Samuel Parris motioned to the hags. The stout one came forward holding a large chalice made of bone, intricately etched with figures and symbols. It produced a solid *thunk* as Samuel Parris dropped the stone into it. Next, he selected one of the many drawstring bags, all of different colors, which the sisters had laid out during their preparations.

"George, will you be so good as to read the rest of the recipe?" Parris addressed the youngest member of the group, a burly, red-faced man who, although dressed in the style of the current period, sported a head of golden curls that suggested a twenty-first century stylist.

George picked up the heavy book the man in the wig had used as a hymnal, thumbed through it briefly until he found the correct page, then read aloud: "Antimony—three drops."

Samuel Parris took an eye dropper, dipped it into the silver bag, drew the fluid, and put three drops into the bone chalice.

George continued: "Six grams of mercury."

Again, Parris chose a drawstring bag and added the measurement to the chalice. Next came sulphur and Seed of Gold, followed by Adamic earth and salt. Each time, the preacher would extract a sample from a different bag, adding it by degrees to the concoction in the chalice.

At last, the large man looked up from the book, his self-satisfied round face grinning like a gargoyle. "The last ingredient is the House of Spirit."

"That should make it go down smoothly!" The oily voice of the man with the pock-marked face seemed to be the catalyst that set the others off in a flurry of conversation.

"Silence, please!" Reverend Parris raised his hand after pouring a liberal amount of liquid into the chalice from a dark green long-necked bottle provided by the smallest hag. "We now have before us"—he held the elaborate chalice up with both hands as if it were a hard-won trophy—"the correct combination of elements to produce what men throughout the ages have tried to capture. Gentlemen, I give you the *Universal Essence*."

Hawk drew in his breath. "The third stone," he said, his voice almost a whisper. "They've managed to create the *Stone of the Wise*."

"The elixir of eternal life!" crowed the Reverend Samuel Parris, as he held the chalice toward the night sky.

The hags began to shriek and clap their hands; "'Tis time! 'Tis time!" they chanted. "His Majesty is nigh! All hail the Powerful, the Strong! All hail Lord Astaroth!

The witches hopped up and down as if a parade were about to begin, and the men at the table shook hands all around, clapping each other soundly on the back.

Then the ground began to shake, but this time it was much different than when the buildings had risen. Rather than splitting open, the ground pulled and twisted as if tearing itself in two, causing a deep ravine. The four of us had to jump back as the gap in the ground widened, cutting us off from the circle and the men who now stood looking past us, toward where the hags pointed as they hopped about with glee. Suddenly, the rumbling stopped, leaving a chasm deep and wide enough to swallow a bus.

As the four of us turned to see what drew their attention, an enormous dark shape flew out of the night sky with a triumphant cry. We watched as Avnova soared over our heads. Down from the gathering clouds she came, landing lightly on the scythe next to the Badb Sisters' cauldron. The great hawk flapped her wings once and then settled on the thin blade like a spectator awaiting the opening ceremonies of a sporting event. Thunderous hooves and carriage wheels announced the arrival of still more company.

I do not know what caused me to look down into the ravine at that moment, but what I saw at the bottom of that ditch nearly caused me to lose my footing and plunge headfirst into it.

There in the moonlight, like a mound of forgotten ivory, lay the jumbled bones of a mass grave. Skulls lay grinning up at the night sky, their empty eye sockets a testament to hopelessness. Though horrified by the gruesome sight, I could not tear my eyes away. As if spellbound, I began to count the bodies. I paused at number eight when I realized one of its hands was missing—and the other was moving.

In morbid fascination, I watched it rise until it hung suspended, its forefinger pointing directly at me.

"Watch out!" Thomas pulled on my arm.

If he had not grabbed me at that moment, throwing me to the ground, I am sure the trembling earth would have given way under our feet, and we both would have toppled over the edge and joined the bones waiting at the bottom. Thomas' tackle forced the air out of my lungs with a loud *whoosh* that left me gasping as I struggled to regain my breath. Besides being tall, he was muscular and solid and probably outweighed me by at least fifty pounds. Even though I fought to get up, he still held me down, and I quickly realized why, as two enormous carriage wheels rolled by, inches from where we lay.

The smell of fire, as if someone had just lit a charcoal grill, immediately filled my lungs, causing me to hack and cough. When the carriage passed, Thomas helped me to my feet. Hawk and Jeff stood off in the distance, out of harm's way, as the ornate horsedrawn carriage rolled past at a brisk clip. Instead of slowing as it approached the gaping crevice, the horses picked up speed. But they were no ordinary carriage horses. These equine giants had one difference: their feet threw off flames, leaving trails of fire in their wake.

Thomas and I rejoined Hawk and Jeff, watching in amazement as the demonic horses pulled the tall black carriage with its two cloaked passengers across the deep ravine, leaving a bridge of burning coals behind it.

When it reached the ring where the six men stood, the carriage came to a stop and the two occupants stepped down, leaving the hags to lead the horses around to the back of Hathorne House.

Samuel Parris and the taller of the two wigged men stepped forward to greet the new arrivals, one small and the other a giant of a man who towered above the others. When they threw back the hoods of their cloaks, it was as if someone had suddenly flipped a switch and turned the air from cold to subzero.

Avnova let out a single cry from her perch on the scythe, as if to warn us to beware, but it was unnecessary. The marks that I had gotten on both my arms while lost in the Rings began to burn as if they had never healed, but this time it was different. This time, I could see who was responsible. This time, I was meeting him face to face across a chasm that might have been miles wide or mere inches—it didn't much matter because now, I knew my enemy.

Jeff and Hawk said, "Mr. Roth?" at the same time Thomas spoke another name. Even though he physically resembled our math teacher and probably the person Thomas had spoken of as well, the figure that stood before us now was no mere mortal. As he raised his head from within his hood and met my eyes, his reflected an endless appetite for all things loathsome and vile. Like windows to an endless pit, they burned with an insatiable desire to destroy.

His partner stood beside him, the wind blowing his red hair up so that it made him look like his head was on fire. He stepped forward to the edge of the ditch, just in front of the bridge of hot coals. "Hello, Children of Avnova!" he called, as if we were standing across the distance of many miles instead of mere yards. "Let me introduce—"

"I know who he is," I said, surprising myself by cutting him off. "We have met before."

A slow, cold smile spread across the face of the darkly handsome man I knew as Astaroth, and he inclined his head in mock acknowledgement.

"Gentlemen, we must be getting on with the ceremony." Samuel Parris stepped forward like the old fussbudget he obviously was, but the man with the flaming hair brushed him aside like an afterthought. With narrowed eyes, he lifted his pointed chin and glared at me. "I was about to introduce *myself* before you cut me off," he said in his whiny, sharp voice. "I am Mr. Barbatos, personal assistant to His Royal Highness, Lord Astaroth." The little man straightened his spine and puffed out his chest like an offended sparrow. I half expected him to flap his wings and preen.

Astaroth's smile widened, revealing sharp, feral teeth behind the blade-thin lips, as he turned to Samuel Parris who, by this time, had spotted Thomas standing in the shadows. Clearly dismayed by the fact that his son was about to observe what was surely a secret ceremony, the reverend ordered Thomas to go home at once. When Thomas refused, his father turned to Astaroth, as if seeking guidance with this most difficult aspect of being a parent—a defiant child.

"Let the boy stay," Astaroth said, without taking his eyes from me. "We will conclude the proceedings in short order." The big man turned, then made his way into the circle, where he stopped at the table.

"Where is the scale?" he demanded. All three hags jumped as if shot by an electrical charge and scurried off into the darkness. Almost immediately, they returned carrying a large brass scale. It consisted of a single post with an arm that balanced on a narrow ring at the top. Two brass plates hung suspended by three chains on either side of the arm. The hags placed it in the middle of the table, and Mr. Barbatos took his position behind it, like a caller at a bingo game.

As he opened his mouth to speak, a shrill birdcall pierced the frigid night and was answered by Avnova. Justice the raven flew out of the darkness, gliding gently to a stop on top of the scale.

"All is ready!" shouted the hags, in unison. "Let the trial begin!"

Like a bored adult at a children's party, Astaroth stood to one side, arms folded. The expression on his face plainly said, *This is a waste of time—these children are of no consequence. Just sign the document and be done with it.*

The man Samuel Parris had addressed as Cotton Mather emerged from the house with a long, narrow wooden box. Laying it on one end of the table, he opened it and took out a rolled-up document, which he spread out on the tablecloth, then placed one of the drawstring bags on each corner to keep it from rolling back up. The other men gathered around like greedy blackbirds, eager to partake of a feast.

Mr. Barbatos brought the meeting to order by rapping on the table with a small gavel. "Hear ye, hear ye," he intoned. "Let it be known that the Bargain hath been struck this night of November 11, 1701, between these men"—Mr. Barbatos plucked up the silver bell and rang it once after saying each man's name—" the Honorable Judge Jonathan Corwin; the Honorable Judge John Hathorne; Sheriff of Salem Village, George Corwin; the Very Reverend Samuel Parris; the Esteemed Reverend Cotton Mather; and his father, the Very Reverend Increase Mather."

As his name was called, each man took his place at the table. The tallest hag set an inkpot with a quill pen next to the vellum document, the ends of which flapped and tossed under the weight of the drawstring bags, threatening to fly away at any moment in the stiff, cold breeze.

"There is, however, one codicil that needs to be addressed in order to finalize this covenant." Barbatos stared across the crevice to where the four of us stood, side by side. "The One known as The Prediction must be present and willing to test the weight of her soul against one feather from the wing of the hawk known as Avnova." Barbatos' lips twisted into a nasty grimace—a mockery of a smile. "But if The Prediction fails to appear at the foretold time"—he threw a pointed look at the gap separating me from the proceedings—"or if The Prediction fails the test of souls, then the Bargain will be signed and sealed by all named within."

Murmurs of excitement rippled through the group of men as they shifted with anticipation.

"Furthermore," Barbatos continued, holding up his hand for silence, "with the signing of the Bargain, each man will be given a sip of the Stone of the Wise, thus ensuring each one's immortality, in addition to those positions of power currently enjoyed by all"—Barbatos smiled knowingly toward the men, lined up like mercenary children at a nightmarish birthday party—"in exchange for the souls of those who, over the centuries, have fallen victim to those present for whatever reason. But if the scales should balance"—the men focused their full attention upon the little red-haired man—"the Bargain will be broken and all gains forfeited, as stated clearly in the document before you. In addition, your souls will be forfeit as well and, after being judged by the boiling of the Badb Sisters' cauldron, will become the property of His Majesty, Lord Astaroth."

As Barbatos recited the last part of the Bargain, all six men in black turned toward where I now stood, next to the bridge of hot coals. Summoning my courage, I walked to the edge of the ravine—Hawk, Jeff, and Thomas joining me—as the details of the Bargain were read. Looking at each man, I watched the history of their long, miserable lives play out as if their eyes were movie projectors, flashing the past three hundred years like a twisted tribute to their vile deeds.

From some, I saw slaves, shackled to poles, being sold and forced to live like livestock; huge ships filled with human cargo as obscene amounts of money changed hands at their expense. I saw families torn apart as children were sold and traded for other commodities. Another's eyes revealed scenes of sweatshops packed with women and children, who would perish because the company owner refused to provide for the likelihood of fire. I saw the rise of millionaires from the labors of stooped Chinese workers as they built a railroad system that laced the country from end to end. In yet another, I glimpsed the hollow eyes of immigrants, forced to live in squalid tenements while the sweat of their backs allowed employers to build mansions and summer homes they whimsically called "cottages." On and on, each face, each pair of eyes, reflected the centuries of power and corruption each man had lived and now thirsted for, as if it were the very water of life.

Like someone who steps out of darkness into a brightly lit room, it became clear to me that if this Bargain, this dreadful pact entered into by six power-hungry men on a cold November night in tiny Salem Village, was sealed, the abuses of power over the past three centuries would not only continue but worsen. I thought about Annie and the others buried on this godforsaken hill and the ones who lay at my feet, discarded and forgotten; the strong profiting at the expense of the weak.

I turned to Thomas. "I don't know how I am supposed to do this—weigh my soul, that is—but first I have to find a way across the ravine." I looked at the bridge of coals glowing in the night like an iridescent orange ribbon.

Barbatos' smarmy voice rang out over the divide. "Is there anyone here tonight who wishes to be recognized?"

I stepped forward. "I do!"

"Who speaks out in answer?" he called, as if I were invisible.

"I do!" I shouted. "You know, *me*—The Prediction?"

Astaroth raised his eyebrows at my arrogance.

"November, be careful," Hawk said, wheeling himself up next to me. "Remember, your soul can't be off by as much as a sigh. I'm not so sure anger is a good thing right now."

I ignored him and shouted out again, "I would love to come to your little soul-weighing party over there, but I have a bit of a problem."

"And just what might that be?" Barbatos taunted.

"Well, I can't seem to figure out a way to get across that … burning bridge!" I was barely containing my temper and my language.

"Oh, dear, and the hour is so late!" Barbatos' false sympathy made me grit my teeth. "If you decide that it is too much trouble to come to the weighing of the souls, then the Bargain shall stand by default." Barbatos' laughter was joined by the men at the table, but Astaroth looked thoughtful.

I bit my lip in frustration.

"Well? Have you made a decision? Time is running out," Cotton Mather jeered.

"November, ask him if someone else can carry your soul to the scales," Hawk said.

"What do you mean?" I turned toward him.

"I can make it across the bridge," he said, staring at the smoking coals with determination. "At least, I'm pretty sure this wheelchair can."

"It can, Em," Jeff piped up. "Aunty Gin had both the Dune Buggy and this spare specially outfitted with silicone tires that can withstand extreme heat and cold. But," Jeff continued, "what's Hawk supposed to carry? I mean, how do you just take off your soul and weigh it?"

"You know, don't you, November." Hawk's narrowed eyes scrutinized my face. "You know what it is you need to weigh." When I didn't say anything, he went on. "Remember when we were in the woods, and I had to go to the bathroom? Remember what you said?" He didn't wait for my answer. "Aunty Gin always says, *heed the rule of three—what ye put forth comes back to thee.* So I'm going to give you back your words." He held out his hand. "*Just trust?*"

I looked at the boy sitting in his wheelchair, and for the first time, actually *saw* him. Hawk wasn't a fragile figure to be protected—or worse yet, pitied. I had always thought the wheelchair meant weakness or dependency—a kind of slow death. With the clarity of a sunbeam breaking through the clouds, I realized that I didn't need to rescue Hawk from some unknown fate—I needed him to rescue me.

***

Pushing the hair back from my forehead I plucked the snowy white feather that had been growing there since I had gotten lost in the Rings. I placed it in Hawk's outstretched hand, then turned back to Barbatos.

"You don't need me!" I shouted. "It is my soul that must be weighed, and it's on its way right now."

I held my breath as Hawk steered the wheelchair onto the tracks of the burning coals. Thomas, Jeff, and I joined hands as we watched the slender form of Hawk—the bravest of us all—make his way slowly across the chasm of death.

Chapter Thirty

Double, double, toil and trouble; Fire burn, and cauldron bubble.

Fillet of a fenny snake, in the cauldron boil and bake …

—William Shakespeare, *The Witches' Spell*

"This is highly irregular!" shouted Barbatos. "Wait! Wait until the members of the committee convene!"

But Hawk either didn't hear him or was blatantly disregarding his orders. With grim determination, he continued to push the wheels of his chair slowly over the burning embers toward the other side.

Astaroth shifted uncomfortably as his assistant turned to the others, who busily examined the document for any mention of this type of irregularity. Justice the raven hopped first on one foot, then the other, like an excited fan at a playoff.

After a few minutes, Cotton Mather looked up, shaking his head at Barbatos. "There are no provisions for anything other than the soul," he stated. "The contract says only that *the soul* of The Prediction must be weighed against the feather from Avnova." He looked toward the bird, who calmly returned his stare.

Without a sound, the giant hawk lifted her wings and flapped them three times in rapid succession, causing a single feather to drift down and onto one of the plates of the scale, tipping it a fraction.

"Half is done—half is here!" squawked Justice, as Hawk wheeled over to the table and handed the white feather to the black bird. Taking it in his beak, Justice hopped on top of the scale, and I felt Jeff and Thomas squeeze my hands as he laid the feather, ever so gently, on the empty plate. The scale now tipped back and forth, each plate dipping and then rising for what seemed an eternity, before finally coming to a stop with both plates evenly aligned.

Justice cried out, "The scales are balanced! The soul is pure!"

I let out the breath I didn't realize I had been holding—and then chaos broke out. As if the front gates had been thrown open on the prison they had inhabited for so long, the souls of the bodies in the ravine and in those graves without names on the hill rose from the ground with a jubilance that swelled until it filled the dark skies. Like a long-silenced choir, the voices sang out with a mixture of relief and wonder.

"*Radikal!*" Jeff said, as we stood, hands clasped, necks craned, watching the incredible spectacle before us. The souls first appeared as long wisps of smoke, then flew up, turning into pale gray doves as they threw off their earthly constraints. With the eagerness of the long-confined, they entered the sparkling white clouds that filled the night with white light. Their song was one of freedom and release, and one from the ravine flew past close enough for me to hear: "Thank you, my child."

As the doves made their way noisily toward the light, Jeff pointed to what was happening across the ravine. The hags had gone into action at the same moment the souls had taken flight, and now they stoked the fire under the cauldron, rushing from the building to the boiling pot like demented caterers. Barbatos herded the men in black into the middle of the circle to stand before the bubbling cauldron, and Astaroth stood just outside the fracas like a magistrate at a public trial. Ignoring the goings-on overhead, those in the circle wasted no time getting on with the business at hand.

We watched Hawk pull up to the table. Justice grabbed Avnova's feather, then the white one, in his beak. He jumped down from the scale and hopped toward Hawk, where he deposited both in Hawk's outstretched hand before taking wing into the night.

Holding the feathers close to his body with one hand, Hawk spun the wheelchair around with the other and started back across the chasm, his arm pumping like a piston. As the last of the doves flew into the light, Hawk steered his chair toward us.

"Thought you might need this." He held the white feather out to me as he leaned forward to catch his breath.

Upon touching it, I was suddenly aware of just how empty I had become. It was like the feeling you sometimes get when you don't realize how hungry you are until you start eating. As my hand closed over the snowy feather, it dissolved, and I felt all the hollow places within me fill. It was only a momentary thing, but it made me realize that my soul was not something I ever wanted to *bargain* again.

"*From the cauldron of Moirae* …" the tall hag's voice rang out. She dipped the staff with the blue crystal into the boiling pot and began to stir it round and round, as if it were a gigantic pot of soup. Her sisters joined her as she chanted:

"Thaukt will wail
With dry tears
Badb's bale-fire
Let Astaroth keep his own."

The leaping flames curled up the sides of the black pot, causing the long faces of the doomed six gathered round it to look even more grim. Barbatos stood off to one side as the sisters invoked the name of his superior, prompting Astaroth to step forward.

The tall witch, Nemain, leaning over and staring into the pot as she chanted, now stood straight.

"The fate of the souls before Badb's cauldron has been decided," she announced. Removing the staff from the cauldron, Nemain deliberately looked at each man individually before pronouncing sentence. "The six who have been so named in the document before them"—she nodded toward the signed Bargain that still lay on the table—"shall live out their natural lives within this time period. At the moment of their deaths, their souls shall be collected by Morrigan, Queen of the Ghosts, and rendered into the possession of Lord Astaroth." The witch paused and the round sister, Morrigan, stepped forward, opened her mouth, and began singing with the high beautiful voice of an evening lark:

"Hallowed Woman of the Earth,
We give this gift to you.
For Grandmother Moirae, riding forth this night,
Look kindly on what we do,

Mother Holle, beldame of the wheel,
Spin us the wyrd we await.
Moirae, keeper of the cauldron
Your pronouncement seals the fate!"

As Morrigan sang, each of the six men began shrinking, turning into black moths. The tiny winged creatures hovered around the firelight until the singing ceased. Then, as if blown by a sudden gust of wind, they flew off into the darkness.

Thomas cried out as he watched his father transform into an insect and flutter away in the night breeze. He stood, holding his hand to his mouth, as if the gesture could somehow keep him from falling apart completely before full sentence had been pronounced.

Nemain's voice rang out again at the conclusion of Morrigan's song: "The aforementioned signers of the broken Bargain will return to their earthly bodies and earthly homes this night, there to enjoy what days they may have upon this earth, until such time they depart from it and their souls are turned over to His Majesty." She turned to her sisters and together they chanted:

"And so shall it be,
And so shall it be."

I turned to Thomas, standing there with arms at his sides, his face the picture of misery. "I am so sorry," I said, simply. And I was. Sorrier than he could ever know, not so much for having been a part of his father's fate but because he had witnessed it.

Jeff laid a hand on Thomas' shoulder. "Hey, it's not like he's gone or anything. He'll probably be at home when you get there."

"Yeah," Hawk added. "I had a peek at the Bargain while I was at the table, and it says that the men will return to their own time period to live out their lives, without any awareness of having lived beyond this time."

Thomas squared his shoulders. "I am not sorry that Father has met with his punishment—this, he hath brought upon himself. My sorrow is for the sins of the whole of them, those things done that cannot be undone." His gaze went to the ravine. "Those who hath died—"

"Thomas, think about why you are here," I said, causing him to stop in mid-sentence. "I mean, don't you think it's possible that you were meant to see the handiwork of that group of men so that your generation doesn't repeat it? Now that you know who was behind the betrayal of those killed," I said, pointing toward the chasm, "and more important, *why* they did it, you can make sure *not* to follow in their footsteps, and maybe you can be the first one in this village to take steps toward seeing that it never happens anywhere else."

As I spoke, I saw something come alive in Thomas' eyes, the seed of an idea that would take hold and grow, ultimately shaping the man he would become.

"Thou art wise, Doe, and thy words are true," he began, but he was cut short by rumbling, like approaching thunder. Turning toward the source, I saw Astaroth had left the table, where the hags busily cleared away the remains of the assembly, and now stood at the edge of the ravine, his head lowered, looking directly at me.

He was the source of the sound that stilled the night air with a power that seemed capable of silencing Nature herself.

Stepping away from Thomas, I motioned to my cousins to stay back as I walked toward the edge of the precipice. I had not taken three steps when Astaroth leaped up and over the chasm, landing mere feet in front of me.

Before I had time to react, he began to transform. I watched in awe as first his feet burst free from his highly polished designer shoes to become the hooves of a steer. His shoulders humped, causing his cape to lift and fall back to reveal huge, intricately boned black wings that sprouted up from his shoulder blades and spread to an incredible width. The muscles in his thighs swelled, ripping the seams of his trousers, as a long, heavy black tail swung up like a bullwhip, then hit the ground with a crack that left a fissure in the dirt. Like an award-winning weight lifter, the gigantic mutating creature's abdomen was taut and tightly muscled.

But it was his head that made me gasp and reflexively step back. Pointed ears now topped a high-boned faced. Enlarged nostrils on a thick snub nose rose above a sharp chin. It was the face of a bat. The blue black hair streaming down his rippled back was the only thing that had not changed, and now, as I looked into the almond-shaped eyes that glowed like the fires of Hades, I knew that I was seeing the real thing at last. I was looking into the face of the dark angel known as Astaroth.

"You pathetic little girl." The words came out in a snarl. "Do you actually think you have won?"

I stepped back as Astaroth, now towering to a monstrous height, came toward me. His hooves clacked like hard-heeled boots on the frozen ground. He stopped and spread his arms wide, as if to engulf the sky. "*Behold, all that is mine!*" He roared like a lion standing over its prey. "Those few souls you managed to deprive me of this night are nothing … *NOTHING!*"

The night grew even darker and a spectacle began to play out across the heavens. Scene after scene flashed across the black sky—I saw thousands of ships packed with human cargo, their soul-tearing cries echoing over the span of hundreds of years; centuries of war and religious atrocities, followed by more recent scenes of inner-city drug deals, gang wars, and horrific acts of terrorism; crime bosses, thieves, and predators profiting and plying their evil at the expense of the weak and innocent—on and on it went like a parade of all things obscene and vile. There was so much misery, so much inhumanity and hateful cruelty that I could not bear to look, and I turned my head away.

"Seen enough?" His voice had now become quiet and silky as he leaned down just above my head. "That is just a small part of my empire." Almost a whisper now: "Every one … every time there is a transaction, a compromise of the … *spirit,* shall we say … each one of the millions of unfortunate choices that transpire around this ol' whirling ball of water and dirt, I get the spoils. So you see, *November*, the Pre-dic-tion"—he pronounced every syllable in the last word—"you are nothing more than a bothersome gnat. And as such, you can and *shall* be eliminated. And as for your family …" His laughter sounded like bones being ground to dust. "The Children of Avnova—they will pay next."

I snapped my head up, eyes locking with those endless pits of black fire burning in Astaroth's face. His mouth split in a twisted grimace, a parody of a smile. "Yes, let's see, perhaps I'll start with those two unwitting souls in the South of France. The one you call Frank is an easy enough target, but the other one—I think you call her Mom—oh, yes, she will be a challenge, but then I do so love a challenge."

I don't know when it began but I felt suddenly saturated by something more than mere anger, although I was white-hot with that. This was similar to when I was lost in the Rings and thought I was going to throw up. But instead of making me queasy, this was a kind of "filling up," as if at any moment I could explode and shatter into a million pieces.

As Astaroth said the word *Mom*, I reached overload, and without realizing it was my voice, I heard the word *No-o-o!* break the silence surrounding Astaroth's desiccated voice. I raised my arms, the fingers of both hands pointing directly at the demonic figure, and felt my body give a huge shudder, as wide bolts of bright white light emanated from my fingertips. Like the rings that result from a pebble thrown in a pond, the light radiated outward, engulfing everything in its path, until blinding brilliance was all that could be seen. I continued to scream without taking a breath and, somewhere deep inside, I marveled at my ability to sustain it. I was one with the brilliance—one with eternity.

I don't know how long I stood there, but eventually, the last of the powerful white light drained from my body. I lowered my arms and looked around me. It was as though I was inside an incandescent bulb. Then, everything went black.

***

I knew I was dreaming, and yet it didn't matter; dreams can sometimes be more real than waking life. Thomas and I were beside a lake. The sun reflected so brightly off the water, it was almost impossible to keep my eyes open. I closed them and leaned back into his embrace.

"I have waited so long for thy return." He kissed the top of my head.

"But I'm here now." His long hair brushed my arms as I turned and put them around his neck.

Thomas reached back and grasped my hand, placing it over his heart. "Ye and I share one heart, Doe." His warm eyes searched mine. "And nothing, neither time, nor man, nor demon can change that." And then he kissed me and I hoped I'd never wake up.

***

I opened my eyes to see Justice perched on a crossbeam in the rafters of The Croft. Jeff and Hawk sat beside the fireplace, talking quietly. I drifted off for a moment and when I next opened them, Thomas had joined the brothers by the fire and sat cross-legged with a wooden box on his lap.

"Me see ye hast returned to us." Tituba's soft accent interrupted the boys' conversation, causing them to hurry over to where I lay on the rope bed in the corner of The Croft.

"November!" Both cousins started talking at once, but Tituba shooed them back like so many chattering birds.

"Now, now, there will be time for talkin' later." The small brown woman with the bright red scarf wound round her head helped me to a sitting position. She held out a small chipped bowl containing a fragrant beverage, and I was struck once again by how much she looked like Aunty Gin.

"Drink it, child," Tituba instructed, "quickly, while it has strength."

I did as I was told but I could not help feeling like a helpless infant, as all three boys stared at me from the foot of the bed.

The result of the warm liquid was almost immediate. I could feel the strength returning to my body, and as I drained the last of it and handed the bowl back to Tituba, I felt more like my old self again.

"Ah, some color returning to thy cheeks," Tituba observed, as I swung my feet over the side of the cot. "Thou hast given us quite a scare.

"What happened?" I asked, running my hands over my face. Although I felt fine, I had the disconnected feeling of having been asleep for a very long time.

"You were *off the charts,* November!" Jeff blurted, and Hawk nodded his agreement.

"Astaroth threatened our family," I said, sitting back down on the bed as the memory of events just before my blackout began to return. "I just wanted to stop him, wanted him to *shut up* and go away."

"Well, he did that, all right," Hawk said, grinning. At my questioning look, he continued, "You don't remember? You pointed both your hands right at his big ol' hairy chest, and you zapped him so hard with a bolt of lightning that he and those witch-crows and Hathorne House, and *everything*"—Hawk threw his hands wide—"everything on the hill was blown into who-knows-where by your white light."

"Indeed, for a few moments, 'twas all that could be seen," Thomas volunteered.

As the full memory of Astaroth's threats washed over me, I jumped to my feet. "He is going after my mother and Frank," I said. "Astaroth said they were next." I looked around wildly as if there was some way in 1701 that I could make contact with them, warn them to be careful. "We have to go back—to our own time. I have to warn my parents," I said to Jeff and Hawk. It was as if they knew something I didn't and were holding out on me.

"And so you shall," came a familiar male voice, as a white-haired gentleman entered The Croft.

"Sir Edmund!" Hawk and I cried, as the scientist, followed by Ambrosine, made his way into the tiny room.

"But how—?" Hawk began, as Sir Edmund shook his hand.

"All will be explained, I assure you," Sir Edmund answered, as he turned to Jeff and Thomas who looked somewhat bewildered. "And who have we here?"

I introduced both boys to Sir Edmund Halley, who heartily shook hands with each of them.

Thomas' mouth fell open. "*The* Sir Edmund Halley?" he said in awe. "Thou art the most famous scientist in all the world! I have studied thy works in magnetism. It is most truly an honor, sir!" Thomas practically pumped the man's arm off in his enthusiasm.

Extracting his hand from the star-struck Thomas, Sir Edmund turned to Hawk. "Well, if you will remember," he said, "I told you when last we met that I am a traveler. And of course, this is the time period in which I was born and have lived most of my life, although not on this continent."

Ambrosine produced a chair from a corner of the room, and Sir Edmund gratefully accepted it. Jeff and Thomas plopped down on the floor at his feet, and I sat on the bed, as Ambrosine and Tituba set about making some refreshments for their newest guest.

"Not long ago, I was passing through the Room of Rings and heard Hob talking to his mother about having sent Ambrosine, along with the two young travelers, to Salem Village." Sir Edmund accepted a mismatched cup and saucer from Ambrosine with a nod of thanks. "Of course, I thought immediately of you two." He indicated Hawk and me. "It seems that your two aunts, November, had come back through the Rings by using your Point of Zero cards, and Hob and his mother were simply beside themselves with worry as to what to do about it." He took a sip of the hot liquid before continuing.

"Well, of course I suggested that I bring some new ones to you. You see, Ambrosine and I are old friends." He glanced over at our hostess, who returned his smile. "I have done extensive studies on the Elfin kingdom, and Ambrosine was one of my first interviewees, so I knew where to find her in this time and place. And I must say, it is wonderful to see The Croft again after such a long time!" Sir Edmund looked around at the cozy cottage with familiar fondness. "And there is Justice! Hello, my old friend!" he called to the raven in the rafters, who flapped his wings in greeting.

Sir Edmund took another sip from the cup and cleared his throat. "Well, need I say, Hob and Adorabelle hastily set about making new cards and I was soon on my way. However," he paused and his face grew grave, "I'm afraid the Keeper of the Rings and his mother did not realize there were four of you."

"What are you saying?" I asked.

"What I am saying is that I have only brought three Point of Zero cards. And while normally it would not be a problem for me to return and get another, I have commitments that preclude my going back through the Rings for some time." Sir Edmund started to rise with his cup, and Tituba was instantly at his side, allowing him to stay seated.

Jeff, Hawk, and I looked at each other.

"You and Hawk go back—I'll stay," Jeff said.

I started to protest but was cut off by Ambrosine.

"That will not be necessary, Jeffrey," she said, coming to stand next to Sir Edmund. "I am not returning."

Tituba stopped rinsing cups and turned to look at the tall woman with the flowing red hair.

"What do you mean?" I asked. "You are our guide."

"And what about your renewal?" put in Hawk. "I mean, Hob said you were very close to renewing."

Ambrosine dried her hands on a roughly spun cotton towel as she took a seat on the bed next to me. "It has been a very long time since I have been back in this place—my home." She looked around with the satisfaction of one who has found her place of belonging. "And I now know that renewal is not what is best for me. This is best for me." She waved her arm, indicating the cottage and its surroundings. "Here I will stay until such time that I cease to exist."

Sir Edmund's kind eyes were a mixture of admiration and sorrow as he said, "What Ambrosine does not say is that if she chooses to stay in this place, rather than go back, she will forfeit the opportunity to renew, thereby giving up her immortality." He looked at Ambrosine with a gentle smile: "You will become mortal, won't you, my dear."

Ambrosine nodded once and then lifted her head high. "And that is how it must be. I cannot bear to leave this place again." She looked at Tituba, then said, "Besides, now that the Bargain is no more, there is much work to be done to help repair the wrongs committed against the good people of this village."

Tituba's smile showed great admiration for her friend.

"Well," Sir Edmund said briskly, as he got to his feet, "then it is settled, and you three need to be getting back to your own time." He started for the door, but Thomas touched my arm as the others filed outside.

"Wait—please," Thomas said. "There be one more thing." He motioned for me to join him beside the fireplace.

Sir Edmund indicated that he would wait for us outside. "But do not tarry," he warned, as he closed the door behind him. "We must be on our way, and soon."

Joining Thomas, I saw that he had fetched the box he had been holding when I first opened my eyes, and now he held it out. It looked like the same box he had shown Hawk and me in the clearing when we first arrived in Salem Village, but this box had a bright brass clasp, held in place with a small, sturdy padlock. Heart-shaped, with a solid bar that swiveled over the keyhole, it was made of iron and looked impenetrable.

"I know not what lies within this," Thomas said, looking down at it. "It is sure my father and the other men of the council will no longer remember it at all. On the night of the signing of the Bargain, the two strangers placed it on the table as a gift to those who would agree to sign the document." Thomas swallowed hard as the memory of that night returned, his eyes haunted as he told the story. "My father and his company did not know this, but I doth secreted myself in the cloakroom. After each man had made his mark on the document, they gathered by the fireside to drink a toast." He paused and bit his lip, as if to gather his courage to continue his tale. "Whilst no one looked on, I slipped out of hiding. When I came to the table, *two* boxes were revealed to me—one that held the documents being presented by the two strangers, and this one. I believed that if I took them both, the terrible Bargain being struck that night would not be fulfilled.

"I carried the boxes outside, intending to place them both in the ground beneath the sapling that had been planted in the meeting house yard only a few months before. But there was only room for the smallest of the boxes beneath the roots, and it was snowing mightily that night. The ground was frozen and … well, I just took this one and hid it under the woodpile behind our house—but Tituba found it. I ran here to The Croft after ye fainted, Doe," Thomas said, "because I knew Tituba and Ambrosine would know what to do. While Ambrosine and Candlelight went to fetch thee on Hathorne Hill, Tituba told me to run home and fetch the box. I know it is too big and heavy to take wither thou goest," he said, "but whatever lies within no longer belongs in this time. And whatever mischief it represents will do no good here. But I believe it will be of great value where ye go." Thomas took a golden skeleton key suspended on a leather strap from around his neck. He took my hand in his, causing my stomach to do a funny little flip-flop. I wasn't sure if it was because I recognized the key or because of the warmth of his skin against mine.

"That's the key we used to open the door to the Elfin kingdom." I said, as Thomas leaned forward and placed the leather necklace over my head.

"'Tis the very same." His eyes met mine as I raised my head. "And remember what I told ye about it?" His face was so close to mine I could feel the breath of his words.

"It will keep me safe," I answered.

"And return thee safely to me."

His lips on mine felt as natural as morning sun through a window. The warmth of that kiss would stay with me forever.

Thomas sat back, still holding my hand. "Keep this key, Doe, and I shall be waiting for thee on the other side of time."

"I don't want to go," I began, but Thomas shook his head and looked down at the rough-hewn box.

"I shall bury this, this very morn, within the foundation of the new Putnam house. It lies directly north of the sapling. Look for it there."

"But in my time there are so many buildings, and the tree might be long gone—how am I ever going to find—"

"I am afraid there is no time to ponder that question," Sir Edmund said from the open doorway. "Ambrosine has readied the Point of Zero, and you really must be on your way."

Thomas placed the box on the hearth and together, he and I left The Croft to join Ambrosine, Sir Edmund, and my cousins.

I didn't want to say good-bye, but it was obvious that my cousins were ready to go home. After hugs all around, we three stood side-by-side, as our countdown to Point of Zero began and the wavering POZ windows appeared.

Before inserting my card, I took one last look at Ambrosine, Tituba, and Thomas, standing together. I touched the key hanging round my neck, and Thomas held up his hand in a final wave, as Tituba blew us a kiss.

"Go in love and light, little ones," she called, as we inserted our cards and stepped into the colorful folds of the Rings.

Chapter Thirty-one

And so I got home safely. I didn't drop the eggs, my nose had grown no longer, and my legs were still my legs. I didn't lose my penny, or tumble in a ditch—so mind you smile and say 'Good Day' when you meet a Witch.

—Eleanor Farjeon, *W is for Witch*

"HALLOO! HALLOO!" SHOUTED HOB, AS ONE BY one, Jeff, Hawk, and I were pulled from the Rings. The nervous energy of the elf gave Jeff pause but as soon I made introductions, he began to relax. I suppose the mere mention of elves, much less seeing one again, would be a bit unnerving for Jeff for some time to come. But the sheer joy of Hob's greeting was enough to show even the most wary traveler that he had nothing to fear from this elf.

Gushing and fawning and telling us how worried he had been, Hob ushered us like a clucking hen out of the Room of Rings and into his living quarters, where Adorabelle and her daughter, Abella, picked up where he left off. After scrutinizing us to make sure we were okay, they made such a fuss about the fact that we had given our cards away that I felt like I was standing in the principal's office, being reprimanded for sharing the answers to my homework. They pressed drinks upon us, clucking and cooing, until they finally agreed that we were fit to travel beyond the Room of Rings to make our way back home.

"What day is this?" Jeff asked, as we sat at the table drinking sweet tea and eating soft, sugary cookies that looked like tiny waffles.

Adorabelle consulted one of the many calendars on the wall next to the stove. "Well, you, young man, have been gone more than six months, according to the Elfin calendar. However, in your time it is

9:31 ante meridiem, on November 12, in the year of the Gregorian calendar."

"What?" Jeff said.

"It's nine-thirty in the morning on November 12th," Hawk translated. "By their time, you were in the Elfin realm for six months, but in our time, you've only been gone four days."

Jeff shook his head, trying to sort that out, when the outer door swung open and a hearty voice said, "And with just enough time to get home for breakfast!"

The tip of a tall red hat entered the room first, followed by the blue-coated figure of Dynnis striding toward us, his rosy face split in a broad grin, and his arms open wide in welcome. "You did it, my young friends. Well done!" he exclaimed. "I have to tell you that when I left you at the door of the Elfin Mound as a child, I worried that I would not see you again. And I also must say that having to live all those hundreds of years without knowing what became of you was difficult, to say the least! And so you must tell me all the details while we walk."

After expressing our thanks to Adorabelle and Abella, Dynnis lead the way out of Hob's cozy living room and into the narrow chamber. Glancing up uneasily, I hoped none of the Shriekers still lingered, and I doubted that I would ever look at a bat the same way again.

With the certainty of a guide dog, Dynnis led us through the moldering old asylum, choosing corridors with ramps to accommodate the wheelchair, as Hawk, then I, related what had happened since we last saw him. Before we knew it, we could see sunlight streaming through the entrance to the double doors of the administration building.

"Light at the end of the tunnel!" Jeff's use of the cliché expressed my feeling exactly. I grabbed the handles of Hawk's chair and the three of us broke into a run. Jeff pulled into the lead, slamming both doors open as we all rushed into the welcoming daylight and skidded to a stop, as Hawk's chair bumped into Jeff, who hopped on one foot in order to avoid pitching headfirst down the front steps.

As if we'd practiced it, Mr. Whoozi-What's' golf cart pulled up just as we burst through the front doors, but instead of jumping out and yelling at us, the big man seemed to be busy containing a squirming puppy.

He called out, "Hey! You kids know who owns this dog?"

Jeff and I made our way down the steps while Hawk took the ramp. As I approached the golf cart, I could see the puppy was a very young bloodhound. It looked like the one I used to puppy-sit for when my neighbors back in Phoenix went on vacation.

As I stroked the pup's head, Mr. Whoozi-What's surprised me by plopping him in my arms.

"Allergies," he said, drawing in a sharp breath before letting loose with an explosive sneeze. He produced a tissue from the pocket of his uniform and blew loudly into it, then stuffed it back in his pocket. "I'll tell you what. I won't make a big deal about the fact that I caught you three coming out of there." He indicated the double doors we'd just exited. "In exchange, you take that … that animal and find out who it belongs to." He sneezed again and wiped his teary eyes. "I'll even throw in a ride home."

We exchanged glances as the puppy wiggled once and then happily settled itself in my arms, as if to say, *Sounds good to me.*

"Deal," we said in unison.

Dynnis had done his disappearing act upon Mr. Whoozi-What's' arrival, but I was sure he followed, hopping from bush to bush, as the golf cart sped away from the asylum toward Aunt Marsha's house.

I checked the puppy as we rode along and discovered he had no collar and that *it* was a *he.* The fact that he had no collar or tag was going to make it tough to figure out where he had come from.

As we made our way onto Preston Street, Hawk asked Mr. Whoozi-What's, "Have you lived in Danvers long?"

"All my life," he answered. "Why do you ask?"

"I was just wondering if you've ever heard of the Putnam family. I mean, I know the school is named after them and that they were one of the original families and all, but I've always wanted to know where they lived or if their house is still standing."

"The old Putnam house?" Mr. Whoozi-What's replied. "Sure, it's still there. I would have thought you already knew that—since it's the house you're living in." He brought the golf cart to a halt in front of Aunt Marsha's house and turned to us. "That is one of the oldest structures in Danvers," he said, indicating the tan three-story. "Been standing since the early 1700s. If you kids are really interested in learning more about the people who first founded Salem Village, there are a lot of books on the subject at the local historical society."

"Thanks," Hawk said, as Jeff and Mr. Whoozi-What's helped him into his chair.

"Yes, thank you. You've no idea how much we appreciate your help," Jeff said, shaking Mr. Whoozi-What's' hand.

The older man narrowed his eyes suspiciously as he took his hand back. "Yeah, well, you kids need to stay out of that old asylum. I'll let it go this time, as long as you keep your part of the bargain and find that puppy a good home."

The Bargain? We all looked at each other and laughed. We promised we would do both, and Whoozi-What's jumped back into the golf cart and sped off back toward Danvers Asylum with a wave of his hand.

Holding the puppy close, I dashed up the ramp behind my cousins and into the welcoming arms of Aunty Gin and Aunt Marsha. As I explained about the puppy, Aunty Gin went into the hall closet and returned with a large cardboard box and some newspaper. After putting the tiny creature inside, she set about offering it some water and dry crackers.

Aunt Marsha insisted that we sit down and tell them everything that had happened after they left Hathorne Hill. Her eyes clouded with worry when I repeated Astaroth's threat to my parents.

"I'm putting in an international call right now," she said, heading for the phone. A few minutes later, she returned to the room, saying the overseas operator reported no answer, but they would keep trying and would put the call through as soon as someone could be contacted. "They assured me they will call us when they've reached your parents," Aunt Marsha said.

"And now, the best part." Hawk, who had been squirming worse than the puppy in order to contain his excitement, blurted. "Before we left, Thomas showed us a box he had taken from the Meeting House table the night the Bargain was signed. He'd kept it hidden in the woodpile behind his house without ever opening it. But he gave November the key and told her he was going to bury it in the foundation of the new Putnam house."

Hawk paused and Jeff took over. "And do you know what the coolest part is?"

Both ladies shook their heads and Hawk cut in. "The coolest thing is that *this* is the Putnam house!"

"I knew that," Aunt Marsha said.

"What? You knew that, and you never told us?" Hawk accused.

"I didn't think you'd care," Aunt Marsha returned defensively.

"Oh, well, what difference does it make?" Jeff waved a dismissive hand. "The thing is, the box is probably buried in our foundation at this very minute."

I thought of Thomas' promise. "And even though it was only a little while ago to us, it's been waiting in that foundation for more than three hundred years," I added.

"Well, let's go find it!" shouted Aunty Gin, and the rest of us followed her out the door and into the yard.

Pushing aside dead weeds, we scanned the heavy stones that made up the foundation of the building. Each of us took a section of one side of the house to search, but after a long bout of pushing and prodding, the stones yielded nothing. Although the sun shone brightly, the air was cold in the shadow of the house, and as I stood rubbing my arms, I heard the puppy crying in the living room. Leaving the others to their task, I brought him outside, setting him down on the lawn in case he needed to go.

As I knelt down, the tiny, long-eared pup hopped around playfully and began sniffing the pocket of my jeans. "I know it's been awhile since I've had a shower," I laughed, "but I hope I don't stink too badly."

In response, the little guy dashed away, his ears trailing in the tall grass. Without hesitation, he made a beeline right to the corner of the building. Stopping dead at the foundation of the house, he sat down and began to bay as if he had just treed a cat.

"What's the matter with him?" Aunt Marsha began, but Hawk interrupted.

"Look!" he said, pointing to the foundation where the puppy now dug furiously.

Jeff brushed the weeds away and there, shining in the morning sunlight, was the imprint of a feather, long ago imbedded in a newly formed cornerstone.

"Avnova's feather." I didn't realize I had spoken aloud until I saw Jeff and Hawk staring at me. Together, we gazed in awe at the symbol Thomas had left as a clue.

The stone moved so easily when Jeff pushed on the imprinted feather, that it was hard to believe it had stood in place for so many centuries. Within minutes, my cousin and Aunty Gin had pulled it free. Jeff reached in, and I thought about the black widow spider and the Wild Hunt.

"I have it!" Jeff cried, and once again, Aunty Gin lent a hand as together they pulled the heavy box out and into the sunlight of the twenty-first century.

When we had all returned to the living room, I deposited the puppy back in his box, and Hawk said, "Well, November, you have the key so I guess you better do the honors."

Taking it from around my neck, I set to work. As old as the padlock was, it sprang open with amazing ease.

The ticking of the grandfather clock was all that could be heard as I eased the lid up. I heard the intake of several breaths as its contents were revealed, glittering brightly in a shaft of sunlight streaming through the front window.

"*One square stone, inlaid on the great foundation stone will give forth a luster, as if so many bright suns ...*" Hawk quoted. "That's what the document in the other box was referring to—the cornerstone!"

I sat back in stunned silence, and Jeff bent forward.

"Gold!" he said. He lifted a handful of the quarter-sized coins filling the box.

Everybody started talking at once, and I leaned in for a better look. There had to be hundreds of them—gold coins like the one we had found in the first box—like the one the witches of the Wild Hunt had given me, and I had used to pay the old elf.

"Gold guineas bearing the bust of King Charles II," Dynnis said next to my ear, and I turned to see him sitting beside me on the sofa.

"I think it's time you introduced us to your friend," Aunt Marsha said, getting up from where she knelt next to the coffee table. She smiled and extended her hand to Dynnis, who gladly accepted it and that of Aunty Gin.

Just then the phone rang. Aunt Marsha answered it and, after speaking briefly, held it out to me.

My mother's voice filled me with a mixture of relief and longing.

"November, is everything all right?" Mom asked, her concern traveling plainly through the fiber-optic cables.

"Yeah, it's good. I just wanted to hear your voice. I miss you, Mom," I said, then added, "Is Frank okay?"

"Yes, honey, we're both fine, and we miss you, too. Are you sure you're really okay?" The disembodied voice paused before continuing. "Because I can come home, you know, if you need me to come back."

"No. No, Mom, I'm fine really. I just needed to know you were, too," I said.

"Well, if you're sure you're okay." She didn't sound convinced. "So. What have you been doing? Anything exciting happen lately?"

"Uh … well, I got a puppy." Now why had I said that? The puppy wasn't mine. Most likely, at this very moment, his owners were out looking for him.

"No one is looking for that puppy. He was dumped by the side of the road this morning," Dynnis said, as he passed by on his way to the kitchen.

"A puppy! Oh, November, are you sure that's okay with your aunts?" My mother was all business now. "I don't want you imposing anything like that on them."

"Oh, they don't mind," I began, but she cut me off.

"Put Marsha on the line after we finish our conversation. I need to hear it from her that you are not overstepping your boundaries."

The rest of the conversation was brief, and after exchanging I-love-you's and promising I would be better about e-mailing, I handed the phone to Aunt Marsha.

"What's so funny?" Hawk asked, when his mother rejoined the group.

Still chuckling, she said, "Arleen told me to be careful not to let November put one over on me and Aunty Gin. In fact, her exact words were, '*You know, November has a way of getting what she wants. I swear, sometimes I think that girl would argue with the devil!*'" She and the others dissolved into laughter, and the puppy joined in by jumping up on the side of the cardboard box and howling.

Leaving them to enjoy their joke, I picked up the tiny pup.

"You need to go for a walk," I told him, retrieving my leather necklace with the golden key and slipping it over my head as I closed the front door behind me.

"November, go to the tree." Thomas' voice was so clear that I almost dropped the wiggling animal. I thought I was starting to slide into that other time. In fact, I tried to, and for a brief second, I almost succeeded. The houses around me dissolved, and the wavering figure of Thomas appeared for an instant before vanishing.

"Thomas—wait!" I cried, but he was gone, and I was standing in the middle of my aunts' yard.

"Go to the sapling." The voice was very faint now. "Look beneath and then above." Then silence.

Getting a firmer grip on the puppy, I headed for Mr. Whoozi-What's' front yard.

***

The old black oak stood leafless in the cold November morning. And I knew by now that Mr. Whoozi-What's would be asleep after his night shift at the asylum.

I placed the puppy on the ground, and he happily scampered around, sniffing all the wondrous smells of the out-of-doors. I got on my knees at the base of the tree, where it had all first begun. The hole beneath the root was still there. The puppy ran up and stuck his head in, then began to dig. Pushing him aside, I reached in, and my hand closed on a small, smooth object. When I had removed it and brushed some of the dirt away, I saw it was a heart-shaped ceramic jewel case, hand-painted with a dove on the lid.

After several tries, I managed to pry it open with a stick. Inside, I found a folded piece of paper, brown and fragile with age. As I lifted it carefully out, something fell to the ground. A coin—the coin the witches of the Wild Hunt had given me, the one the greedy elf had bitten to see if it was real gold. "*The coin will always return to thee, no matter how ye spend it or give it away,*" Tituba had said.

Gently unfolding the note, I read Thomas' words, written in a penmanship taught long, long ago.

Time can never part
Those who share
One heart

"Look beneath and above," he had said. I picked up the puppy and got to my feet. There, high up on the trunk, carved deep into the thick bark of the old oak was the outline of a heart with the initials TP and NA:

Reaching up, I ran my hand over each one, gently tracing the letters Thomas had so carefully carved all those years ago.

Then I read the final line on the paper …

I shall await thee, my Doe.

Epilogue

Six Months Later

"Everything is settled, then," Alvis Lacour said to the man on the other end of the phone line. "My sister and her family will be coming to New Orleans on the twenty-first in order to finalize the will and help me inspect the property."

"And will they need accommodations?" asked the soft voice.

"Oh, no. No, they'll be staying with me and my wife at the plantation house. Going to have a family reunion of sorts. I mean, it's not as if there aren't enough bedrooms," Alvis chuckled.

"Indeed," came the voice from Louisiana. "So, may I expect to see you …"—he paused as he consulted his calendar—"on Friday, the twenty-second, then?"

When Alvis agreed, the smooth, well-modulated voice continued. "Excellent. I look forward to meeting you and your … family at that time. Until then, adieu."

Alvis hung up the phone and turned to his wife. "It's all set. We're all going to meet at the lawyer's office, and after the papers are signed, we'll go see what the old girls have left us."

As Willa Lacour stepped into his arms, Alvis smiled over her head. "Won't it be fun to see Ginny and Marsha and the kids again? I can't wait—we're going to have a grand old time!"

***

The lawyer replaced the designer phone in its cradle and turned to his employer. "Everything is arranged," he said.

The big man sitting behind the Hermann Miller desk, his fingers forming a tent as he gazed out the eighth floor window of his office, spun his chair around to face his red-haired companion. “And the girl?” His deep voice sounded like the growl of a large cat.

“She and her parents will both be coming,” the lawyer answered.

A slow smile spread across the handsome face, and for a brief second, something resembling small flames burned in the depths of the black eyes.

“Thank you, Mr. Barbatos,” he purred. “Well done.”

The End